He's sworn to protect her, but can he save her from himself?

Danika Rubystone has hated the minstrels ever since her mother ran away with one. As Princess, she's duty bound to marry Valorian, a minstrel from the House of Song. But problems in the kingdom are mounting. With her father dead she's the sole heir to an imperiled throne, and wyverns attack Ebonvale's southern shores. But after Danika finds a lone survivor of a wyvern's attack who holds the key to protecting the kingdom and she finally meets the enchantingly sly Valorian, everything changes.

As Ebonvale's Royal Guard sails with the minstrels to smite the uprising of wyverns, Danika dances a line between sticking by duty like her father, or following her wild heart like her mother

Books by Aubrie Dionne

Nebula's Music
Messenger In the Mist
Minstrel's Serenade

Published by Kensington Publishing Corporation

Minstrel's Serenade

Aubrie Dionne

LYRICAL PRESS
Kensington Publishing Corp.
www.kensingtonbooks.com

First Electronic Edition: July 2014
eISBN-13: 978-1-61650-5509-9
eISBN-10: 1-61650-550-8

First Print Edition: July 2014
ISBN-13: 978-1-61650-605-6
ISBN-10: 1-61650-605-9

To every fan of fantasy and romance. Never stop dreaming.

Chapter 1

Fire's Mark

"No lady should see what evil lies beyond the ridge." Bron blocked the exit of the carriage with a great wall of muscle, sweat and dark skin. Plumes of smoke rose like great fingers brushing the sky behind his broad shoulders.

Danika focused on the strength in his dark eyes. "Nonsense. Every ruler must bear witness to the devastation afflicting her people so she can make the right decisions to protect her kingdom."

Bron's stance didn't change.

She narrowed her eyes; bodyguard or not, he had to follow her orders. She could force him to let her pass, but, maybe this one time she'd play his game. "So she can enact the most deserving form of revenge."

"That's more like it." Bron smiled, thick lips curving. "Spoken like a true warrior."

"Flattery will get you nowhere. Let me through."

He sighed with a gentle rise and fall of his broad chest, ran his hand over his shaved head, and stepped aside. "If you insist, Princess."

She placed her fingers in his war-hardened hand and allowed him to guide her to the blackened earth. The air stank of soot and ash, searing her eyes and the smooth skin on her cheeks. She blinked through the wave of heat and summoned her courage. "Show me the site of the greatest devastation."

"As you wish, Princess. The smoke spooks the horses, so we'll have to trek up the cliff on foot."

"Walking doesn't frighten me." She'd worn her thigh-high riding boots underneath her damask underskirt for such an occasion. She ripped the top layer of silks off, revealing the same leather leggings warriors wore under their tunics.

Bron averted his eyes. When his gaze returned to her, he seemed to appraise her with newfound interest.

She stashed the frills in the carriage, hiding the burning flush in her cheeks. Surely the heat had raised her temperature. She refused to blame Bron's attention. "Lead me to Shaletown."

"Or what's left of it."

Bron picked his way through charred trunks, presenting his hand whenever the footing grew treacherous. Although the ground steamed and the soles of her feet burned, she made her way on her own, refusing his offers. As the new ruler of Ebonvale, she had to show strength in a time when fear spread like the plague of the dead.

They crested the ridge and she covered her mouth with her sleeve. The blackened village lay before them as dead man's land. People had walked the cobblestones that morning going about their everyday business, unaware of the impending devastation. Anger boiled inside her, followed by a black void of loss sucking her dry.

Danika cleared her parched throat. "Has anyone searched for survivors?"

She knew the answer before Bron opened his mouth.

"No, my lady. The clouds from the blaze obscure the sky and the wyverns may still hover, waiting for stragglers. Besides, the chance of any surviving such devastation…"

She scanned the remains from her raven perch, balancing her boot on the stump of a sizzled tree. The brick foundation of a tavern stood without its thatched roof or bluewood walls. Black stains streaked across the town square where the fire's breath licked its way through. Skeletons littered the ash, their black-splotched finger bones grasping through the soot to seek salvation. This kingdom belonged to her now, and she couldn't let the provinces fall to ruin because of a swarm of vermin from the south.

Her heart raced as ire shot up through her chest, splitting her apart. "How could they destroy innocent people?"

"They're beasts, Your Highness. There's no logical reasoning to their onslaught."

"But we've stayed clear of Scalehaven. Unless something lured them to our lands?"

Bron shrugged as if the wyverns' attack were inevitable. "The beasts' population brims with hatchlings. Scouts have reported the yearlings as far north as Brimmore's Bay." His voice danced, careful and light, as if he wanted to protect her from the truth.

She ran her mother's satin scarf across her blistering forehead. Sweat stained the pink fabric red. "My father would know what to do."

Bron's gaze dropped to the ash as if her words defeated him.

Danika cursed her weak tongue. She knew better than to speak of the late king in front of him.

He met her gaze once again. "I have full faith in your rule."

Helplessness trickled through her, threatening to weaken her knees. Danika pulled away, straightening her back against the rising channels of smoke blotting the sky. She wanted to lean into him and borrow his strength, but such a gesture led toward a doomed future. To choose such a lowly man, albeit the Chief of Arms, when so many more lucrative prospects remained, would place her kingdom in further jeopardy. Especially in times as dark as these.

A blur of earthy brown scrambled between an overturned carriage and the remnants of the smithy. Danika's concerns flew from her mind as she focused on the form huddled behind the coal pit.

"There." She thrust her finger into the smoke. "A small child."

Bron grabbed for her arm but the silky fabric of her sleeve slipped through his fingers. She threw herself forward, stumbling down the cliff's side.

"Princess, no!"

Her arms flailed as she scrambled between slabs of malachite, the sharp edges exposed by the wyverns' breath. Halfway down, a keen wail rode the wind, slicing her ears. Black ribbons flickered on the horizon.

"Danika, stop! They're coming back!"

She jumped the final five feet and landed on her hands and knees beside the smithy. So many had died. If she could save just one...

The boy cowered with his arms covering his head.

"Boy! Come here." She waved to him but his eyes were shut as tight as a noblewoman's purse.

"Horred's Grave." She'd have to sprint to make it. She skirted a pile of flaming wood and jumped over the wall, the broken glass tearing her bell-shaped sleeves like wyvern's teeth. She stumbled forward on her hand and knees, ripping the fabric to free herself.

A bronze plate three sizes too big hung on the boy's sagging shoulders. Had the armor shielded him? Surely not. The fire would heat the metal to near melting, sizzling a layer of skin.

As she ran toward him, he turned in the direction of her footsteps and peeked through narrow eyelids. He must have recognized her, because his eyes widened as big as two chicken eggs in a face covered in thick, black ash. Surprisingly, he had no burns.

"Follow me." She hoisted him up, and they scuttled through a hole blazed into the foundation.

The boy tugged on her arm to hide underneath the anvil. "It's too late. They're here."

Danika fought him as she glanced at the sky. The ribbons grew thicker, spiraling through the air like glittering pennants on Festival Day. The pattern of swirls mesmerized her as the horde unfurled.

She blinked, tearing her gaze away. "We can still make it."

The boy had stopped battling her, hypnotized by the sky. "It's too late."

"No." She yanked him around and screamed her throat raw. "Run!"

As they neared the cliff, Bron stood above them like a chiseled statue of a war god, unsheathing his golden claymore. A pang of worry pierced her stomach like a dagger. He'd stayed behind to distract the wyverns' attention to cover their escape.

Why had she been so foolish?

The first wyvern landed with a gush of wings on the outskirts of the village behind them, while a second flew straight toward Bron. Danika climbed, knowing full well she might have sent the two-time war veteran to his death. She lifted the boy and pushed him up the hill.

"Burrow's Bucket! I can climb by myself." He swiped her away and paused, throwing off the breastplate before scrambling up the crag. Danika grabbed at weeds, pulling them out as she struggled for a handhold. Although she should have focused all her energy on climbing, she gazed up at Bron.

The wyvern dove and lunged, smacking jaws longer than Bron's claymore. Bron ducked and swung, sinuous muscles bunching and stretching. He missed its shimmering hide by inches. The warrior excelled in hand-to-hand combat, but if the wyvern ignited its belly of fire, he'd have no defense.

"Over here." The boy had found a path up the incline. He reached down over a ridge and grabbed her hand, trying to pull her up. His scrawny arms shook as Danika slid through his sooty fingers. Her heels skidded backward until they hit a rock. "Don't wait for me. Go!"

The boy dangled his arm, waving her to him. "Come on."

She could make it. She took a step back and ran, leaping toward the ridge and catching a bramble. The boy grasped her arm. Thank the gods for all the secret training Bron had given her. Danika hefted herself over the edge. She grabbed the boy's hand and they scrambled toward the carriage.

She glanced at the place where Bron had stood. Nothing remained except a darkening sky with wyverns writhing through the air. "B-Bron." Panic rose inside her, along with a feeling of sheer loneliness. What if he'd died for her impulsiveness?

"I'm here, Princess," he thundered from behind the carriage. He'd rigged the horses and collected the reins in his hand.

The boy jumped in without a word. Danika shot Bron a look that would have killed an ordinary man.

"I thought you'd died."

"Princess, you know better than to traipse off while wyverns rule the sky."

Danika gestured to the boy kicking his heels against the carriage seat. "I couldn't leave him."

"So be it." He threw a tarp over a lump of steaming scales, shining oily green black in the twilight. "You have a new trophy for your mead hall."

"Honestly, I prefer the wall bare." Disgusted by death, she jumped in the carriage.

Frenzied screeches filled the sky behind them like mad raven calls.

"Hi-ya!" Bron whipped the reins and the horses galloped forward. Danika pressed her cheek to the glass. The wyverns became threads in the darkening sky. Her castle had a bastion of archers, but there were many more beasts than in her nightmares. Her stomach sank to her knees. In time, the writhing masses would overcome Ebonvale's ramparts as well.

Chapter 2

Lyric Poem

Danika awoke to the squealing wheels of the carriage as they rounded patchy lumps in the road. What under-tended alleyway had Bron chosen? Groggy from slumber, she checked on the boy. He'd fallen asleep curled on the cushions. After wiping away a smear of ash on his cheek, she reached over him and drew back the velvet curtains. The last rays of dim light filtered in and she almost lost her stomach. Blue-tinged trees loomed overhead. Gray moss draped from the drooping branches in wisps, like shrouds of the dead.

Anger and frustration rumbled inside her. She could never leave Bron alone without expecting him to defy orders. Danika slid the front window open and stuck out her head. "Bron, why in Helena's Goblet are we traipsing through Bluewood Pines?"

"I see you've woken." Bron twisted his thick lips in a small half-smile, the scar on his right cheek shining like a badge.

"Woken is correct, but to what?"

"Relative safety. The wyverns cut off our escape. Those sky worms are smarter than you think. They let us get away, Princess."

The woods swirled around her. "I don't understand."

He shook his head. "You're lucky I still have my eagle eye. Another swarm waited for us across the bridge. I saw black flickers in the sky as we crested the main road. Although I'm flattered, you overestimate my abilities to protect you. I can take down one, but an entire swarm would incinerate us in heartbeats."

"This isn't our territory."

"They'll never know we're here."

"The carriage squeals like a newborn pig."

His over-confidence normally drew her in, but in times like these she wished he had more humility. He'd risked his reputation for her whimsy, smuggling her out of the castle to spy. But to lead them into the Minstrels' Forest of Song?

He shrugged. "Better to ward off the wild boars."

She sniffed the heavy tang in the air. "We reek of wyvern blood."

Bron grinned. "Let the smell be a warning to all."

A low humming throbbed around them. She groaned. The names she would have called Bron if she'd been another man and not a princess were infinite, each one worse than the last. "Speak of the devil. Here they are now."

Bron pulled back on the reins, halting both horses. He grabbed the hilt of his claymore. "You think they'd have better things to do with their time. Pansy-ass finger plucking crooners…"

The sound drowned out his voice as the drone swelled into a multi-chordal ostinato. The song wove gentle fingers around Danika's mind, reaching to her innermost emotions, soothing her into a state of fabricated bliss. "No."

She turned to Bron for strength, but he fought against the tones as well, the muscles in his hand weakening, turning limp. No wonder these men quelled the wyverns' attacks. "Bron, never mind the sword. Whip the reins."

"Too late now." His voice grew soft and velvety, something she'd never heard before and enjoyed far too much.

Danika tore through the carriage door and jumped onto the mossy road as the horses collapsed on their bellies. She knelt beside them, massaging their legs, urging them to stand. Black eyes lolled in their heads. The song swelled in her ears, and she put her hands up to her ears to block the sound.

A hooded shadow emerged from the mossy wisps, flanked by four others on either side. As the man stepped into the light, silver eyes caught her attention. A hand-painted lute lay strapped across his lean chest. Filigree patterns swirled around the strings much like the fire wyverns in the sky.

Bron jumped from the carriage and flexed his right arm to grab his sword. The music turned dissonant, tones pushing against themselves to delve deep inside her heart and make her ache for something unreachable. Bron fought against it, scrambling for the hilt. The dissonance rose and then resolved like a flower opening its petals, and he stumbled, falling to his knees.

The leader flicked back his hood with long, thin fingers. Swirly, deer-brown hair cascaded around his ears. He stepped up to Bron and his voice flowed like warm honey. "What brings you here?"

Bron grumbled and Danika spoke up before her bodyguard muttered something that would get them both in trouble. "We seek an alternate route. Wyverns swarm above the road to my castle."

"Your castle?" The minstrel raised a hand and the men singing behind him softened to a low hum. Danika gave Bron a stern look and he bowed his head, allowing her to take the lead.

She rose, dusting off her hands. "Yes. I am Princess Danika Rubystone, daughter of the late King Artemus Rubystone, chosen ruler of the people of Ebonvale."

The minstrel blinked and took in a sharp breath before bowing low. "Princess Danika, my apologies. Why haven't you answered any of my letters?"

Bron gave her a questioning furrow of eyebrows, and Danika almost swallowed her tongue. "You're Valorian, Prince of the House of Song?"

He lifted his head, wavy hair falling back to reveal sleek cheekbones. The sharp edges on his nose and chin could have cut through silk. "I am."

Burrow's Bucket! Her skin heated. Maybe if she'd known how handsome he was, she would have written a reply.

"Come, let us take you to the House of Song. Night approaches, and the fire wyverns will no doubt rule the sky until dawn." Every word he spoke resonated like a lyrical poem.

Bron rose to his feet. He stood a head taller than the minstrels, looking like an ogre amongst fairies. "That's not necessary. I'm capable of transporting the princess home safely."

"Bron, wait." Danika had snubbed the minstrels for too long, bent on deferring their offers to unite kingdoms. She'd learned stubbornness and independence from her father, but dire times called for unexpected measures. These song spinners might prove a useful ally. High time to take them up on at least one offer. Her heart tore to disappoint Bron, but she had a kingdom to think about and a hungry little boy in the backseat.

"I don't question your abilities, Bron, but Valorian and I have some catching up to do." She bowed to Valorian. "If you'd be so kind as to awaken my horses?"

He smiled as if deeply pleased. "Certainly."

Valorian waved his hand and the pulse of music quickened into a jig. The men behind him strummed their lutes in undulating rhythms. The horses rose and Danika slipped into her carriage. Bron cursed under his breath. Would he disobey? Her heart hung in between beats until the carriage rocked as he climbed aboard.

Moments later, the horses whinnied and the carriage tugged forward into the burgeoning night. What had she gotten herself into?

"Are we there?" The boy rubbed his eyes, righting himself on the velvety seat.

"We've taken a detour." He'd probably squiggle away if she wrapped her arms around him. She couldn't imagine who he'd lost in the attack and she knew not to ask.

He gazed out the carriage window and his eyes widened. "Where are we going?"

"To the House of Song." She smiled, trying to get his mind off the horrors of the day. "You're one lucky little boy. Not everyone from Ebonvale gets to see the House of Song." Although she didn't mention it, luck had favored him more than once. He'd survived the fire wyverns' wrath. Was it because of the breastplate? Danika pursed her lips. Pushing him so soon after the tragedy was cruel. She'd let him be a boy again before bombarding him with questions.

He shrugged and remained silent. Like any boy, he was hard to impress.

"I'm Danika." She extended her hand.

"I know." The boy stared at her ivory skin and flaxen hair, traits her mother had brought to their kingdom from the south. He didn't move. "I've seen you in the parades."

"And you are?"

He murmured the name, "Nip."

"Nip?" She'd try not to judge. "What an interesting name for a boy." It sounded as if he'd pinch her arms when she looked away.

Nip sniffed. "Ma named me after the cold--she had me in a blizzard."

His mother. Probably dead.

Her eyes stung with unleashed tears. Maybe if she'd attacked the wyverns after her father passed away, the boy's village would still be standing, and he'd be cooking with his Ma right now. "I'm sorry about what happened."

He nodded but made no further comments. Endless hurt shone in his brown eyes, as if he hid within himself. Even a princess' offerings couldn't help. She couldn't reach out and make the horrors go away. Nothing would bring back what he'd lost.

She'd make those worms pay, even if gleaning revenge meant allying with the House of Song.

Danika squeezed her palms until her muscles ached. She would find a way to rid their infestation, even if it meant taking a boat to Scalehaven Isle herself and sinking the entire island chain. The wyverns were vermin, just like the rats in the wheat sheds and the crop-eating locusts. Except, if Bron's wisdom rang true, these pests had a mind of their own. The wyverns' possible sentience frightened her more than their fire breath or pin-sharp teeth.

Her thoughts wandered to dark places until the boy spoke again.

"Thank you for saving me, Danika."

"'Twas the least I could do. Remember, you saved me, too."

The carriage followed a winding road, crawling up a steep embankment. Moss brushed against the walls as if they rode through an old man's beard. Nip stuck his arm out and tugged on a wisp until the end came free, sending glitter motes across the velvet carriage seat.

"What's it made of?" He ran his fingers through the strands as they disintegrated with his touch.

"Magic and music." Danika caught a shimmer of glitter on the tip of her fingernail. "In the Forest of Song, they are one and the same."

Snippets of melodies rode the wind, accompanied by tinkling chords and a low humming buzz. Now and then one particular note would catch itself in her heart and she'd sigh, remembering days long past when her father took her hunting, or when her mother sang a lullaby.

The orchestra of sounds grew louder as they rode into the minstrels' domain until a mighty symphony pounded bass notes in the bottom of Danika's stomach. She glanced at Nip. Would he block his ears? But the boy listened carefully, as if each refrain held the answers to secrets he'd long sought.

The carriage rose from the mist of the forest and turned a bend.

"Whoa." Bron's voice echoed as a dissonance against the backdrop of harmonious sounds. The horses slowed, giving Danika and Nip time to take in the scene spread before them. Gabled cottages, nestled in long-stemmed grassy hills, shone pearly white in the rising moon.

When the carriage door squeaked open Danika expected Bron's paw-like palm and met Valorian instead. He offered a long-fingered hand to help her from the carriage. She slid her fingers into his, feeling his cool, soft skin.

"Follow me."

She eyed Bron as he untied the horses. He bowed his head in deference, failing to meet her eyes. A pang of guilt swept through her. How could she leave him to be a second hand? Valorian pulled her forward, and she had no choice but to leave Bron behind. Nip followed behind her and Bron took up the rear with both horses in tow.

Valorian led her past ivy-laced village gates. The cottages glowed warm honey light onto the pebble stone as the denizens prepared their evening meal. Every structure resonated with a different chord, each one more beautiful than the last. The plunk of a harpsichord accompanied their steps, followed by the trill of a flute and the swell of a fiddle. A solemn chant became a meandering melody and then turned into a lilting lullaby. Did the residents ever tire from making music? Surely they must sleep and allow silence to descend.

"Music protects this village," Valorian explained as if he'd heard her question. "We must churn out sound at all hours, each sentinel taking turns."

They followed the main thoroughfare to a domed cathedral at the town center. Crystal flutes hung from the ramparts, tinkling in the evening breeze. Once in a while, the wind hit the mouthpiece in the right angle, sounding a breathy note.

Danika had imagined the House of Song as a giant cottage, or a vast and insurmountable fortress. But now, seeing the legend for the first time, the House of Song couldn't possibly be anything besides a reverberating dome. The vault echoed the music like a massive speaker, resonating as each note careened through the lofty ceiling.

Diaphanous moonlight shone through the pinnacle of the glass dome, illuminating a throne made from bluewood sitting on a stage surrounded by feathers. On the throne sat a middle-aged man blowing scales on a wooden flute. As he played, sparrows flew in twirling arcs above his head.

Danika froze, unwilling to interrupt the tranquil scene, but Valorian gently pulled her forward. Eagerness shone in his metallic eyes, as if he'd introduce her as his new bride and not someone who'd trespassed in their forest.

The King of Song paused on a low note, the sound echoing before tapering off into the ceiling. The sparrows settled on rafters above his head as he turned to greet the odd procession. Bron had tied the horses to a lamppost near a gushing fountain where they could drink. He stood behind her and Valorian. The boy hid in their shadow.

"Father, may I introduce Danika Rubystone, Princess of Ebonvale, and her retinue."

Valorian turned to Danika, "And may I introduce to you, King Troubadir, my father."

King Troubadir set his wooden flute upon the throne's arm with a click. "This is a long anticipated meeting, dear Princess. Come, take a seat."

He gestured to a row of satin pillows circling a low table on the stage. Valorian led Danika up three marble steps. Releasing his arm, she adjusted her skirts and positioned herself on the nearest cushion. After she nodded to Bron and Nip, they did the same. Bron sat at the opposite end of the table, where he had the greatest tactical advantage should he need the use of his claymore. Nip stayed by her side, pleasing Danika more than words could say. Valorian lit several lanterns of painted glass and took a seat by his father.

A servant appeared, carrying a tray with steaming tea and an ale loaf. Nip whipped his hand out and fingered the largest piece. He stuffed his soot-streaked face until his cheeks stuck out. Danika watched the king's expression, ready to correct the boy, but the older man smiled. "Help yourselves. You've endured a long journey, no doubt."

Bron sniffed the tea and took a hesitant sip. He nodded to Danika before she lifted the ivory chalice to her lips. She inhaled the scent of wilderberries and tasted sweetness.

"Thank you, Your Highness, for such wondrous refreshment. Indeed, we've had a difficult journey. The wyverns have risen from the south, invading Shaletown, and I'm eager to return to my stronghold."

"Surely, you are." Troubadir sipped his tea and crumbled a piece of ale loaf in his fingertips. "My audience will not detain you at length. However, I suggest you stay the night at least. The Forest of Song is protected by enchantments, but some beasts roam free, undeterred."

Danika flicked her gaze over to Bron and the warrior nodded his acquiescence. She buttered a piece of ale loaf with a tiny silver knife. "So be it."

Troubadir's lips stretched into a pleasant smile. "My servants will arrange your chambers shortly." The smile faded as soon as it appeared. "Now, to discuss the urgent matters at hand. We are both aware of the uprising of wyverns, as proven by your witness of Shaletown's attack."

Danika glanced over at Nip but the remainder of the ale loaf distracted him.

"I do not wish to sit here and talk of the past." She raised her eyebrows, gesturing to the soot-covered boy.

"Of course. My mistake." He sipped his tea. "Let us talk of the future. I propose an alliance between Ebonvale and the House of Song."

Danika stiffened. Her father had warned her for years not to trust the song spinners. He had due cause for his concerns. They could change a person's mind with only a few plucked notes. Dabbling with the minstrels was akin to stoking a fire.

She narrowed her eyes. "With such superb defenses, why would you need our alliance?"

"Excellent question, Princess. Why, indeed?" He stroked his beard, the silver and gold strands catching the lantern light.

"We've lasted hundreds of years, sequestered within the bluewood forest with not as much as a skirmish with the wyverns. Our songs protect our village, much like the famous archers of Ebonvale."

The king waved over the nearest server and focused his attention on Nip. "Son, why don't you follow my friend, Mira. She can show you our collection of leather-bone drums."

"I'm fine here, sir." The boy crossed his arms. Troubadir cast a glance at Danika, but the princess didn't trust these minstrels. Better if the boy stayed with her. She shook her head.

"You are a brave boy." The king paused, placing a piece of ale loaf on a china plate, untouched. Each plate had five staff lines painted with dotted eighth notes across the rim. Which song did each plate hold? Did the un-played notes bless their food or taint it?

Troubadir sighed. "Our time of peace is at an end. Scouts have come from as far as Brimmore's Bay claiming stories of a massive Mother-Beast, a leviathan of the sky."

Nonsense. Danika shot a glance at Bron. The warrior leaned forward, eyes alert as if the king piqued his attention. Danika ruffled her dress, thinking. If Bron paid these ridiculous claims heed, then she'd sit still long enough to hear him out. She nodded for the king to continue.

"They say her tail spans the length of three warships, her wings spread the size of Shaletown's borders. Her neck alone stretches farther than any of these bluewoods."

Danika breathed in to contradict him, but he held up a long forefinger.

"Worse yet, one puff of her breath melts anything in its path within a mile's radius. Traders from Kilra claim the beast took out the city of Talis within heartbeats."

His gaze flickered around the shadows, as if the beast would spring from any lantern flame. "Her eggs gestate while we speak. She's building an army, a massive legion of sky worms capable of singeing this entire continent before any one of my minstrels could complete a stanza."

So quick to respond before, Danika could not summon a retort. His words stirred a sick current of bile in her stomach, and she regretted gulping down so much ale loaf. The boy sat in silence beside her. She should have sent him away with Mira.

"Do you have any proof of these claims?" Bron's muscles tensed.

Troubadir spread his arm across the china plates and crusts and gazed down, wearing a sad smile of inevitability.

"Holy Helena's Goblet." Danika fell backward and caught herself on her elbows.

Bron jumped up at the same time, and the boy sat wide-eyed, running his hands along the oily surface.

"This isn't a table," her voice croaked.

A surface of blue-black, as shiny as a marble and as thick as her leg, glittered with swirls of hidden colors when she tilted her head. They'd eaten their dinner on a single scale--a mere shedding from a mighty beast.

Troubadir wasted no time. "Our only hope is to travel to her isle and defeat her before she lays claim to this land."

Bron shifted, his leather tunic creaking like an old floor. "Swarms of wyverns with a giant mother-ass viper in charge--sounds like suicide to me."

Danika gasped in enough breath to recover a partial amount of her wits. "Our soldiers are not equipped to handle such fire. No armor can withstand such an onslaught."

"Pa's armor can." Nip's boyish voice resonated in the great dome.

Danika stared at him open-mouthed.

Nip stood, looking both proud and sad. "He was pounding a leg shin when the wyverns came."

"The breastplate." Danika nodded. "You wore a piece of armor when I first found you."

Nip swallowed hard. "I wanted Pa to wear it. I told him to, but he placed the breastplate over my head. As I tried to wiggle free, a puff of smoke pushed me backward into the wall. Ma screamed, then the roof came crashing in and everything became so hot, I feared my skin would melt."

Nip slumped down and Danika reached for him, pulling him against her. "You're here now. That's what matters."

"And it seems your father has found the answer." Troubadir bent down to meet the child's eyes.

"Where did he get the metal? How did he forge it?"

Shivering, the boy hid his face in Danika's skirts.

"Don't pester him," she snapped. "He's lost so much."

Valorian stepped in, putting a hand on her arm. "My apologies, Princess, but we must know, and we don't have much time."

An entire kingdom rested on the memories of a soot-streaked boy. Danika nodded, wiping away a stray tear on his cheek. She pulled Nip away and knelt in front of him, holding his shoulders in both hands. "Where did your father get the metal? Tell me his secret."

Nip's eyes shone bright with fear. He shook his head.

"Please, Nip. We need the answer now more than ever."

He whimpered. "Deep down in tunnels. The albinos traded the metal for rice."

"Darkenbite." Bron hissed under his breath and spat on the floor. "A damned and foul place."

"Do you think they have more of it?" Danika smoothed over his hair, ignoring Bron. "Do you think they'll still trade?"

Nip nodded, curls bobbing above his eyes.

"That settles it." Danika rose from the floor and met Troubadir's anxious gaze. "We'll need all the rice you can muster. We're traveling to Darkenbite at dawn's break to retrieve more of that precious metal. I'll employ every blacksmith in Ebonvale to pound it into armor. Once we're equipped, I'll send word to your minstrels. Together, we'll ride out over the Sea of Urchins and battle this untamed She-Beast with the greatest army ever to sail the fourteen seas."

She extended her hand to the king, hoping an army would be sufficient, hoping he didn't push for her hand to Valorian as well. "Deal?"

Troubadir raised his head, his thin nose pointing up.

Danika refused to allow herself a glance at Valorian. Who knew the kinds of thoughts smoldering in his head?

"You have yourself a bargain, Princess."

"Good. Please take us to your guest chambers. Nip is tired, and Bron needs his rest if he's to drive the carriage in the morning."

"Negotiations such as these can make anyone tired. Valorian, guide these kind people to their quarters."

"Most certainly, Father." Valorian gestured to the entranceway. "Follow me."

Danika reached for Nip's hand but he shrugged her away. She'd have to accept Valorian's arm instead. Slipping her fingers around his wrist, she allowed him to lead her into the night. Bron grumbled under his breath behind her as he and Nip followed. Danika resisted the urge to turn around and give him a look.

Did Darkenbite frustrate him? Or did he find Valorian's affections annoying?

Surely, he thought of Darkenbite. How could the Chief of Arms, appointed as her bodyguard by her father before his death, harbor feelings toward a princess? Seven years her elder and five ranks below her, he had as much of a chance as a prisoner in their dungeon cells. *Remember that.*

Danika breathed in slowly to calm herself. Long journeys such as these blurred the ranks, but they'd return to Ebonvale soon enough. Her throne and all the expectations along with it awaited her.

Valorian brought them to a pair of bluewood cottages set apart from the village, resting in a moonlit glade behind the domed House of Song. "The one on the right is for your counterparts. This one, over here is for you."

True to his position, Danika's bodyguard didn't budge. His dark shadow at her shoulder reassured her.

"Very well, then." Valorian slipped her hand into his and brought her fingers to his lips. His kiss fell soft on her skin. "Tomorrow then, Princess." He bowed to Bron and Nip. "Warrior, and son."

Valorian disappeared into the shadows while a lone flute trilled on the wind.

Bron bowed to Danika and turned to leave. "Come on, little dragon slayer. Best we get some rest."

The night seemed unfinished, like she'd struck a dissonant chord with no resolution. A sudden longing to speak with Bron came over her, as if the answering note lay with him. "Bron, wait."

He raised an eyebrow and gestured for Nip to go in without him. The boy scurried to the front porch and slipped in the door. Bron returned his attention to her.

"Yes, Princess?"

"Watch over the boy for me. I do not trust these minstrels. They could have something stuck up their velvety sleeves."

Bron grinned as though amused. "I was beginning to think you didn't need me anymore."

His words hit a chord in her heart and it vibrated along with the distant hum of song. Danika touched his arm and his skin burned hot under her fingertips. "I'll always need you."

They stood frozen while a musical phrase swelled and cadenced behind them. She'd said too much and not enough all at once and her emotions ran unbidden as if Troubadir had slipped wine into her tea. Bron's eyes shone dark with mystery, making her heart beat faster.

"Evening, Princess. We have quite a day ahead of us, and the night's running its course."

"Goodnight." Danika pulled away, embarrassed. She'd guessed wrong. Protection was not love. He was an exceptional bodyguard at most. Biting her lip, she strode to her cottage. Honestly, the more time she spent outside the castle walls, the less princess-like she became. Once this quest came to an end, she'd have to find an appropriate suitor, and Valorian ranked highest on the list.

Cursing her strange emotions, Danika opened her cottage door. She glanced over her shoulder, expecting Bron to have disappeared inside. He stood underneath the moss-draped gable, watching her in return.

Chapter 3

Wyvern's Breath

Bron guarded Danika's retreat to her cottage, her skirts kissing the blades of grass with each delicate step. Her elegance in awkward situations always impressed him, and she'd handled herself like a queen in the negotiations. Her father would have been proud, and Bron was proud as well. She'd grown into a regal woman with a flair for battle and a spitfire tongue. If only his feelings ended with thoughts of protection and pride.

Danika paused on the gabled porch and turned toward him, as if she heard his secrets on the wind. Her meadow-green gaze brought goosebumps to his skin. A sheer vulnerability weakened him until his legs felt like porridge. He was a veteran warrior, for Horred's sake. He'd scaled the Fortress of Angst singlehandedly and defeated the dead army of Sill. Now a woman's gaze threatened to bring him to his knees?

He didn't think she'd look back. She shouldn't.

Bron couldn't break her gaze. He had to make sure Danika entered the cottage safely. Besides, looking away would reveal too much. He nodded slightly, as if he'd meant for her to catch him staring. Danika tore her gaze away and disappeared inside.

He exhaled slowly, calming his nerves. The minstrels' music taunted him, reminding him of the circus he'd visited with his brother, Hule, on Festival Day. The jesters had leered at him, the bells on their three-pointed hats tinkling as they danced and pounded on drums. They made everything in life a mockery, and their disrespect churned his stomach. The Man of Muscles had earned his admiration. He'd lifted a wheel barrel holding two goats over his head. Bron had wanted to be that man, and here he stood now, guarding a princess as the Chief of Arms.

If only he hadn't failed her. The memory of the battlefield left a scar on his heart far greater than the one on his right cheek. The deep tones of a bass lute mirrored his regret. Bron pushed the uncomfortable memories from his thoughts, refusing to play into the song's desperate notes. Music played slippery tricks on his mind, whereas steel made an honest and clean cut. No, this time he wouldn't fail, even if it meant protecting her from himself. Bron smoothed his fingers over the pummel of his claymore, the golden etching hard underneath his callouses like a forgotten language. He skimmed the night and slipped into the cottage without a sound.

Nip sat upright in bed, straight as a broomstick. He hadn't even unlaced his boots.

"Cannot sleep?"

"I want to see it." Nip locked on his eyes, his small mouth set tight.

Bron still reeled from the encounter outside. He collapsed on the cot and pulled off a boot, massaging the sole of his foot. "See what?"

"The wyvern snout. The one you killed."

The warrior paused and rubbed a hand over his shaved head. Tiny prickles of hair dusted the skin, and he needed time with his dagger and a bowl of water. But the lad seemed determined.

"Won't it give you nightmares?"

"I already have 'em." Nip stood and smoothed over his soot-stained tunic. "It'll make 'em go away."

"It's not a pretty thing, child."

Nip's voice rose and he stomped his foot. "I'm not a child. Not anymore."

Bron raised an eyebrow. Surviving the scene that morning would make a man out of a duckling. The boy had a point. But to lay eyes on the dead beast's head so soon after the attack?

"It's late. How about we take a look in the morning?"

Nip swallowed. "I have to see with my own eyes what killed my parents." His chin trembled.

Bron scanned him from the ratty hair on his head to his scuffed boots. Did a hint of warrior shine in those sky blue eyes?

"Troubadir was right about one thing. You are brave." Bron pulled his boot back on. "Come. Let's meet this beast eye to eye."

They skirted the House of Song, careful not to make a sound. Clinking chimes covered their footsteps. The minstrels' music had taken an introspective turn, and a sprinkle of minimalistic notes drifted over droning chords. The denizens had snuffed out most of their golden lights, and the moon lighted the path.

The carriage lay where he'd left it, parked next to the gates of the village. Bron reached down and fingered the tarp covering his latest conquest. The fabric still emanated heat, warming his fingertips in the cool mist. Bron shot a glance at the boy. Nip nodded in determination. The warrior tugged and the tarp slipped off.

A snout three times bigger than a dog's and littered with ivory white teeth snarled out from the carriage's backside. Onyx eyes glared in the moonlight, defying death. Two horns spiraled backward from a ridge of fin-like protrusions.

Nip froze as sulfurous steam from the beast's mouth pooled around his boots. It would take days for the head to cool and the smoke to dissipate.

The stark fear in his expression reminded Bron of himself as a boy. His brother had paid a shiny copper for each of them to look upon a caged harpy. Walking to the curtained bars, he could still remember the musky scent and hear the squeaking of its claws on the planks. At ten, he'd needed Hule's cajoling to get him to open his eyes. When he did, the black-feathered beast seemed more prey than predator. Ever since that day, he knew fear lay in anticipation.

Bron nudged the boy forward gently as a clammy tang, like old seaweed drying in the sun for too long, wafted up. "Don't be afraid."

"Burrow's Bucket! It stinks." Nip covered his mouth with his sleeve.

Bron shook his head. "Remember that smell. Get used to it. 'Tis the reek of death."

Blue-black blood trickled from thorny whiskers, sizzling a hole in the grass. Nip reached out, his fingers brushing over the oily scales. He shuddered, managing to uphold his stance. A scale the size of his hand stuck out from the weave and the boy yanked it off. Bron caught him as he fell backward.

Nip jumped from his arms and stood on his own. He ran his fingertips over the smooth seashell-like surface of the scale as if touching the feather of a god. Stepping back into the shadows, Bron allowed him time to think, to mourn.

"I promise, Ma and Pa, to right this wrong." The boy's eyes watered, and he swiped at them with the back of his hand. His face grew fierce as he held the scale above his head, challenging the night. "Vengeance is mine."

Chapter 4

Break of Dawn

Golden sunlight direct from the heavens refracted within a chain of silver armor. Each soldier gleamed like a Knights and Wizards *game-piece polished to perfection. Danika observed the processional from her balcony, waving her mother's satin scarf in the breeze in tribute. Her father wouldn't approve of her using anything from her mother's untouched room, never mind the fine scarf he'd given the former queen as a token of his undying love. But, it seemed wasteful to let such finery collect dust. Besides, it was all she had of her mother. The former queen had left her with little else. Now, she might lose her father, too. Watery melancholy and deep angst bled together in her heart, creating a whirlpool of anxiety. Why couldn't he stay on his throne?*

She knew him too well to plead. If the dead army of Sill breached their northern expanses, only fields separated the insidious evil from blighting their lands. This mission ranked too high to trust with his generals, and he never watched the action from afar.

King Artemus led the army on his ebony war stallion, flanked by flag holders on either side. Behind him, Bron rode a dove-white charger. A gilded helmet covered his bald head, but Danika recognized the width of his shoulders and the swell of the armor fitted to his muscles. At least Bron would keep him safe.

A nagging concern pressed on her chest, squeezing out her breath. Her fingertips loosened and the scarf fluttered away in the wind. Hadn't this scene happened before? A memory of her father's bluewood coffin draped in Ebonvale's violet-and-green pennants drifted through her mind.

"No."

Her attendants shrieked as she pushed herself through the back row and plunged down the stairs in the tower. Her heel caught on the rug and she kicked off her beaded sandal, sprinting three steps at a time.

"My lady, wait! Come back!" Muriel, her lady-in-waiting, screamed just as Danika flung open the door and met the crowd.

A pang of guilt rolled through her. Muriel was like a sister and to leave her worrying was cruel. Yet, she had to stop her father before he made the mistake that would cost him his life.

People crowded around her, tugging on her lacy clothes. She pushed through the throng of onlookers. "Let me through!"

Elbowing two men as big as bears, she tore herself away from groping hands. A circle of milk-maids leaned over the main road, dropping roses at the soldiers' feet. She squeezed through, stepping on their offerings. An old man placed his cane on the trail of her gown and she ripped her underskirt, kicking the fabric free. When she turned back, a poor chimneysweep, covered in ash, dove for the rich lace.

Danika emerged from the crowd, stumbling onto the pebble stone of the main thoroughfare. She jogged alongside the marching army. Ignoring the soldiers' questioning looks and hoots, she picked up her pace. The brigade went on and on in an endless line. Would she ever find the lead? Their pace quickened and she panted as she struggled to keep up. What if her father had already kicked his horse into a gallop? The hills of Mealee rose before her like the fuzzy backs of giants, and Sill's blackened gates lay just beyond.

Gravel tore the skin of her bare foot and blood ran, warm and sticky, through her toes. Bron's helmet rose a head taller from the ranks and she quickened her pace, her lungs burning raw.

"Father!"

Bron turned in his saddle but she paid him no heed. Danika focused on the golden-etched armor in the lead, as if staring could bore a hole into his back.

"Father, stop!"

A gilded lion's head turned toward her. The visor snapped open and her father's rigid face peeked through. He looked both majestic and timeworn, his sharp features decorated by webs of wrinkles.

Danika tripped and fell to her knees.

Her father tugged his reins and his black horse turned full circle, interrupting the ranks. The soldiers eddied around him like river waves parting before a stone. He dismounted and rushed to her side. His armor chinked as he knelt beside her and laid a hand on her arm. "Why have you left your attendants?"

Time suffocated her, pressing in on all sides. She knew she had only moments before the past replayed the chain of events leading to his demise.

"You'll die in this battle." Her words tainted her tongue.

His eyes were steady, his features as calm as if he knew what his future held. "You must let me go."

"No."

Soldiers marched around them like puppets of fate, their boots stomping the ground in rhythm with her racing heart. King Artemus' voice grew faint. "You're the ruler of Ebonvale now."

She shook her head. "I'm not ready."

"As the woman of the manor, you've been ready for many years."

His armor reflected the sun's rays, blinding her.

She fell back, shielding her eyes. "I need you. The castle is under siege once again."

He stood, gathering his horse's reins in his hands. "You know what to do. Follow your instincts. The answers lie in front of you. All you have to do is pay attention."

He pulled away, leaving Danika on the pebble stones. A horn blasted through the air, the intervals signaling the call to arms. The army surged around her, hoof-beats and footsteps speeding into a blur of movement on all sides.

Emptiness consumed her, her body fell in on itself until it was as though she'd shrivel up like a dead flower. Her father had taken a part of her with him. Would she ever again feel complete?

"Princess." Bron's bass voice broke though the pattering of hooves and feet. "Princess, if you don't come out, I'll have to break in."

Come out where? Danika scanned the crowd. The bodies ran together in a blur of strangers.

"Princess!"

Danika shot upright in bed. Sunlight streamed in through transparent curtains. A loud knock came at her door.

The bluewood muffled Bron's voice. "What if she's not in there? What if the minstrels stole her away? I'm breaking the door in."

"No!" Danika stumbled from the bed, her legs catching on the sheets. She kicked the satin off and stumbled forward. A broken door would only stir up animosity in her newly formed alliance. She turned the handle and whipped the wood back just as Bron held up the blunt end of his claymore.

"Princess?" Bron's eyes widened in surprise. He looked away, sheathing his sword. Nip stood by him, holding his own makeshift wooden weapon.

Danika realized she wore only her underdress. The lacy trim barely covered the swell of her breasts and the wind blew the hem up past her knees. Goosebumps prickled her ivory skin, but her cheeks burned as hot as blood. Trying to regain her composure, she stood up straight as if she wore a full-length gown. "I'm quite all right."

"I can see that." Did Bron's cheeks redden underneath his tan? "We were afraid the minstrels took you away."

"No. I simply overslept."

The remnants of her wretched dream seized her. Why did she always dream of her father?

Bron spoke into the door instead of meeting her gaze, as if looking upon her committed a crime. "The minstrels have arranged for five bushels of rice. We can fit the load in the carriage if you and Nip ride alongside."

"Nip cannot come with us. It's too dangerous for a boy."

Bron grinned as if he'd lost the argument already. "You tell him that."

Danika put her hands on her hips and glared at Nip. The boy clutched his mini-sword in his hand, swinging the blade at thin air. "I can too. You need me to find the albinos. Besides, I know how to barter."

"And how would a young boy who cannot even comb his hair know all this?" Danika raised her brow. She could sniff the stench of a tall tale from the truth.

Nip held his head up high, even though his curly head of hair only came to Danika's silken waist. He sheathed his sword in a loop at his side. "My father told me tales of Darkenbite."

Danika glanced at Bron and tweaked a questioning eyebrow.

The warrior shrugged. "He provided an accurate description of the stalagmites. In other words, he speaks the truth, Princess."

She paused, ruminating over the lesser of two evils. Either leave him with the minstrels, or take him with her to Darkenbite. Both ways presented problems, including possible ransom or the unknown dangers of the caverns. Who knew how well the minstrels would look after him? If they didn't hold him prisoner, they might just allow him to wander off. If Danika brought Nip with her, at least she'd have him in her sights.

"All right, but you answer to me, you hear?" Danika pressed him as if her edict as High Princess had no clout in a boy's eyes.

Nip nodded eagerly, his hair falling into his face. "Right."

"We'll have to get you a haircut along the way."

Nip froze in terror and Bron smiled, running a hand through his floppy hair. "I'll see what I can do, Princess. In the meantime, we'll take our leave to allow you time to change. The weather's cool today, like the gods have turned their backs on us."

"Let them. We don't need their help." Danika bluffed and slapped her nightshift down against the wind. Honestly, her attendants would have a heart attack if they saw her now.

Bron bowed, pulling the boy away. "Come, gallant knight. Let's see what these lute players eat for breakfast."

"Yes, sir." Nip bowed and winked at Danika before skipping to join him.

Chapter 5

Party of Four

A light jig danced on the wind as Danika approached the carriage. She wanted to scream for the song to stop. Not only had she listened to enough music, the playful tones mocked the gravity of the journey ahead. If only she could find the source of the tune, she'd bash in that particular player's lute.

When she arrived, Bron had loaded most of the bags of rice, filling both passenger seats and the underside of the carriage where he'd stored the wyvern's head. He'd already hooked up their horses, and Nip sat in the driver's seat, pretending to whip the reins.

"What about your war trophy? You cannot leave a good wyvern head behind." Danika smiled.

"I gave it to the minstrels." Bron heaved the last bag of rice into the carriage. It plopped on top of the velvety seats, stirring up moss dust. He turned and winked. "Maybe King Troubadir will make another table."

"A horrid table indeed." Danika rolled her eyes. "I cannot even imagine."

"Maybe you can discuss it with him now." Bron gestured over her shoulder.

King Troubadir had arrived, flanked by three minstrels on either side. Their long cloaks brushed the tall grasses behind them. They were dressed in formal robes, flutes hung from silver cords around their waists. Not one of them carried a lute. Valorian hadn't come.

His absence surprised her. Why wouldn't the prince bid them farewell on their journey? Maybe his affections didn't run as deep as she thought. A newfound sense of freedom from obligation poured over her, but an underlying current of disappointment irked her as well. Did no man seek her attentions?

"Good morning, Princess Danika." Troubadir smiled and extended his hand. Danika bowed before him, taking his hand in hers.

"I trust your quarters provided sufficient rest and relaxation."

Behind her, Bron grunted and spoke under his breath, "Maybe a little too much."

Danika cleared her throat to silence him. She didn't need him reminding her of her lay-about late morning nap. She blamed her exhaustion on the previous day's terrors.

"Yes, my cottage exceeded my expectations, indeed." She released his hand, eager to be rid of it.

The king curled his delicate fingers around a crystal flute as if from habit. "Wonderful. As you can see, I've provided more than enough rice."

"My thanks, Your Highness." Danika counted the horses. They needed all four to pull the carriage. Where were her and Nip's mounts?

"Excuse me for a moment, Your Highness." She bowed and strode over to Bron.

He busied himself cleaning the horses' hooves with a silver pick. He glanced over his shoulder. "Yes, Princess?"

"Where are the rest of the horses?"

Bron shrugged. "The king said he'd see to it."

"Doesn't look like he's seen to anything with four legs." Danika huffed and crossed her arms. Time slipped through her fingers and she couldn't wait around for forgetful minstrels. Did they plan to keep her waiting until her kingdom fell to ruin?

Bron straightened, meeting her eye. "Do you want me to talk with him?"

"No. I'll straighten out our arrangements."

"Hi-ya, great stallions, on to battle!" Nip shouted from behind them.

Bron chuckled, "Looks like we have the makings of a great warrior in our midst."

Danika rolled her eyes. "One is enough for me."

"Is it, now?" Bron's gaze darkened.

Did he ask if *he* was enough? The air between them sizzled with anticipation. She studied the curve of his lips, ending with the scar trailing up to his cheek. If only she could reach out and trace the vulnerable skin. Maybe then, she'd touch his soul and guess the thoughts lingering in his head.

Hoof-beats pounded the earth, coming from the village behind them. Danika ripped her gaze away from his unwavering stare. Valorian rode in on a spotted stallion, trailing three auburn horses. He dismounted in a swift arc and led the horses to her side. "Morning, Princess Danika. I've brought you the finest steeds the House of Song has to offer."

He'd already saddled the horses with fine leather and jeweled reins. Their coats gleamed in a flawless shine.

Danika couldn't hide the awe in her voice. "Thank you, Prince Valorian."

"My pleasure." He flashed a smile, silvery eyes catching the sun like an upraised sword.

Danika blinked, trying not to be too mesmerized.

"Can we proceed with this journey?" Bron grumbled. "I doubt the She-Beast waits for tardy warriors."

"Of course." Valorian handed the princess a set of reins, his fingers closing over hers.

Heat traveled from his gentle grip to her face. She looked away. "I have to summon Nip."

He released his hold. "By all means."

She thought she'd have to bargain with Nip to get him out of Bron's seat, but the boy jumped from the carriage and saluted Valorian with a wave.

"Here you are, valiant knight." Valorian hoisted him on his mount and handed him the reins.

"Thank you, sir." Nip settled in the saddle, looking like a toddler on a warhorse.

Danika grew nervous, doubting her decision to have the boy tag along. "You do know how to ride a horse, don't you?"

Nip fumbled with the reins. "Yeah. We had a pet mule named Gracy. I used to ride her in town all the time."

"Excellent practice." Valorian nodded, leading the beast forward.

Danika flared her eyes at the prince in warning and shook her head. "Nip, secure a good hold. The fall to the ground is much farther than from a mule's back."

"I'll make sure he's riding straight." Valorian released his grip and watched Nip steer the first few paces on his own.

Danika opened her mouth to ask how he'd protect Nip all the way from the House of Song when she noticed a travel bag with a goat's stomach strapped on his horse. He wore a different cloak than the others, too, the velvety fabric replaced with smooth, black leather. He meant to travel with them.

"We have no need for your assistance, I assure you, Prince."

"The fate of both our kingdoms dangles on the backs of a princess, her bodyguard and a small boy. Surely, one more hand will aid your quest. Especially a minstrel for protection."

Her mouth tightened with a retort as Valorian swept his arm to the carriage. "Bron can lift an ox, no doubt. Four bags of rice, however, will constrain him, especially when he's supposed to be offering his protection. What if the albinos decide you are a better meal than all that rice?"

"Bron?" Danika questioned him with a glare.

Bron threw the silver pick near his travel bag on his seat. He gave the carriage a long look before answering. He scratched his head. "He's right. If I carry the rice all by myself, I'll be incapacitated. I could take two or three trips wielding my claymore, but time is of the essence, and we still have to lug all the metal back if they'll trade."

Looking at Valorian's long branch-like arms, she doubted he could carry even one bag. Anger mustered inside her and she fought to keep her tongue in check. She didn't want to be babysat by a minstrel. He'd spy on them all the way there. Not to mention the fact he had a certain power over her, no doubt resulting from his magic charms.

Bron walked over to her and offered his arm, "Princess, if we may speak in private?"

"Of course." She glanced at Valorian and King Troubadir. "I'll just be a moment."

Valorian bowed. "Take all the time you need."

She slipped her hand over Bron's round bicep and followed him to a glade beyond the line of bluewoods. A lark trilled above them and flew to a higher perch in the shadows. Danika shot the bird a skeptical eye. Who knew what form of spies lurked in these woods?

She settled on an outcropping of granite. Her fingers shook from rage. So many plans had gone askew these past days. Her father would shun her if he knew she'd allied with the minstrels and yet, even her risky alliance might not be enough to save the kingdom. Now the prince would ride by her side? She closed her eyes to calm herself, the sun warming her skin. When she opened them again, Bron stood across from her, patient as a great bluewood.

Danika swallowed. "You wished to speak with me?"

"Princess, you know I advised your father on war tactics, among other things."

"Yes, and he didn't always listen, did he?" Her voice wavered, thinking back to the day on the battlefield, the day she'd lost him. She hadn't truly forgiven Bron for accepting the king's orders. Bron should have rebelled and protected her father, but then they might have lost the war, and she wouldn't be sitting in the sunlight today. Fate twisted in a circular loop, making her mind spin. She pushed those thoughts of the battle away. She must work with what she had now and not dwell on the past.

Bron breathed in as if she'd stuck his gut with the tip of a sword. "Do you trust me?"

"More than anyone in the world." Her answer flung out of her mouth before she gave it a thought.

Bron's eyes widened. His tone softened. "Then, hear me out."

Danika crossed her arms, long sleeves folding in on themselves. "Very well."

"The prince speaks the truth. As much as I don't like his scrawny velvet-clad ass, I'm not going to put you or Nip in danger for my own prejudices, or yours, for that matter."

She tried to look away but he kept her gaze as if he knew her too well. A vision of her mother's formal veil flitted through her mind. She clutched the memory and tossed it away.

"You have to think rationally, Princess. One more hand or voice, I should say, against the beasts of the forest, the albinos in the cave and the wyverns in the sky, makes sense. Besides, we cannot snub King Troubadir after he provided all that rice. You're sabotaging your own alliance."

"I understand." Danika played with a stray thread from her dress. "I do allow my prejudices to intervene."

"As would any human." Bron stepped forward until he stood within an arm's reach. He moved his hand and his fingers twitched in the open air between them as if they yearned to touch her. His face softened and he licked his thick lips. He pulled his hand back, resting the palm on his hilt. "'Tis what makes you a compassionate ruler."

"Like I said before, flattery will get you nowhere." Despite her stern tone, she gazed at him and smiled. "I've considered your counsel and have decided to allow the prince to accompany us."

He bowed his head. "Your wishes are my commands."

"I'm not sure who is commanding who right now." She held out her arm. "Escort me to the carriage. We have a long journey ahead of us, and the sooner we get on with it, the sooner we'll be rid of him."

Bron's voice turned melancholy. "I hope you speak the truth."

* * * *

Amber sunlight trickled through the canopy, lighting their path. The bluewoods gave way to towering pines, and their horses' hooves stirred up needles and cones instead of leaves. The air turned from a humid bath to a refreshing cool breeze as the northern winds picked up. Danika rode with Valorian in the lead. Behind them, Bron drove the carriage with Nip's horse tied alongside. Nip sat beside him, sharpening his wooden sword. She hoped he wouldn't have to use it.

Danika's cheeks burned, and it wasn't from the patchy rays of sun. Valorian stole glances from across the trail as he matched her horse's gait. She forced herself to ignore him, lest he capture her eye and hold her gaze until she rode into a tree.

Minstrel's magic, 'tis all it was.

But, he hadn't sung a note.

By midday, her bowed legs ached and her stomach grumbled. The tang of wet minerals hovered in the air and she drew back on the reins. Her horse slowed, puffing hot air from its nostrils. Valorian mirrored her move like a skilled horseman, following every step. He pulled by her side, his long, angular face drawn with concern. "Something amiss, dear Princess?"

"No. We should take a break. It's a long journey and I don't want to tire out our horses too soon." She refused to speak of the pain in her rear or her parched throat. She'd spent too long cooped up in her castle, making her body weak.

Valorian nodded. "Very well." He dismounted in a smooth arc, his boots landing silently in the undergrowth. He'd tied his silky hair back in a loose ponytail, and a glint of sunlight caught the auburn strands, bringing out the amber highlights. He offered his hand.

She could push Bron's hand away whenever she liked, but to refuse the prince of the House of Song tempted war. Danika slid her gloved hand in his. He gripped her fingers as she swung her leg over her mount and landed beside him, a little too close. The change from the horse's back to the soft undergrowth caught her off balance, and she fell forward, her hands resting on the richly embroidered crimson vest across his chest.

His breath caressed her cheek. "You are an excellent rider, my lady."

She stepped back and turned to her saddlebag to hide the flaming heat in her cheeks and neck. She retrieved her sheepskin and held the spout to her lips, the cool water sliding down her throat. "I thought a rider's eyes are trained to look ahead."

"How can one ignore such elegance and grace?"

She sniffed. How much stock could she put in his honey-laced tongue? "I've trained to ride like a warrior since I was sixteen."

"You must have had an expert teacher."

Just as Valorian spoke, the carriage rounded the bend in the trail and Bron shouted to the horses. "Whoa! Hold back."

The sight of Bron brought Danika relief, and she relaxed her shoulders and curved her lips in a small, secret smile. "I did."

Valorian's perfect arched eyebrows rose as if he missed a jest. Bron pulled alongside them and the carriage creaked to a halt. The warrior nodded at Danika and gave Valorian a skeptical glance as if his skinny minstrel ass couldn't handle the long journey. "What's the reason for the delay?"

"I smell a stream." Danika gestured to the east. Why did she feel the need to step in and defend Valorian against Bron? He was a grown man, and music supposedly ranked more powerful than steel. He could defend himself. "We can refill our water rations. Our horses need a break."

"As you wish, Princess." Bron jumped from the carriage seat, his leather boots stomping the ground in a mini earthquake.

Nip waved his arms impatiently. "Me, too."

Bron lifted the boy from the carriage and set him down beside him. Nip ran to the side of the trail and began swiping the ferns with his sword.

The trees rustled around them, boughs bending to the will of the wind. Danika had never traveled this far north. The forests surrounding Ebonvale had fluffy topped saplings compared to these ancient pines. Danika felt like a porcelain doll.

Bron scanned the area. "We need to hide the carriage and horses."

"Save your strength, man of steel." Valorian chuckled. "My father's rice wouldn't fetch one silver coin on the black market."

Bron crossed his arms, his leather jerkin creaking. "Yes, but a ransomed prince or princess would bring the house down."

Danika didn't know if Bron meant any house or the House of Song. Whatever the intention, Valorian didn't appreciate the jab, or maybe the thought of being an object to pillage. He straightened the sharp collar of his lined riding coat, his silver eyes steeling. "I wouldn't allow anyone to touch the princess."

"Anyone?" Bron stepped toward him with playfulness in his eyes. "Even a sweet-talking, lute-strumming…"

Valorian stepped forward, his long fingers tightened around his lute strap, as if the instrument were a weapon. "Are you inferring a prince from the House of Song would compromise a woman's honor?"

Bron harrumphed. "It's happened in the past."

"Our music doesn't fabricate love. Our songs bring out the true shape of the heart."

Bron growled, stepping toward him. "You're saying our queen had the heart of a betrayer?"

Valorian held his ground, calm and rational. "I'm saying she chose her place."

Emotions whirled in Danika's chest and she shoved them down before they overwhelmed her. The time to argue about her mother's loyalty had passed long ago. If Bron and Valorian continued at this rate, they'd kill each other before they reached Darkenbite.

She grabbed Bron's arm. "Over here. There's a hidden outcropping."

"Saved by the princess." Bron snarled at Valorian and turned to Danika. "I don't care what this minstrel says. We should conceal our trespassing."

The whispering trees sent shivers up her spine. She wasn't about to argue. "You're the bodyguard."

They steered the carriage off the trail and made camp uphill from the road where they could spot any passing travelers. Valorian unlatched a bag of fruit and passed a sweet peach each to Nip and Danika. Bron refused, chewing on jerky.

The warrior said nothing. Danika leaned forward, swallowing a mouthful of sweet peach juice. "How did King Troubadir acquire such a massive scale?"

Valorian had finished eating and swung his lute over his shoulder to rest against his flat stomach that could or could not contain chiseled abs. Danika didn't need to know.

He strummed a tentative chord. "The table?"

Danika nodded, leaning on the trunk of a massive black pine. The cool, mossy bark soothed her aching back.

His fingertips plucked a series of melancholy notes. Two high chimes then a low bass drone. "Traders from Brimmore's Bay brought the scale in. They said the monstrosity washed up on their shores."

"Makes sense with the tide rushing up from Scalehaven." Danika ran her tongue over her front teeth, still tasting sugar. "Have you talked with anyone who's actually seen the She-Beast?"

Tension grew in Valorian's melody. "No one has seen her up close and lived to tell the tale. The reports come from witnesses on the shore. They see the worm's writhing outline on the horizon. They say her body resembles a corkscrew unfurling infinitely long, cutting the sky in half."

Danika refused to let fear in. Village bumpkins were known to exaggerate their accounts. "And how do you plan to vanquish her?"

Valorian struck a dissonant note and the lute rang throughout the woods. "I have reason to believe these fire worms are intelligent, and if they are, my minstrels will find a way to use our songs to quell their raging breath. But, our music cannot kill. Our songs open one's heart to the emotions residing within." He gazed at Bron. "I'll need your bodyguard's steel to strike her when her guard is down."

The note dissipated into silence. Danika nodded. "'Tis a good plan."

Bron shifted his weight, stretching his massive legs across the pine needles. "Only if the She-Beast and her kin can understand the music's meaning."

His song finished, Valorian strapped his lute to his back. "Music is a universal language understood by all."

Bron unsheathed his dagger and used the tip to clean his teeth. "What if these fireworms don't care for music?"

Valorian smiled like he'd won the game. "Everyone cares for music, even a newborn baby or an elder too old to remember anything else. The trick is finding the right chords to strike to find their innermost desires and open their heart. All I need is the protection to get near enough for my music to reach these fireworms' scaly ears."

Bron sheathed his dagger. "Consider it done."

A foul wind tickled Danika's nose and she covered her face with her sleeve.

Valorian stood. "It seems my song of warning has been ignored."

Bron took a deep whiff, his dark eyes staring at the trees in a menacing challenge.

"What is the meaning of this ill-fated breeze?" Danika pulled Nip to her side.

"Grab the horses and prepare the carriage." Bron drew out his claymore. The steel reflected the dark silhouettes of the pines, framed with patches of shadows. "We're being followed."

Chapter 6

A Perceptive Boy

They rode as swift as the wind blowing across the sea and silent as an unspoken secret. As a farmer's son, Bron's experience lay in hauling heavy shipments in carriages, and he knew the maximum speed of the horses and the berth the wheels needed for each bend in the trail. When they'd rested, he'd rubbed woodwork oil on the joints to keep the wheels from creaking like toads in the bog.

Bron kept checking over his shoulder but the forest refused to surrender its secrets. Since camp, the air held no trace of hunters. They rode into the wind, and anything trailing them would have the advantage. Bron had only smelled that redolent stench once in his life, and that time it meant trouble. So, why did he wonder if he'd suffered from some paranoid delusion?

It was because the princess' life hung in the balance, and he did not-- would not--fail again. Even if it meant he played the fool.

Valorian had made a jest of his urge to hide the carriage, and surely the pretentious minstrel thought Bron's assumption of someone, or something, hunting them to be superfluous as well.

God's willing, the long-haired pretty boy was right.

Bron would rather be proven wrong by Valorian than have anything or anyone endanger the mission.

Valorian rode side by side with the princess, like two love birds acquainting themselves. A thorn twisted in Bron's side, and he did what he did best: ignored the pain. Ushering Danika into Valorian's arms was the right move for the kingdom, and if everything the minstrel said rang true, his hand in marriage would keep her and Ebonvale safe.

So, why did seeing her with Valorian irk him so?

The memories of the past surged like ghosts, peering over his shoulder. Even now, he felt King Artemus' pain. Bron couldn't protect him from heartache.

The warrior sighed. This was an entirely different situation. Danika wasn't married or even promised to anyone else. She was free to give her hand to whomever she chose. Or whomever provided Ebonvale with the best protection.

They passed under an overhanging bough and Bron ducked, pulling Nip down with him. Just in case. Needles rained on top of them, prickling Bron's neck as they brushed the lowest branch.

"Horred's Temple! That was close." Nip's eyes widened as he turned back to see the branch whipping in the air.

Bron ruffled the boy's hair, threading out the needles with his awkward sausage-thick fingers, better for wielding a weapon than a gentle caress. Then he swiped his own neck. "Where does a boy your age learn such language?" If he'd spoken that curse in his house, his father would have stuffed soap in his mouth.

Nip shrugged. "Pill."

Bron raised an eyebrow in question.

"My older brother."

"Of course." No other name would complement Nip's so well. Bron wondered where potty-mouthed Pill was now then remembered the blackened village they'd left behind. He thought of Hule and thanked Helena his brother lived safely in Oaten's Dell, looking after their aging parents. Fate had been kind to Bron, and he should be more thankful instead of dwelling on unattainable quests.

Nip tugged on Bron's pinky finger. "Are you thinking about the princess?"

Bron blinked and straightened as if Nip had splashed cold water up his nose. "Why do you ask?"

"Because you have the same expression on your face Pa had when Ma was angry with him and he couldn't do anything about it."

Nip's comment amused him. Bron's lips curved into a smile. "Do you think the princess is angry with me?"

Nip shrugged and picked at a splinter in his sword. "Like Pa used to say." His little voice grew grumbly, as if mimicking an older man's. "If she wasn't mad sometimes, she wouldn't care."

"Care about what?" The conversation had shifted into strange territory and an uneasy feeling crawled across Bron's shoulders.

Nip flicked the splinter into the trees. "'Bout you."

Chapter 7

Horn of the Undead

Day gave way to shadowy twilight, and the forest grew dark with lurking threats.

Danika's horse heaved underneath her. Although the minstrels had lent her a fine stead, the stallion slowed with fatigue. Valorian's horse slackened as well, struggling to keep pace in the patches of filtering moonlight. Even Nip's horse dragged its hooves and he had hardly ridden the beast all day.

Surely, whoever followed them couldn't have tracked them this far. Even so, staying to fight would give their horses much needed rest. Either way they'd have to confront their pursuers. Running made Danika feel like a fugitive. She pulled back on the reins as they broke through into a clearing where the white moon illuminated the glade. "Enough."

Valorian followed her lead. He jumped from his horse and offered the stallion water from his sheepskin.

Danika sniffed and pulled up by his side. "The air smells clear."

He held the sheepskin to her horse's steaming muzzle. "You forget we are upwind."

Valorian slid his hand into a secret pocket in his vest and brought out a dagger with an ivory hilt carved with the same spirals that decorated his lute. He handed her the silvery blade. "Be careful."

She had her long sword, but she wasn't about to refuse another weapon. "Thank you." Danika slipped the blade into her boot. Why would a minstrel carry such a weapon? She thought music was all they needed for protection.

Bron caught up and the carriage rumbled to a halt. He leapt from his seat as if he'd awaited this moment all day.

Danika rushed to him, drawn to his strength. "Are they gone?"

A flock of starlings took flight from the forest behind them. All eyes turned toward the darkness between the trees. Bron shrugged. "Better to be safe than slayed. We'll set up a perimeter defense using the carriage and the bags of rice."

Valorian lit torches as Bron stacked the bags against the carriage on either side. Danika grabbed Nip's sword as he swung the blade at the low-hanging branch of a tree. "Get in the carriage and stay there until morning."

"I want to fight." Nip pouted with his lower lip jutting out. He looked so adorable, she had a hard time saying no.

"We need to keep you safe so you can lead us to Darkenbite. Remember, you're our guide."

"I cannot leave Thunderhooves unguarded." Nip struggled to cross his arms and hold his sword.

Danika furrowed her brow. "Who?"

"The boy's horse." Bron unsheathed his claymore and swung the blade in an arc over his head, stretching his muscles.

"I named him myself." Nip stared at her as if she would deny him the ridiculous name. She almost did. He hadn't spent more than half the day on the saddle before he lost interest and wanted to fiddle with his sword. Now he'd give his life for the beast? More likely he used the horse as an excuse.

Danika smoothed the wild hair on the boy's head. "Thunderhooves will be fine with the other horses. This is no place for a little boy, no matter how courageous."

Nip bit his lip. "I'm strong enough."

"Yes, you most definitely are." Valorian handed Nip a pendant with an emerald framed in gold. The stone caught the firelight of the torches, sparkling. "Here. You stay in the carriage and keep this safe from robbers."

Nip's eyes widened. "What is it?"

Valorian smiled. "On the back is the royal crest of the House of Song, a lyrebird. The insignia proves I'm their prince and the rightful heir."

"Whoa!" Nip held the amulet close to his heart. "Don't worry. I'll keep it safe." He ran to the carriage and shut the door.

"You have a kind way with children." Danika gave a gentle smile.

Valorian brought out his lute and grinned. "If only my charms worked on Bron."

Primal hoots from the forest stifled Danika's laugh before the sound left her throat. Bron aimed the tip of his sword into the shadows. "Let them come."

Beside her, Valorian breathed deeply. He strummed an open chord on his lute, opened his mouth and sang. His honeyed tenor voice echoed through the woods, challenging the darkness with light.

"Who so thrives to hunt this night
Rest your wearied souls.
For a sweet languor
In the eve's stillness
Lingers to console."

She drew out her long sword, a miniature replica of her father's blade with the silver pommel formed in a lion's head and three rubies lodged in the hilt. Her blade wasn't as thick as the late king's, but the lighter bulk allowed her swift movement for quick, superficial cuts. As Bron had taught her, she needed all her weight behind her to lodge the tip through a man's heart.

Hulky shapes formed in the shadows. Pairs of red eyes glowed. The air reeked of rotten eggs, rancid sweat and wet dog. Heavy breathing penetrated the night, the sound much like prowling hounds closing in on mouthwatering prey.

"Kobolds." Danika coughed, bracing herself for the fight. Smarter and leaner than trolls, their stench alone could kill a man.

The leaves rustled around them, then silence. Not one of the monsters stirred.

"Why aren't they coming out?" Bron shook his sword at the woods in a challenge.

Danika shouted over the next refrain. "Valorian's music holds them back."

"I bid you flee the flames of foes
Whose sharp blades cut the thickest hide.
This battle cannot be won with numbers,
Spears or forceful pride."

Bron tightened his grip on the hilt. "He cannot sing all night."

Valorian's song had calmed Danika, as well as the beasts in the forest. With steady hands, she gripped her sword and pushed toward the nearest pair of eyes. "Then we'll cut them down one by one while they're spellbound."

She reached the first silhouette and raised her sword. Beside her, a massive shape twice the size of the carriage barreled through the front line and broke into the clearing. Legs like hairy tree trunks stomped the grass and rumbled the food in Danika's stomach.

The kobold carried an axe with a blade as long as Danika was tall, the sharp edge glinting in the moonlight in the places between the smears of dried blood. Human skulls clattered in a chain hanging around his neck. A single horn protruded from his forehead in a sharp, spiraling twist.

Valorian increased his volume, practically shouting the refrain as the beast swiped at her and Bron. They ducked and rolled as the axe hit the first row of trees. Branches crashed around them, one of them falling on the carriage. Danika thought of Nip and prayed to Helena and Horred for the boy to have enough sense to stay put.

"Why isn't the music working?" Danika shouted into Bron's ear. The kobold opened a jaw as wide as his forehead and roared, showing rows of uneven, square teeth.

Bron sighed and leaped up, brandishing his sword to block the princess. "Too dumb to understand?"

"No, look!" Danika pointed to the monster's head. Thick, pink membranes grew over malformed ears. "He's deaf."

Bron swiped his sword and the beast matched his arc with the axe. The weapons clanged, sending sparks through the night like falling stars. Bron's muscles bunched as he held the axe in place. "Just my luck."

Valorian widened his eyes, and Danika waved him behind her. "Keep singing. Hold the others back." She'd handle this.

As Bron pushed his sword against the axe's weight, Danika rounded the kobold and stuck her long sword in its back. The monster wailed and lashed out, sending her flying against the carriage. The force of the fall knocked the wind out of her. Her head hit the carriage wheel and rang with dizziness. The kobold reached behind, trying to dislodge Danika's long sword like a splinter in a slab of meat. The distraction gave Bron the opportunity to lunge with his sword and slice a gash in the kobold's left leg.

The carriage door squeaked open and Nip thrust his hand out. He whispered, "Come inside."

"No." She had to help Bron and keep the monster from reaching Valorian. If he stopped singing the others would flood the clearing and there'd be no trip to Darkenbite. She held up her palm. "Stay there."

When Danika looked back, the kobold had pinned Bron on the ground with his fist and tried to stomp the warrior to death. Bron rolled from its grip, jabbing his sword whenever he had the chance. Each lunge made a superficial cut at best. Valorian kept singing, his fingers turning red as he strummed the metal strings of the lute over and over.

Danika took a deep breath, stood and leaped toward her sword. She grabbed the hilt and hung from the monster's back like a rag doll as the beast waddled back and forth, dancing on top of Bron. A thin dribble of purple black liquid dripped from the cut.

Danika braced her feet against the monster's back and pulled. The sword wouldn't budge.

Behind her, Valorian's words nudged her memory.

"Bestow a gift to the bearer
At the most opportune time.
Out of care, and something more
An ivory relic that once was mine."

Valorian's dagger! Danika swung herself into the air, head over heels. Her feet landed on the blade of her sword. She waved her arms to balance and shuffled toward the monster's back. Grabbing onto the thick hair, she climbed toward its neck.

The odor choked her and she gagged, her stomach threatening to spew the remnants of Valorian's sweet peaches on the creature's back. One thought of Bron flat as a coin hardened her will, and she scrambled down her boot for the dagger. She unsheathed the blade and held it in the air, contemplating the right spot on the wart-infested neck. She'd only get one chance.

Danika drove the tip through the back of the creature's neck, puncturing its wind pipe. The kobold wheezed and its shoulders heaved. Danika held onto the hair on his back as he fell to his knees and then his stomach, sending a crashing thump through the forest, louder than any falling tree. When the echo subsided, only Valorian's melancholy song filled the silence.

Danika pulled herself up from the hairy back. "Bron?" Her voice shook with worry.

"Here." The warrior stood with blood running down one of his arms. He offered his hand. "An impressive feat for a lady."

Danika slipped her hand into his as if it should rest there for all time. "I had a good teacher."

"And a great weapon supplier as well." He leaned down and pulled Valorian's dagger from the beast's neck. Bron studied the markings of the House of Song before handing the dagger to her, ivory hilt first.

She felt like such a betrayer. Danika took the hilt and slid the blade back into her boot. He was her bodyguard, dammit, not her suitor.

A shaft whizzed through the air behind them and Valorian's music abruptly stopped in mid-sentence. Danika whirled around just as Valorian and his lute hit the ground, a feathered arrow lodged in his shoulder.

No, no, no. The gods would not allow it...

She ran to Valorian's side, her heart thumping wildly.

Bron stood in front of them alone, a barrier of muscle, and held up his sword. The forest stirred around them as the beasts awoke from the spell.

Valorian clutched the shaft with his good hand. The arrow had torn his richly embroidered riding vest and stuck right into the muscle. Thank Helena the tip hadn't struck his lung.

Danika placed both her hands on the wound and pressed against the flow of blood. "Hold still. Don't move."

He grasped her hand with his bloodied fingers. Branches creaked in the darkness. A wiry kobold, no bigger than Nip, stepped into the clearing. A sly grin spread through his pasty lips. Bark and pine needles stuck out of his ears. *Clever bastard.*

The kobold fired again, at Bron, and the warrior deflected the arrow like a chicken leg at dinnertime. Laughter erupted from the shadows as the kobold's friends slowly woke up.

Danika gazed down at Valorian and his eyes watered with pain, yet held a determination she hadn't seen before. "I have to sing."

Just as Valorian began a ring of kobolds entered the clearing. Some stood three heads taller than Bron, and others only came up to his knees. They wore patches of leather around their groins and various-sized teeth around their necks. Some had one horn, whereas others had two or three sprouting from their heads like defiant fingers.

The horses whinnied, gazing skittishly around them. The lead pair pulled on their harnesses. Thunderhooves snorted with unease. Danika glanced at the carriage. Would Nip stay put?

"Red streaks adorn
The starling's breast.
As he flies the twilight skies,
You think you've won
Oh, foul hunter

But the game has just begun."

Valorian's voice, although still sweet, shook from pain, and there were no chords to support it. Valorian's voice fell to a whisper on the second verse. The kobolds hesitated long enough for Bron to get a good swipe then pounced on him in a horde. The warrior pulled them off, one after another, flinging their broken bodies into the forest. For every kobold he tore down, another three came at him. They bit his legs, jabbed at his eyes and climbed up his back, scratching his bald head.

Behind her, they climbed on the horses. Thunderhooves reared, kicking two with his front hooves, but another three took their place, this time holding sharp daggers.

Danika's heart tore in two. If she left Valorian he'd bleed to death, but if she stayed, the sheer number of kobolds would overwhelm Bron.

Either way, their mission had failed. The kingdom would fall to the fires of the She-Beast, and man would no longer reign in this world.

The call of a low horn echoed over the battle in a long, primal swell, tearing the bottom from Danika's heart. She'd know that sound anywhere. The call belonged to the dead army of Sill.

The kobolds stopped at once, their ears perked to the sky. Bron kicked the closest ones away and scanned the trees.

Danika had thought the night couldn't get any worse. Fate had misled her.

The horn blew again as if answering everyone's question in an ugly bleat. The kobolds cried and scampered into the forest, leaving them alone in the clearing. The wind picked up, sending boughs creaking and pine needles rustling as if the forest breathed in anticipation.

Bron turned to Danika with sorrow in his eyes. A thousand stolen glances could not deliver the pain and longing in that one gaze meant only for her.

Danika mouthed the words, unable to speak. "It cannot be."

Chapter 8

Woman of the Forest

The woods parted and a single figure in a tattered ebony robe strode into the clearing with purposeful steps. Danika's heart climbed to her throat and she swallowed her fear, reminding herself Ebonvale's army had defeated the necromancer king in a campaign lasting all of her preteen years. Her father had died preventing the dead from walking in the land of the living. Had the king perished in vain?

No festering army followed the figure as it claimed the center of the circle, placing a long, knobbed staff into the earth with a black, gloved hand no bigger than Danika's. The figure raised an arm, tan as treated leather, from the folds of fabric and spread an upturned palm, the universal gesture showing he or she meant no harm. Blood pulsed in the veins running down the arm, and the skin, though wrinkled from the sun, was unbroken and not infected. This was no leader of the dead.

Yet, Danika spotted the bone horn hanging from the figure's neck on a thick chord of twined human hair. A skull with horns on either side had been carved into the bell, the crest of Sill.

Bron glanced at Danika with a questioning gaze. He tapped his fingers on the claymore's hilt.

This figure had saved their lives. They would be worse than the kobolds if they attacked.

No. They owed this specter a life debt. Danika shook her head. Bron lowered the tip of his sword, and a single drip of black blood oozed to the ground.

The figure threw back its hood. Wayward, windblown blond hair streaked with white frizzled outward in a halo around a foxlike face wearied by wrinkles and time. One eye, green as the forest in midsummer's sun, stared back at them with curiosity. White film covered the other eye in a thick, cloudy cataract. Wrinkles webbed across her once beautiful face and age spots mottled every inch of her skin.

Danika blinked in disbelief.

Impossible.

If time had sped thirty years in the future, she'd be staring at herself.

It couldn't be. She'd left for Jamal with her minstrel lover. Danika still had the letter, scribbled in hasty strokes, apologizing and bidding farewell. Yet, only one woman possessed a horn of the dead, given to her by her husband after he'd won the first battle with the army of Sill.

Bron dropped to his knees. He bowed his head before the old woman, reaffirming what Danika knew in the crux of her heart. "My Queen."

"Bronford Thoridian of Oaten's Dell." The former queen of Ebonvale placed a hand on his shoulder. "A brave and lionhearted man you've turned out to be."

Her gaze roamed to Danika, the sparkling green eye watery with melancholy. "My dear daughter, you are more glorious than I ever imagined."

Anger, hatred, guilt and regret poured into Danika's soul in a foul brew. She could hardly bear to ask her runaway mother for assistance. However, Valorian lay beneath her hands with an ashen face laced in sweat.

"Please." Danika took in a shaky breath. "We need your aid."

The former queen glanced at Valorian and her green eye grew dark and hard as flagstone. She scanned the shivering woods. "You're lucky you wandered into my hunting snares." She reached underneath a mossy log and pulled a dead hare from a trap. "They'll return in larger numbers. If you want to live, come with me."

Danika nodded to Bron. "Let's get moving."

She tied her scarf around the minstrel's shoulder in a sling, then rose to survey the damage. Two of the horses lay on patches of blood-stained pine needles, their throats cut. Danika's heart dropped as she recognized one of them as Thunderhooves. Hadn't Nip lost enough?

Bron stood beside her making the sign of Helena's sword. "They fought bravely."

Danika turned away from the bloody sight. "Make sure the boy does not see this."

"He's too smart for his own good." Bron shook his head and pulled a jagged, hilted dagger from the horse's flank. He studied the serrated blade with disgust and threw it into the woods. "He'll know soon enough."

Danika grabbed his arm. "Please. Not now."

Bron nodded. "So be it." He lifted the tree from the carriage and Nip's round face peered out the glass window. The warrior blocked the view of the dead horses with his massive waist.

Thank Helena Bron had a soft side. Danika stood and wiped the blood from her hands on her riding pants. Bron held his hand to the carriage window. "Stay in there. We must get Valorian to safety."

"Is everyone safe?" Nip peered around him, and Danika moved to block the view.

"Valorian needs your help." Bron placed his hand on the door so Nip wouldn't open it. "Stay there and we'll bring him in." An edge of authority cut through his voice, strong enough to keep the boy inside.

Bron helped Danika lift the minstrel from the ground and to the carriage. They opened the door and carried him to the velvet seat next to Nip.

"Will he be secure?" She placed her hand on Valorian's forehead. His skin burned hot as fire.

Bron nodded and returned to the rice bags, stacking them on top of the carriage. "I'll make certain to ride carefully and avoid bumps, if I can."

"Hold this tightly." Danika took Nip's hand and placed his palm on Valorian's wound. "Do not let go."

Nip nodded as he stared at the blood blossoming through the fabric with wide eyes.

She moved to close the carriage door. Valorian caught her hand with his own, his metallic eyes lucid. "My Princess."

She was not his princess, but he'd risked his life for their cause, and may soon lose it. "Yes?"

"You fought bravely."

"As did you." She froze, locking her gaze with his. The words from his song came back to her. He'd given her that dagger *out of care and something more.* What did he mean by something more? If he died, she'd never know.

Valorian released his hold on her wrist. He smoothed his fingers over her silken scarf wrapped around his chest. "Thank you, Danika."

"'Twas the least I could do for saving all our lives." Danika placed her hand over his and squeezed. She'd underestimated his strength and the power of his music.

Bron cleared his throat behind her and Danika pulled away and closed the door. She mounted her horse. Bron had secured Valorian's horse in place of the carriage horse they'd lost. Her mother stared at her from the center of the clearing, wistfulness etched in the fine wrinkles around her mouth.

Reminiscing had no place in this quest. Danika shot her an impatient glance. "The scent of the horses' blood will draw all manner of predatory beasts. How long?"

"'Twill take an hour at most."

"Then we shouldn't waste our breath. Lead us forward." Danika spurred her horse.

They would have never survived the attack if that massive abomination with malformed ears had attacked at the same time as the other kobolds. Valorian had risked his life keeping them alive. Time for her to save his.

* * * *

The forest changed from a looming threat full of shadows to a fragrant grove of cherrywoods. Their reddish-tinged leaves and low-hanging branches provided a cozy orchard escape. As they passed the low branches, hollow wood chimes clinked around them, creating a calming tinkle of peace and tranquility.

"There must be a thousand of 'um." Nip spoke behind Danika but the princess didn't turn around. She couldn't tell how far her mother could hear and she couldn't open her heart to care. Valorian's recovery consumed her every concern.

"That's how she's lived here all these years," Bron murmured. "Protected by a minstrel's charms."

A bitter taste tainted Danika's mouth. A minstrel. Of course.

A cottage made from bluewoods tilted at an angle against a hilltop cleared for a patch of wildflowers and a garden. A flagstone chimney puffed with gray smoke on the southern side.

Danika hadn't known what to expect, but certainly not this humble hovel perched in the middle of nowhere slanting against a knoll. Born in the affluent, jeweled city of Jamal, her mother had come from riches. She'd compromised for Ebonvale's inner keep, never mind this sorry beggar's cabin.

"You may tie your horses here." Her mother gestured to a fence near a water fountain at the bottom of the hill. She stepped onto a gabled porch as if the cracked wood were a palace and opened the front door. Golden light cast by a simmering fireplace and hanging lanterns spilled around them. "Bring the minstrel to me."

Bron jumped from the carriage and helped Danika off her horse. "I'll see to the horses after we usher Valorian inside."

"Thank you, Bron." Danika hurried to the carriage door, afraid of what she'd find. They'd ridden for a full hour, as her mother had advised, and Valorian's condition could have deteriorated.

Swallowing bile, she opened the door. Valorian remained where they'd left him, splayed over the bags of rice. He met her gaze and offered a weak smile. Compassion overflowed her heart. "Come with me, we'll get you healed up in no time."

Beside him, Nip clamped his hand over the wound. "I didn't let go."

"Good. You did a superb job." Tears burned Danika's eyes. For such a good lad, he had dreadful luck. She couldn't keep the truth from him for much longer. Soon he'd leave the carriage and count two fewer horses, one of them his.

But first she must tend to Valorian. She placed a hand on his shoulder as Bron came up behind them. "Stay here while we get Valorian situated."

Nip nodded.

Dear Helena, make the boy listen. "That's an order."

Danika and Bron carried Valorian into the cottage. They placed him on a low bed of straw covered in rough linen. Gone were her mother's fancy embroidered pillows. The queen had ordered her handmaidens to arrange and rearrange them on her bed back in Ebonvale. Danika shook off a memory of her mother slapping her sticky hand as a child when she tried to touch a shiny, golden cushion with indigo tassels from Jamal.

Memories came in a flood and Danika swiped at them like bats, turning them all away. She had to focus on Valorian. He wandered in and out of consciousness as blood soaked the scarf she'd tied around him.

Bron paced back and forth in the small room. "I'll get the boy."

"Bron." Danika touched his arm in warning.

"He has to know." Bron pulled away. "In times like these, boys turn to men sooner than later."

Danika nodded, frowning. If only she could protect Nip from the truth.

Her mother carried over jars of ointment and bandages from a storage room in the back. She knelt beside Valorian and untied the makeshift tourniquet.

Suspicion clouded Danika's mind. "Since when are you a healer?"

Her mother didn't even glance up. "Since I've lived alone in these woods. Necessity is the greatest teacher."

Alone? Where was her minstrel lover? The man she had loved more than Danika and her father?

The prince of the House of Song glanced up and held out a shaking hand. "You can call me Valorian."

Her mother took his hand in her knobby fingers. Complex emotion sped through her eyes.

Danika leaned forward. Was she remembering her minstrel?

"My name is Sybil."

"I know." Valorian closed his eyes as Sybil pressed an ointment into the cut. His response almost knocked Danika backward. Did he know her or know of her? She'd heard rumors the House of Song arranged for her mother and the minstrel to meet and even enabled their escape. If Valorian's family had been a part of this, she could never link her kingdom with such thieves.

Was she getting carried away? The former queen had left a legacy of infamy back in Ebonvale. Perhaps Valorian just knew the tale.

Behind her, the cottage door opened and Bron stepped in. "Come." He took Danika's arm as if sensing the tumultuous feelings storming inside her. "The boy needs you and I have to tend to the horses."

Danika allowed Bron to escort her to the front porch. The new day had brightened the sky to a dull slate canvas. Nip sat on the last step, staring at the ground.

Danika sat beside him. "I'm sorry about your horse."

He shrugged and sniffed. Tears streaked his freckled cheeks. "It always happens this way."

Danika nudged closer to him, afraid to scare him away if she came on too strong. She wasn't his mother even though the longer she spent with him, the more she wanted to be. "What do you mean?"

He picked a strand of long grass from the ground and tied it into a knot. "Before the wyverns came, Ma asked me to stay inside with her and help her bake sweetbread. Instead I ran into town to see the butcher's new pair of goats. I never saw her again."

Danika took his hand. She'd never held such a small hand before. So small, smaller than her hand when she'd lost her mother. The need to comfort him overwhelmed her. "'Tis not your fault."

"Maybe not. But I should have helped her with the bread. Just like I should have stayed with Thunderhooves. It was the last time I'd ride him." He threw the knotted grass on the ground. "Whenever I make the wrong choice, the gods take things away from me."

She smoothed his curly hair behind his ear. "Gods do not punish little boys for being little boys. All you can do is appreciate what you have before it's gone."

"I have nothing."

She squeezed his hand. "You have me."

Nip leaned against her. She sat holding him and watching Bron clean the horses. The boy fell asleep and she carried him inside. Valorian tossed in a feverish sleep, lying in fresh bandages. Her mother clanged bottles in the back, perhaps creating some new herbal remedy to help him. Danika placed Nip on a cushion on the floor. She should stay by Valorian but the small cottage suffocated her. She needed fresh air. She denied the thought that she needed Bron.

* * * *

Twilight had given way to early rays of golden sun. She put both arms on the splintered balcony as Bron brought their horses to the fountain and cleaned their hooves.

He glanced at her over his shoulder. "You were right to ask her aid."

Danika squeezed the railing, the wood slivers pricking her skin. "I don't trust her."

"You have every right not to." He threw a clod of mud under one of the cherrywoods and went back to work picking her horse's hooves.

"Why do you still bow before her?" Danika couldn't hide the hurt in her voice.

"Because I took an oath to protect and obey every member of the Ebonvale household. She is still my ward, but that doesn't mean I don't harbor the same feelings racing through your heart. Do not forget, I was there, too, Princess. I witnessed the pain she caused you and your father."

Pain that was still as raw as the day she'd read that dreadful note.

"You must find a way to forgive her or at least give her a second chance. Even if your heart forbids it." Bron had finished with the horses' hooves and walked to the balcony, gazing at her like a lover reciting a poem. "'Twill benefit your sanity and peace of mind. She is lending you aid. She saved us. Maybe she wants to set her wrongs right."

"They will never be set right. She cannot give me back the ten years I lost with her."

"So, use the time you have left."

Danika harrumphed and turned her head away to the gray morning sky, ravens circling the dark part of the forest from whence they'd come. The time she had left? While their kingdom hung in the balance, rekindling her relationship with her estranged mother would be the last path she would choose.

Bron's touch brought her out of her musing. He reached up and laced his thick fingers through hers. "Stubborn to a fault. That's my princess."

Her gaze traveled to his, locking in place. It was the first time she'd truly seen him since the start of their journey. The first time she'd let him in. My Princess. Valorian had called her the same thing. But, coming from Bron, it excited her in dangerous ways.

His hot touch lent her strength, a different kind of strength than Valorian's songs. Danika blushed and guilt overcame her for having such feelings while the minstrel lay wounded. Her gaze wandered to his shoulder caked in dried blood.

"Dear heavens. I forgot you're hurt."

Bron shrugged, eyeing the wound as if it were an insect bite. "A kobold's dagger is like a butter knife."

"A butter knife?" That same dagger had killed a horse. She took her hand back and gestured toward the door. "You should clean the wound all the same. Follow me and I'll see you get the attention you need."

"As you wish, Princess." Wistfulness lightened Bron's voice.

Longing tempted Danika to look back. No, Valorian needed her. Instead, she pushed open the cottage door and allowed the golden light to burn away the secrets in the morning mist outside.

Sybil sat on the foot of the bed, cleaning the bloodied scarf she'd once left behind for Danika in a reed bucket full of soapy water.

Guilt overwhelmed her. Valorian lay in pain while she spoke of secret longings with Bron. Danika knelt by the minstrel's side, sliding her fingers over his hand. "How is he?"

Sybil glanced up and down again quickly, as if afraid to meet Danika's searing gaze for too long. "He's lost a lot of blood, but he'll survive. He'll have to rest for a day or two, and he won't regain full mobility for another week or so."

Danika breathed in relief. "Will he be able to play his lute?"

Her mother nodded. "Although, I don't wish to hear it. Too many memories."

The comment piqued Danika's interest. Had her mother's minstrel lover died? She quelled her curiosity. With Bron needing attention, talking of the past would only slow her mother's nursing down. Danika gestured for Bron to come forward. "Can you tend to one more?"

"For Bronford, I would do anything." Sybil's face cracked into a smile. "Come here, my son."

Bron must have felt like a son to Sybil because she'd recruited him when Danika was ten and he sixteen. Danika remembered Bron competing in the tournament and her mother bestowing him with a gold medal of honor. The competition must have been one of the most meaningful days in Bron's life. He must share her mixed emotions concerning Sybil. Although, forgiveness came easier to him.

Bron walked over and knelt near her mother, bowing his head. "My Queen."

"No need to address me so formally here." She gestured for him to rise and peeled back his leather jerkin. "Please, call me Sybil."

Bron's face set in a grim line. Danika doubted he'd ever address a former queen so casually. His loyal heart would never allow such a dishonor. She could learn from his steadfast nature. He'd spoken the truth earlier. If only she could allow herself the luxury of taking his advice.

Chapter 9

Brilliant Sun

Bron gazed into the former queen's face. A regal woman still lived behind the mask of freckles, age spots and a clouded left eye. Every now and then, when she pursed her lips or straightened her neck with commanding poise, the queen shone through.

"Hold still." Sybil dabbed at the cut in his shoulder. "This should heal nicely. You'll have another proud scar."

"I'll add it to my collection." Bron smiled, wondering how a woman with so much elegance, power and grace could fall to such lowly means. But, beyond her impeccable composure, he needed to know if the path she'd chosen for her life contented her. He owed her at least that much consideration. If unhappiness plagued her, he owed her a means of escape.

The beggar should always remember the hand that threw him the first coin.

Years ago, the queen had elevated him from poverty to distinction. Now the festival tables were turned and he held the hand full of coins.

A cooling sensation spread down Bron's arm and throughout his body as Sybil spread ointment over his shoulder. His blood had run hot ever since he sensed the kobolds proximity, and now he finally allowed his body to relax.

"Time for rest." Sybil pulled out another cushion and dragged it next to Nip.

She gestured for Bron to sit and he followed her instructions, letting the weariness of the day overtake him. "Close your eyes and let the medicine work its miracle."

"The princess?"

"She's outside. I'll find a bed for her as well." Sybil's voice grew authoritative. "You take excellent care of her, but sometimes you must refuel your own wells. Rest, my son."

"Yes, ma'am." Bron settled with his back against the wall and his long legs stretched out in front of him. His mind wandered back into memories he hadn't visited in a long time.

Bron wove in and out of the crowded thoroughfares of Ebonvale's inner district, following Hule's head of golden curls. The limitless wave of people pushed both boys forward in a relentless tide. He could have turned back at the city gates, or even before they hitched a ride on a manure wagon from Oaten's Dell to the capitol. Not now.

Bron stifled his anxieties as he ducked under cages of vibrant birds and skirted a fruit stall reeking of overripe plums. He'd come for a reason, a dream, and the sheer number of people would not sway him, even if he was accustomed to cows outnumbering people.

His gaze strayed to a soothsayer sitting in a wicker chair on the corner of the road. Her layers of floral skirts rustled in the breeze as her blind eyes rolled through the crowd and settled on him. She fingered a scratched onyx stone tied around the hollow of her neck and mouthed the words "chosen one." A shiver ran across Bron's shoulders. He averted his gaze, and sure as Helena's aim the old woman hadn't meant him. A farm boy vying for a place in the Royal Guard wasn't chosen for anything, unless she meant ridicule. He turned back to the crowd and Hule was gone.

Horred's Gambit! His eyes shouldn't have wandered. He needed his older brother by his side to reach the second round. Anxiety rushed up his spine. What if he had to enter the arena alone? He ground his teeth together. Then he'd fight hard, just the same as if Hule stood with him.

A hand closed on his shoulder and he whirled around thinking a thief reached for his good sword. Hule's freckled face stared back at him, his eyes sparkling with amusement and something more: hope. "Come on, Bronnie! We're almost there."

Behind his brother's face, the rafters of the coliseum rose, reminding him of his bottom place on the hierarchal chain. Bron jolted forward, following Hule through a back entrance where guards herded other boys their age. The underside of the rafters stunk like pigeons' nests and mold. Bron covered his mouth with his bare arm, smelling the scent of the cool river he'd bathed in that morning to make a good impression.

Last year the contestants had to fight each other for the honors, and the year before, they had to complete an obstacle course guarded with

*tigers from the queen's home city of Jamal. Bron couldn't imagine what
the king had dreamed up for this year.*

*The same thoughts must have burdened Hule, because he turned to his
brother with the first signs of nervousness creeping into his round face.
"What do you think they've planned for us?"*

*Bron shrugged, trying not to let his imagination rule his heart.
"Whatever it is, we stick together, right?"*

*"Right." Hule put his hand on Bron's shoulder. Although Bron was
younger by four years, he'd already reached his brother's height and
surpassed Hule's chest width. Lifting all those carts filled with goats had
paid off. Both boys rivaled the competition, but farm-town hicks had a
disadvantage over the professionally trained, elite charter-school boys
from the city. Some fathers paid members of the Royal Guard to train
their sons, while Hule and Bron's father taught them how to plant for the
optimal season's bounty each year.*

*Bron clenched his fists, eyeing another boy's jeweled armor, as sleek
and smooth as the surface of the lake by his home.*

*"Don't let their shiny asses shake you." Hule clapped his brother on
the back. "It's what's inside that counts."*

*Although Hule exuded confidence, his brother returned empty-handed
every year, besides the gashes in his skull and bruises on his arms and
legs. Bron wasn't going back to the farm like his brother. His muscles
itched to learn swordplay. He couldn't handle another season of plowing
fields.*

*Hule opened the travel sacks he'd carried on his back and handed
Bron the plate armor they'd made by banging together scraps from old
pots and shovels. The dinged surface wasn't pretty, but Bron had faith the
thick metal would hold up against most blows.*

*The doors to the stadium creaked open, and the boys shuffled into the
blinding brightness of the sun. The city boys' armor gleamed like gods.
Bron and Hule's unpolished patchwork shone dull slate gray, like the
cloudy eye of a storm.*

*"Gives you character," their father had said after stumbling in on
them trying out their armor before they left. "Shows them where you come
from." Then again, he knew his father wanted them to stay in the safety
of their home.*

Safe and tedious.

*Bron imagined them as maelstroms waiting to strike. He couldn't wait
to put the first dent in one of those flawless armor plates. His fingers
danced upon the hilt of his sword.*

Hule nudged his arm. "Look there! The king and queen."

Bron shielded his eyes and gazed up at a platform protruding from the rows of onlookers. The king and queen stood dressed in Ebonvale's colors of deep purple and green, waving to the crowd. The sun caught a head of golden hair between them, and Bron spotted the princess for the first time.

"Probably more spoiled than old milk left out in the sun all day during mid-summer." Hule cursed beside him. "I'd like to pull her golden hair."

Bron had the opposite reaction. To him, she represented everything fair and innocent in the world. He wanted to protect her like a dandelion growing in a newly planted field. In time, the other plants would shoot up around her greedily, stealing her sun.

A horn blew, churning the oats that had coalesced in Bron's stomach. Bron and Hule turned around as an army marched into the stadium across from the group of hopefuls. The soldiers wore tattered black robes with tails dragging through the grass, collecting mud. They held serrated spears and long bows made from blackwood and horsehair. Hoods covered their faces, and dark fabric concealed every limb from fingertip to shoulder. They exuded the stench of death.

Bron's stomach dropped to the grass as the crowd gasped in shock. He'd only heard stories from the tradesmen traveling by the farm from the North Country. He'd never seen the undead with his own eyes. How could the king control them? He would never sell his soul to become a necromancer.

"Don't be frightened. They're not real." Hule pointed to a lock of brown hair fluttering out of one of the hoods. "They must have rolled in the butcher's entrails. The Royal Guard is in disguise."

Betrayal blazed in Bron's heart and he felt like a fool. Only the king's court would devise such deceit. His mother had warned him of political intrigue and enemies pretending to be your closest friend. Never would he have imagined a ploy this size meant to frighten the new recruits.

A second horn blew and the army broke into a sprint. Bron turned his anger into determination. Undead or not, these were real opponents and he still had to fight. Gaining momentum, Bron steeled his nerves and unsheathed his long sword.

Hule's pace increased and his brother ran ahead of him. "For glory!"

The world moved as fast as lightning as Bron struggled to stay with Hule. They hit the oncoming army in a clash of metal, grunts and sweat. Bron collided with one of the robed figures, the reek of old blood and decay filling his lungs. He pushed, straining his muscles against the other man's force. He matched Bron's strength well, and they stood in each other's grip like two statues while the battle raged around them.

Bron's fingers yanked the fabric back, and the man's hood fell from his face. He was older than Hule but younger than their father, with sneering lips, a crooked long nose and eagle-sharp eyes.

"You've got some strength in you, boy." The man clenched his teeth and tightened his grip on Bron's upper bicep.

Hule pulled that move on him all the time. Bron feigned weakness and dropped his sword, allowing the man to push his right side back. Bron released his grip and delivered a blow to the man's jaw, sending him sprawling backward. In one move, he swiped up his sword and stuck the tip near the man's throat.

His attacker's eyes widened in disbelief.

"A point for this young man." The Chief of Arms had spotted them locked in the position of conquered and conqueror. He signaled for Bron to release the man; Bron nodded in compliance and lifted his sword. The man on the ground rolled away and rejoined his group.

Bron bowed before the general, thinking of all the stories his dad used to tell him at bedtime about this man's lofty deeds. He'd never seen the Chief of Arms this close. His boulder-like jaw and swollen chest made him more intimidating in person. The hawk-nosed man studied him, running a hand through his head of flowing silver hair.

"Well done, son." The Chief of Arms held out a bronze medal.

Bron reached for the dangling prize. A familiar voice cried out from behind him, tearing his heart in two. Not Hule. It couldn't be Hule. He stopped, craning his neck.

Out of the corner of his vision, a robed figure a head taller than him sent his brother flying through the air. Hule hit the ground hard, unmoving. The tournament participants weren't supposed to fight until the death. However, accidental casualties happened every year. Bron couldn't take that chance. He bolted toward his brother.

Robed figures stood in his way and he crashed through them, using his momentum and his weight to send each one to the ground. The attacker stood over his brother, swinging a spiked ball on a chain over his head. His arm arched and the angle changed, the ball grazing the air over his brother's gut.

"No!" Bron reached out with his sword and sliced through the chain, sending the ball spiraling through the air. The attacker grinned at him with the perfect white teeth only seen in the city and brought out his long

sword, glittering with gemstones. His blue eyes sparkled. "Want to be a hero?"

Ignoring his comment, Bron lunged, and their swords clashed, raining sparks. Bron slid his sword down the length of the attacker's blade. Once free, he whirled around and sparred low, allowing the attacker's sword to skim the hair on his head. A lock of his honey blond hair fluttered to the ground as his blade cut a gash in the man's lower leg. The man stumbled back in shock. He regained his footing and swung toward Bron's gut. Bron leaped sideways and the blade sailed through clear air. The man brought his fist down on Bron's back and the ground came up in the blink of an eye, grass prickling his cheek.

Bron rolled instinctively as the tip of the sword sliced the grass where he'd fallen. He kicked the man's leg out from under him and the man fell on top of him. His weight knocked the air from Bron's lungs. Bron struggled to throw the man off, muscles burning with nothing left to give.

This was it. He'd failed.

Bron's cheeks heated with shame. Hule lay on the ground. He'd come home disappointed each year. His mother shouted in joy each time Hule returned alive. The soothsayer's words came back to him, cooling the burning pressure in his arms. *Chosen one.*

No. It could not end this way.

The attacker's spittle and sweat dripped on Bron's face, dribbling down his neck. Bron blinked the droplets away and heaved, pushing the man over. Before he could regain his footing, Bron scrambled upright and sat on top of him, pinning his legs. Chest pumping with exertion, he brought his sword to the man's throat. *"En garde."*

The man grinned back at him. Somehow, he knew Bron wouldn't deliver a fatal blow.

A horn blew, signaling the end of the battle. Carefully, Bron allowed him to rise, making sure the man wouldn't try anything. He ran off with the others, leaving Bron with Hule still lying on the ground.

"Hule!" Bron stumbled to his knees. He rolled Hule over, wiping grit from his brother's face. "Please, brother. Do not desert me."

Hule coughed and opened his eyes. "Have we lost again?"

Relief flowed through Bron, and he brought Hule's head to his chest, hugging him close. Thank Helena he'd been there the year Hule needed him. They would both return alive to Oaten's Dell. "It matters not."

The royal guard departed, and healers dragged the wounded boys away. Those with medals stood in line to report to the Chief of Arms. Bron thought of his prize dangling before him, but he couldn't stand in line with *nothing like a beggar. The Chief of Arms probably wouldn't remember him in all the chaos.*

Hule struggled to stand. Bron hefted him up, balancing him on his shoulder.

"We return to Oaten's Dell." Resignation weighted Hule's words.

"Hold fast, young warriors." A woman's voice, as keen as a birdcall and as sweet as nectar cut through the air. The men parted. A regal lady with a silken gown flowing over the battlefield like the clouds of heaven stepped into view. A three-pointed crown caught prisms of the brilliant midday sun. She strode to them, staring at Bron as if he were the only man on that battlefield. It was the first time anyone had ever referred to him as a warrior and not a farmer, and from the queen, no less.

She extended her arm toward him, the bell-shaped sleeve draping to the grass. "What is your name, son?"

Sweaty, tired and caked with grime, Bron struggled to meet her sharp eyes. "Bronford Thoridian of Oaten's Dell, Your Highness."

"Well, young Bronford, I watched you from afar. You have exhibited great strength, bravery and fortitude this day, attributes warranting a bronze medal or two. Most of all, you showed us loyalty and selflessness, giving up your medal to protect your brother."

Hule whispered in his ear. "She speaks the truth?"

Bron nodded to Hule and put a finger to his lips. Not wanting to disrespect, he turned back to the queen.

"These qualities are worthy of the highest honor this tournament has to offer." She dangled a golden pendant from her fingers. "Go on, take it. This prize is yours and yours alone. Bronford Thoridian, you have bypassed the subsequent rounds. You are now a member of the Royal Guard."

Bron stepped to the queen and she dropped the pendant in his palm. With her delicate touch, she closed his thick fingers over the prize and kissed his bloodied knuckles. Behind him, Hule hollered in excitement.

Bron's entire body shook. A flock of magpies fluttered in his stomach. "Words escape me."

The queen's lips curled on one side. "You don't need them. Your strength speaks for you."

She turned and her handmaidens followed her back to the podium like ducklings. Bron opened his palm and stared at the emblem carved into the gold, the seal of Ebonvale, a sword resting against a shield. The moment hung in the air like a dream, and Bron knew he'd remember this day and the queen's favor for the rest of his life.

"What will you do now?" Hule peered over his shoulder.

Bron put the chain around his neck, his skin tingling at the cool touch of gold. "I will stay and learn how to fight."

Chapter 10

Fickle Winds

Danika woke to birdsong and the sweet fragrance of cherrywood blossoms in the late morning sun. Although her mother had offered a straw bed inside the cottage, Danika had chosen the creaking porch swing, allowing the wind to rock her to sleep.

Her first thought shot to Valorian and she jolted upright, causing the swing's hinges to screech.

"Be calm, my dear." Sybil sat on the top porch step holding two cups of steaming broth. Had she watched over her all night?

Stifling a current of irritation, Danika sat up, clinging to a quilt draped over her legs. Her mother must have placed the fabric over her sometime in the night. Shedding any peace offering came as her first instinct. However, the morning air had an edge of chill and her leggings were thin. "Is Valorian all right?"

"I checked on him not long ago. He sleeps, as does everyone else in your traveling party."

Disbelief and mistrust still crackled in the air between them. She creased her eyes. "Even Bron?"

"Yes, the warrior needs his rest, too. He works hard to make sure you are safe."

"Bron is an excellent bodyguard, aye." Danika looked away, afraid her flaming cheeks would give her away.

Her mother tapped her shoulder. "Here, have a cup of braised hare."

"You cook as well?" Danika hadn't seen her mother lift a pinky finger in the kitchen, never mind gut and clean game from the forest.

"Necessity dictates my actions, dear." She spread her arms over the wilderness stretching beyond her orchard. "How else would I survive?"

How her mother had survived one night in the woods without her satin pillows, Danika had no idea. She took the chipped cup in her hands and allowed the heat to warm her cold fingers. Eyeing the liquid skeptically, Danika blew the steam over the rim. Probably tasted like bathing water. She took a deep breath and sipped, tasting salt, rosemary and thyme. Her brow rose. "'Tis good."

Sybil waved away her compliment. "It's nothing like Jamal's exotic maritime cuisine, or even Ebonvale's fire-broiled venison, but the broth sustains me nonetheless."

A day ago, Danika would have thought her mother would need an entire kitchen and wait staff to sustain her. Her mother's new streak of resourcefulness impressed her.

Sybil sat beside her on the swing and they creaked backward with the redistributed weight. Trying to fathom this newfangled concept of her woodland mother, Danika dangled her legs in the air and took another sip of the broth.

Her mother held her own cup, unmoving. "You've always craved adventure over courtly balls. Now, your wish has come true. I should have let you follow your own path instead of pushing you onto mine."

Danika stopped in mid-sip and swallowed hard. "If you've come to me this morn to apologize, I'm not ready to hear it." She couldn't hide the growl from her voice.

Sybil tucked a wayward strand of gray hair behind her ear and sighed sorrowfully. "Not to apologize--for I can never make up for what I've done." The edge returned to her expression. "I need to warn you."

Danika choked and coughed, almost spilling her broth. "Warn me?" What could her mother possibly know about her and her mission? How dare the former queen assume higher authority when she lived in a hovel, forcing Danika to run the kingdom alone?

"So you do not make the same mistake."

"Which mistake?" Danika shot back with a glare. Abandoning her daughter, running away, placing her own needs before the kingdom's?

"Marrying out of duty and not for love."

Danika clamped her mouth shut. She hadn't expected that answer.

Sybil set her cup of broth on the wooden planks of the porch and folded her hands in her lap. "I accepted your father's marriage proposal as a young and naïve girl. Jamal needed an ally to protect the Bluefin channel from the pirates stalking the seas, and King Artemus' growing army provided the shield Jamal needed to secure its trade routes to

Ebonvale. I couldn't argue with the logic. Ebonvale would protect my family's domain and ensure its success."

Danika ran her fingers over the rim of her cup. "Duty to one's kingdom must come first."

"Or so your father told you." Sybil's voice condemned. "I wanted more. Fifteen years my senior, the king remained kind but distant, treating me as a special pet. I could never replace his first wife, the beautiful Islador. She exhausted the treasury in the first six months of her reign and provided him with no heirs, dying of sickness a year after they were married. Yet, in his mind, she embodied perfection, and how can you compete with an ideal?"

Danika shrugged, wondering why she'd never heard her mother's side of the story.

"He showed more attention to the handmaidens than me. I wanted a youthful man who honored me for my true self, someone to grow old with and experience life together. Not a man closed off by grief, hungry for battle and the long leaves his war campaign provided."

Danika shifted on the swing to face her mother. If she didn't ask now, she'd never know the truth. "What happened to him?"

Sybil's gaze dropped to her hands. She unwove her fingers and wove them again as if casting a spell or undoing one. Many emotions passed through her good eye: fondness, melancholy, pain. "I met Crescenti when he came to Ebonvale's court to sing of King Artemus' lofty deeds. His voice wooed me with its sweetness and I admired his clever wit. When the king left for the border to quell a recent spate of undead attacks, Crescenti consoled me. He stole my heart and I thought I'd taken his in return."

Thought? Danika's mind raced. Did fate twist her mother's wrong against herself? Did Crescenti betray her mother in love?

Sybil wrung her hands together as if grinding wheat. "After we left Ebonvale, Crescenti took me back to the House of Song. He thought we'd be welcomed with open arms, able to live with the minstrels for the rest of our lives. However, our arrangement horrified King Troubadir. Not only did he condemn our pairing, he exiled us from the House of Song forever."

Danika bit her lip. King Troubadir sided with Ebonvale? She thought the minstrels had planned the pairing, like conniving thieves. But, Valorian's father didn't stand for her mother's indiscretion. She'd been wrong about Valorian and his family. Prejudice had misled her in a great many things.

Sybil's hand motions ceased, and she sat back in resignation, studying her weathered skin. "Crescenti couldn't handle the infamy and the embarrassment our love caused. He left me in these woods. I couldn't go back to Ebonvale, or Jamal, so I decided to stay here and make a life for myself. I've lived in these woods ever since."

Danika's emotions swirled with confusion between her love for her father and a new compassion for her mother. She'd never heard the tale of a husband absent both in mind and body. She'd only seen her doting father weaving daisies through her hair and reading her bedtime stories of Helena's and Horred's conquests. Still, her mother hadn't fulfilled her duty, and she had shirked her responsibilities for a handsome face. Underneath Danika's newfound sympathies lay an undying loyalty to her father. She tightened her fingers around the cup. "My father saved our kingdom by sending the dead army back to Sill."

Sybil fingered the horn around her neck. "Yes, his precious crusade. Do you truly believe everything he sacrificed will hold them back forever, or has he only angered a force beyond any man's control?"

Disquiet shot through Danika's heart. Surely the dead army wouldn't attack again. With King Artemus dead, who would lead Ebonvale's Royal Guard to victory?

Bron. The certainty soothed her worrying heart. Bron's strength rivaled her father's by twofold. Could they fend off the dead army and the wyverns at the same time?

"I didn't mean to disturb you, my dear daughter." Sybil put her wrinkled, knobby-knuckled hand over Danika's arm. "'Twas only a thought to keep in the back of your mind so you don't grow smug in that lofty castle. I merely aim to warn you against my pitfalls. You have a weighty decision to make, and I see two worthy suitors in your future. Make certain the one you choose is the one you love."

Sybil's words left Danika speechless. Two suitors? Valorian's intent was clear as the surface of a lake, yet how could her mother possibly know the furtive cravings in her wild heart? Danika met her mother's gaze in confusion and desperation.

Sybil patted her arm and stood. "Perhaps you do not yet see it and this conversation is premature. When the time comes, think of my recklessness and let my actions be a warning…" She swung her arm out to encompass the landscape around her cottage. "To guide you to a better path than this dead end."

The door creaked open, and Bron emerged, breaking the thick atmosphere of woe her mother's tale had spun. He bowed to the queen and then to Danika, his eyes averted from her simple underdress. "My Queen and Princess, I apologize for any interruption."

Mortification froze Danika to stone. Had he overheard their conversation?

Sybil touched Bron's shoulder, gesturing for him to rise. "Nonsense, Bronford. Our talk has come to a natural end."

Bron nodded, then looked to Danika. "Valorian awakes. He wishes to speak with you."

"Of course." Danika bolted up and used the quilt to cover herself. "Allow me to freshen my appearance. I'll be there in a moment." As she walked by her mother, Sybil grabbed her arm with a knowing look. Her mother's eyes darted to Bron and back to her. "Remember what we spoke of."

Danika pulled her arm away. Bron's proximity tingled the hairs on her neck. If only he knew. The result would be disastrous. She shot her mother a reprimanding glance. Why not shout to Bron how she considered him in the running for her hand? "Dear mother, how could I forget?"

Danika washed her face and arms using the cold well water. Wanting a more thorough bath, she beat the dust from her riding tunic and pulled the leather over her head. She checked her reflection and smoothed her blond hair. As a reigning princess and ruler of Ebonvale, she refused to start looking ragged like her mother.

Danika entered the cottage and joined the others. Nip and Bron sat together, sipping broth. Valorian lay propped against the wall, his legs spread before him. He smiled when she entered and beckoned her with a wave of his hand.

Danika sat on the edge of the bed and took his hand. "How are you this morn?"

"Healing." He winced as he tried to lean closer to her. "Sore, but alive thanks to your mother's talents."

Embarrassment rose, and she shrugged the emotion away. Valorian would see her for who she was--warts and all. He already knew her family history if his father had exiled her mother and her minstrel lover. Yet Valorian still wanted her. Even now, sore from an arrow wound, he risked discomfort to be two inches closer. Was it from duty or something more?

Danika pulled away. Bron sat in the corner, watching their every move like a raven hawk. She couldn't bear to show Valorian favoritism in front of the warrior who'd pledged his life to protect her and her family. Her mother had spoken the truth. She did have a weighty decision on the horizon.

But not this day.

Their quest to Darkenbite hung over their heads, shadowing every move as a perilous, unavoidable fate. Only after they had defeated the She-Beast would she confront the truth within her heart.

Chapter 11

Farewell Bidding

"En garde!" Nip lunged forward and his wooden sword clacked against the tree branch Bron held in his hand.

Bron allowed the boy to push him back against a cherrywood, pretending to be taken off guard. "Excellent. Now, what must you do next?"

"Go for the heart!" Nip swung his sword toward Bron's chest. The warrior deflected the blow, and the sword swung skyward, the hilt flying from the boy's hands. Nip swore and scrambled after it.

When Nip turned back to Bron, the warrior had extended the branch so the leaves at the end tickled Nip's nose. He yearned to let the boy win every time, but a false sense of triumph would teach him nothing, and real battles loomed. "You're dead."

"Horred's Gambit." Nip pushed the branch away and kicked a rock.

"Never sacrifice your guard for a venture as risky as extending your entire reach to pierce another's man's chest. You're taking the bait like rainbow trout in a stream."

Nip nodded and sniffed. "I'll never be a warrior like you. I'll never kill a wyvern or avenge my family. Or Thunderhooves. I couldn't save them."

"Hold your griffon's tails, little one." Bron ruffled his hair, thinking back to his own training and his reasons for choosing the warrior's life. "If you become a warrior, you'll save more people than you could ever count. You may even save someone you love. All you need is courage and someone to believe in you." Bron crouched down to eye level. "You have both."

The boy wiped his eyes. "Who believed in you?"

Bron's gaze lingered on the cottage hugging the hillside. "A very special lady. Someone who recognized not only who I was but who I could grow up to be."

"Who's gonna do that for me?" Nip swung his sword at an overhanging branch and the tree rained pink blossoms around them.

The hairs on Bron's arms stood on end. This moment meant everything to Nip. His actions would define the course of the boy's life with a push in the right direction. This orchard was Nip's tournament coliseum, and he needed a figure that mattered to lend him hope. Bron walked over and placed a gentle hand on his shoulder. If a queen could bother herself with a farmhand, then a warrior could kneel before a lost boy. "I am."

Bron knelt before him in the piles of pink blossoms as though he knelt before a future king. "A warrior's life is one of selfless sacrifice. You swear to protect and defend without retribution, giving your life to keep those around you safe. 'Tis not an easy path, but it holds great worth and satisfaction. If this is what you desire, I'd like to offer you an apprenticeship."

Nip chewed on his lower lip. "What would I do?"

"Learn how to fight, follow in my footsteps, maybe one day, join the Royal Guard, like I did as a boy."

The boy's eyes lit with fire. "You are certain?"

Bron nodded and pointed to the boy's chest. "The only uncertainty lies here. You must vanquish your self-doubt if you choose to accept."

Nip breathed in, his small chest rising as if he seriously considered Bron's challenge and all the implications that came with it. The boy had to crave adventure in his heart, or his sword would never strike true.

Nip held his breath for several seconds before releasing it. "I accept."

Bron nodded and pulled the boy close to him. Nip froze in the warrior's arms. Slowly, he wrapped his arms around Bron's neck and hugged him back.

Movement on the cottage porch caught Bron's attention and he straightened, loosening his hold.

"What is it?" Nip stood on his tiptoes, peering between the cherrywood branches.

Bron stepped forward, pulling the boy with him. "The queen. She's beckoning." His body tensed. Had the kobolds found them? Had Valorian's condition taken a turn for the worse? Was Danika all right?

Bron's heart pounded in his chest as he lifted the boy and ran through the orchard. Sybil's placid face came into view, telling him nothing. As queen, she'd learned to hide behind a mask of confidence. Could she be employing such a tactic now?

Bron reached the stairs and lowered the boy to the ground. He sank to one knee. "My Queen."

"Sybil. You must call me Sybil."

Bron nodded. He'd never utter such a blasphemy as long as he lived. "What is the matter?"

"It's Valorian." Sybil waved her hand to the cottage.

A thousand thoughts crossed Bron's heart.

Sybil's face cracked into a pensive frown. "He's able to ride. Danika wishes to leave immediately."

Bron nodded, relief mixed with more complicated emotions. He would never wish harm upon the minstrel, yet hearing of Valorian's continuing presence once again built a barricade in his heart.

Idiot. He knew the princess must marry the minstrel. Besides, she'd never want a lug of a bodyguard, someone the kingdom would frown upon to her dying day. Fate had chosen, and this time it wasn't him.

Why couldn't he let her go?

Sybil's frail hand rested upon his shoulder. "Time will tell. You must wait until destiny's path reveals itself. 'Tis a long journey you attempt. Many turns can happen along the way."

Bron glanced at her with confusion swirling in his head. "What do you speak of?"

"A matter close to your heart." She gestured for him to rise, a motion she'd done a thousand times in the past in the marble throne room. "Come. You must prepare."

Bron extended his arm and took her hand, pulling her back before she reached the cottage door. The former queen whirled around in defiance. Never had Bron acted so boldly.

"Come with us."

Sybil slumped forward, looking even older than last night, when her medicines had given her purpose. "I cannot."

Bron wouldn't give up. He moved his hand down her arm and held her palm. "I know the princess will come around. We could appoint you Regent to the Princess, Dame of the Handmaidens, or Matriarch to Ebonvale. I know it's not near what you had--"

"It's too much." She shook her head. "Too excessive for an old miser like me. I've chosen my path, and my accommodations are just. I could never return to face all those raging tongues and spiteful stares." She gazed at her tattered shawl and leathery skin. "Not like this."

Her condition tore a hole in Bron's heart. He could not make her come, not if she didn't wish it. Besides, she spoke only truth. Ridicule and infamy awaited her if she returned to Ebonvale. She was wise to favor such a peaceful ending to her sorrowful life.

"Very well." He released her, wishing he could give her more. She'd given him the world.

Sybil grabbed his hand back. "That doesn't mean I'm not saddened to see you depart. Bronford Thoridian, you served me well those many years back, and you will continue to do so."

"How can I when you are half a world away?"

Sybil stepped toward him. She brought his hand to his heart and whispered, "Take care of Danika. Although she's lost confidence in me, she's all I have left that's bright in this world."

His heart beat steadily against the palm of his hand, sound as his loyalty. "You have no need to ask."

* * * *

The caravan left the orchard as pink petals rained, covering their horses' tracks. Danika took her place by Valorian's side, the two rulers leading the path into the dark forest. Bron sat in his rightful place with Nip, driving the carriage and watching her back. To stand with her would mean he'd abandon his post as protector, and Bron would never sunder a sworn oath.

Danika didn't look back. Whether she kept her distance from the warrior, or wanted to leave her mother's sorry tale behind her, he couldn't presume. Sybil's time-corrupted face haunted him as he waved his last farewell. It felt cruel to leave her, but he'd be just as cruel to drag her back to everything she'd willingly left behind.

As the damp, moss-laden boughs cooled his bare shoulders, Bron decided to focus on the future and not the past. He turned to Nip. "What drove your father to venture so deep into the forest?"

Nip sighed, tying and untying a knot Bron had taught him with a scrap of twill. "It's a long story."

Bron gestured to the overhanging boughs before them, the morning's mist still clinging to the ground, obscuring their path. The heady scent of pine filled the air as the wheels bled the needles below them and cracked through seed cones. "We have a long time to waste. I know it's hard to speak of your family, but 'tis a passage you must cross. Whether 'tis now or as a young man, you must confront your past to free your heart for future endeavors."

Nip sat in silence, bouncing as the carriage creaked over roots and upturned rocks. Just when Bron thought he'd have to give the boy more time, Nip muttered, "He came through our village in the middle of the night, all hooded as if the light from the moon and stars burned his skin."

Nip tightened the knot, his tiny hands turning red. "No one wanted to take him in. The Ox's Horn closed its doors, and Telli told him she'd booked every room in her inn for the night. My pa and I were walking back from the dock. He'd just paid for a shipment of silver from Jamal. The hooded man had missed the last ferry across the bay and he begged us to take him in. Said the morning light would do him in."

Bron glanced at Danika's horse's flank as the beast disappeared behind a curve in the path. He whipped the reins to quicken the pace. Sybil had taught them a safer route rarely used by the kobolds. Yet, Bron still sniffed the dank air, searching for their rancid stench. "Interesting." He'd never heard of an albino leaving the caves of Darkenbite--they feared morning's first light. "Did the man say where he traveled to?"

"Naw." Nip placed the knot beside him on the seat. "Or if he did, I don't remember."

Danika's horse came back into view and Bron relaxed. "Did your father take him in?"

"He said he could stay in our smithy. The man thanked us all the way back to our house. Pa invited him for dinner and the man refused. He feared our hearth's light. So, my ma made him a big bowl of rice and I took the food to him. The lanterns were all out when I went into the smithy, and he sat in complete darkness."

Nip pretended to grab his eyes with his fingers. "I was afraid at first, but Pa said he wouldn't hurt me. Pa always had a good gut feeling about people, like he could sense evil in a man from ten feet away. He told me to trust my instinct, and if a person was kindhearted, to do everything in my power to lend them aid."

"Your pa sounds like an honorable man."

Nip's chest swelled as he straightened his back and shoulders. "He was the best man in Shaletown. Everyone thought so. He used to make swords as gifts for those who couldn't afford to pay."

"A true hero, indeed."

Nip's eyes reddened, and he wiped at them like an annoyance. "Anyhow. The man asked me to leave the rice at the door. I placed the bowl on the floor, but not before I glimpsed his face in the candlelight."

Nip wrinkled his nose. "Pasty white skin, like sourdough, covered his face. He stared at me with eyes big as goose eggs with blue veins running through 'em. Thick whiskers with tiny feelers on the ends twitched on either side of his mouth as he studied me."

Bron had never seen an albino, but the boy's description fit the stories he'd heard. "All those generations living underground has given them... exceptional traits."

"That's one truth I won't argue." Nip chuckled.

"Did the man tell your father about the caves?"

"No. He left us a medallion made out of a metal Pa had never seen before. It's silver with a pinkish hue to it, like armor in the sunset. One day while Pa stirred his mixture in the cauldron, I played with the strange man's medallion, hanging the chain from the rafters above his head. The metal slipped from my fingers and dropped in the cauldron, blending with the liquid steel. Pa never liked to waste anything, so he made plate armor out of it. Turned out to be stronger than anything he'd made before."

"Did you wear this armor when the wyverns attacked?"

Nip nodded and chewed his lower lip. His eyes grew dark and remote, as if he hid inside himself.

Bron had to have answers to save the kingdom. "You're certain the armor saved you from the flames?"

"Certain as the sun rises." Nip picked at the knot, loosening the twill. "Pa knew the wyverns were coming. He journeyed all the way out here to protect us. Since the man ate all the rice me Ma had given him, Pa took every bag we had and traded. He came back with a bar of silver-pink metal: enough to outfit our entire family. The wyverns attacked a few days later, and he hadn't had enough time. If only he'd had another day or so, he could have at least made enough armor to save my brother or Ma."

Guilt poured through Bron. Why had he pushed the boy so far? "My apologies, son."

Nip sat in silence until the daylight waned and the shadows spread around them. The terrain grew rocky, and the horses struggled to pull the carriage up inclines in the path weaving through the foothills. Through the canopy, the mountains grew, towering over them like the backs of giants.

They emerged from the forest to the banks of a great, placid lake. Twilight cast the water in a silvery glow and mist rolled off its shores. Bron parked the carriage, leaving Nip to guard the horses while he caught up to Danika and Valorian as they explored the eastern shore.

Danika nodded when he arrived through the mist. Valorian picked his way through the rocky shore to refill both their goat skins.

Bron bowed before her, as if they stood in the throne room and she on the throne. "I trust your journey was peaceful."

Danika nodded and spoke loud enough the minstrel could overhear. "How's the boy?" Apparently, she wanted Valorian's presence addressed.

He wasn't about to shout Nip's problems on the wind. Bron's voice remained low and soft, intended only for her ears. "His spirits are low. We talked of his family and how his father learned of the albinos and this new mineral."

Danika stepped toward him. "Why delve into something that brings him such sorrow?"

"For the safety of the kingdom, Your Highness. I must know for certain they have what we seek if we're going to risk our lives for this cause." *Her life. She was too important to Ebonvale--and to him--to lose.*

Danika crossed her arms, looked away and sighed. Questioning the boy was necessary, but he didn't like making the princess angry or proving her wrong. "He's a strong lad. He's agreed to become my apprentice, and to be a true warrior he has to confront his past."

"Your apprentice?" Danika's eyes lit up and her tone changed from belligerent to hopeful. "You're taking him in?"

Bron nodded, surprised by her reaction. He thought she'd be angry with him. Instead, she beamed like a proud mother.

"He'll live with us at Ebonvale Castle and train along with the rest of the Royal Guard. I'm aware how young he is. I'll look after him personally." He hoped she didn't think of his failure with her father. This could be his chance at redemption, a way to show the princess he could protect those she loved.

Danika stepped toward him and placed her hands on his chest. Her eyes blazed with intensity. "I know you will."

Bron breathed deeply. Her proximity alighted fire through his blood, and he had to use all of his strength to hold his stance and stop himself from pulling her against him. His head leaned down, closing the space between them. His gaze focused on her pink, moist lips, slightly open and inviting.

Valorian cleared his throat. Danika whirled around, breaking their contact.

The minstrel studied Bron with new fascination, as if he'd discovered his loyal servant stealing food. "I found the entrance. There's a crack leading into the side of the mountain just beyond the northern shore."

Danika nodded firmly. "Excellent work, Valorian." Her eyes returned to Bron, but the intensity was gone or guarded. Maybe he'd imagined it?

The air cooled between them and for the first time that day, goose bumps stung his skin.

Danika assumed her royal-authority voice, the one she used to cut through the high rafters in the throne room. "We'll make camp for the night then breach the caverns in the morning when we're well rested."

Bron bowed his head, his neck turning hot with shame. What would have happened if Valorian hadn't stopped them? "As you wish, Princess."

"I'll sing throughout the night to keep trespassers at bay." Valorian stepped between them as a barrier of velvet and grace. Somehow, even though they'd ridden all day, he smelled of sweet lavender and peaches, making Bron feel like a sweaty ox. He couldn't believe he had allowed the princess to touch him.

Sweet smelling or not, if Valorian's voice wavered, he risked their safety. Bron challenged him with a twitch of his brow, gesturing to the bandage on his shoulder. "Are you certain you have enough strength?"

Valorian stepped toward him in the place where Danika had stood seconds before. "Shouldn't you tend to the horses, brute?"

The hair on Bron's neck bristled. He stared him down. A bodyguard couldn't challenge a member of royalty. He shouldn't have questioned the minstrel in the first place, but Danika's safety reigned above all else.

Danika pushed herself between them. She cast Bron a pleading look, melting his heart. "I need your strength renewed for the journey tomorrow. Tired muscles cannot carry four bags of rice."

The princess soothed his raging emotions. Bron reined in his swelling pride and bowed. "Of course." He'd allow the princess to have the final say, but that didn't mean he'd sleep without one eye open. "I'll leave you to set up camp."

"Very well." Danika turned to Valorian like a wife appeasing her jilted husband. "Show me this entrance before the darkness engulfs us all."

Bron gritted his teeth and marched back toward the carriage and the place where he belonged.

Chapter 12

Midnight Serenade

Danika wrapped herself in furs and stared at the stars piercing through the thin satiny fabric of her makeshift tent. Bron had caught her off guard when he told her he'd agreed to take the boy in. Considering Nip's lanky frame, stubborn reticence and humble origins, it would be a daunting task to train him for the Royal Guard. However, Bron didn't flinch, accepting his new responsibility with pride. That kind of selflessness delved deep into her heart, deeper than she wanted it to go.

If it weren't for Valorian, she would have kissed Bron. She was sure of it. Even now her mind wandered, wondering what those thick lips tasted like…how it would have felt to wrap her fingers around his strong arms and pull him down to meet her.

Danika slapped her face and forced herself to listen to Valorian's pleasant song. The clear timbre of his high tenor voice soothed her. He'd spoken before of the power of his music and how the minstrels' song only brought out a person's underlying emotions. Still, whenever she opened her heart to the melody, she felt drawn into a spell.

"The full moon doth cast a steady glow
Illuminating truths high and low.
Oh, when will thou heart be true?
For all I can sing of is you."

Blinking, Danika jolted up, her unruly hair skimming the top of the tent. Was this an old ballad or did he sing of her?

Silly girl. Valorian would not reveal his heart so openly. Ever since she was a child, her mother had warned her of thinking the moon, the sun and the stars revolved around her. She belonged to a great universe.

Her existence was a small thread weaving into the tapestry of life. How arrogant to think the lyrics Valorian sang pertained to her alone.

What if he sang of another?

Did jealousy tease her heart? Or simple curiosity? Besides his title as Prince of the House of Song, Valorian's handsomeness rivaled any man in Ebonvale's court. Many women must have sought his charms. What made her so certain she was the prize he wanted? What if he yearned for a lady in the minstrel village whom he wanted but couldn't have because of his station? No, she knew the pangs of hindered love, and she'd never seen those emotions cross his face.

"Tempests churn and rains fall
In this world we see it all.
But a love so pure and true
Can I cultivate it with you?"

Enough! She pulled the furs over her head and his words blurred together. She couldn't fathom how such a melancholy song fended off enemies. Unless the sickly sweetness bled their ears. For once she wished she'd taken Bron's advice. At least his sharp eyes remained closed, allowing her to sleep.

Her mind was like an old bucket, springing another leak of worries before the last was patched. Once she'd blocked Valorian's words from her head, her mind wandered to thoughts of her mother. Part of her wished she'd taken the time to forgive her before they'd left. Now the memory of the former queen standing on that crooked, splintered porch waving them off stuck in her mind without resolution.

Would she ever see her mother again? Could she live with her choice to leave her without forgiveness if their destinies grew apart?

She'd overheard Bron asking her mother to come with them. Danika had known the former queen's answer before it leaked from her old, cracked lips. It was useless to try to save her. She refused outside aid.

Thinking of how she'd battled against Valorian coming with them, Danika realized the cherry blossom didn't fall far from the tree. She'd always pictured herself her father's daughter, but she had a streak of the former queen inside her as well.

Valorian's voice tapered off, and his song changed from words to gentle finger plucks of his lute. Danika turned on her back and closed her eyes. Sleep came like a reluctant visitor, and she lost her worries to the realm of dreams.

The flagstone froze her bare feet as Danika tiptoed through the castle in her nightgown. She wished she'd brought the fur from her bed or slipped on her riding cloak. As a young girl, she got away with scampering around in close to nothing, but her body had changed, and she needed to cover her new curves.

Should she return to her room? The urgency in the whispers below her window and the sound of velvet-clad hooves scuffing in the courtyard told her to make haste, or she'd miss the secrets of the night. The older she'd become, the more she yearned to know of Ebonvale and all its mysteries.

Candlewax dripped across her gown as she scurried down the marble steps. A sweet song wafted on the breeze. The ending cadence comforted her and she fell back against the wall. Her eyes grew heavy and her breathing slow. Slumping to her feet, she gave into the song's lulling turns.

What could be more satisfying than sleep?

Thoughts of the servants finding her in a bare nightgown, snoring on the steps, jolted her awake. She pinched herself to keep alert and hurried down to the landing. Worried about the guards, she peeked around the corner to the antechamber. Both men sat slumped over, fast asleep. They'd given in to the music's charm. Fate danced on her side.

She tiptoed by them and slipped through a crack in the door.

A full moon's glow lit the courtyard in otherworldly iridescence. 'Round the fountain, two figures in hoods packed travel bags on two of Ebonvale's royal stallions, bred to carry the heftiest warriors into battle.

Her father had returned home only yesterday from a triumph in the Northern Pass. Did he leave again so soon without bidding farewell? She crawled toward the fountain on her belly, her neck bristling with anger. He'd done it before. But, to use the court minstrel's sweet song to steal away into the night? That was downright conniving.

The figures came into view and confusion struck her like a knife in her gut. Neither figure was her father. One had his height but not his width. The other had womanly curves.

The taller figure tied a lute to his back. She recognized the delicate paint on the wood. Crescenti. Why had he used his music against the guards? Was he a spy, a thief in disguise, waiting for the right time to make his move? Fear crossed her heart as she realized she'd come alone. She considered running back to wake the guards, but curiosity tempted her forward.

The minstrel pulled the other hooded figure close, wrapping lithe arms around her. A lock of her blond hair flew in the breeze. The taller figure bent down and pressed his face to hers.

Danika rose up from her belly and peered around the mermaid tail spewing water in a steady stream. Was she one of her mother's handmaidens? If so, why meet in secret? Why hide your love?

The taller man spoke. "Come, we must make haste. 'Tis time."

The woman pulled away, wiping her cheeks as if she were crying. She whispered, "I cannot."

The man took her hand in his, pulling her toward the horse. "You must, dearest. If we are ever to be together, if you are ever to find happiness, then you must come with me this night."

Danika pressed her body against the stone fountain to steal a better look, but the figure stood in the moon's shadow.

The woman gazed at the tower above them. "She'll never forgive me."

The minstrel helped her onto a horse. "Did you leave the letter?"

"Yes."

"'Tis all you can do. You've waited as long as responsibility dictates. You've done well raising her. She's almost of age to make her own choices. You must make yours."

The woman signed Helena's sword in the air. "Gods forgive me."

The wind picked up, blowing blond wisps from Danika's braid. The scent of cherrywood blossoms carried on the air.

Danika paused, remembering so many memories of that voice reading to her of Helena's conquests, of that scent mingling with the queen's long robes after she'd gone walking in the orchards.

"Mama?" she murmured. Her heart raced so fast, it might burst out of her chest. They'd argued over her dress fittings the night before, and she hadn't seen her mother since. Surely, her insolence hadn't driven her mother away?

A scraping sound echoed behind her. She whirled around, braid flying. She'd broken the spell of the music by speaking.

The guard wiped his eyes and stood, his sword scraping against the stone wall, and pointed the tip toward the figures. "Who goes there?"

"Hi-ya!" The minstrel yelled, spurring both horses into flight. A cloud of dust covered the courtyard.

"Mama!" Danika raced after her. She ran until the skin on her feet burned. Her gait fell short of the battle horse's long stride. Collapsing on the empty road, Danika hit the ground with her fists, cursing like a warrior.

A regiment of guards ran by her, along with the king. She stumbled to her feet and followed him to the end of the path, where the shadows of night swallowed her mother's horse.

"Sybil!" Her father shouted into the darkness. "In all Helena's Grace, why?"

Empty night pressed in. The melancholy call of skylarks answered his pleas.

"Do you want me to go after them, Your Highness?" The head guard stood in a battle stance, his long sword raised.

"No." Her father's voice cracked. "Let them go." He collapsed beside Danika and held her close.

"I'm sorry, my dear princess. I have failed your mother and, in turn, I have failed you."

His tears fell on Danika as she buried her head in his red velvet robe. She hated her mother for leaving but, at the same time, she feared she might never see her again. All of their arguments seemed petty now. She should have worn her mother's dainty gowns instead of throwing them on the floor in favor of riding leathers.

Bron's voice was the only sound cutting through Danika's grief. He stood above them, crossing his arms below his chest in a solemn pose, like a mourner at a funeral. "I searched her room and found this, Your Highness."

He handed the king a folded sheet of parchment, stamped with the royal crest of Ebonvale, Helena's and Horred's Swords crossed together.

The king sighed and released her. He held out his hand. "At least I'll get some answers."

"It's not addressed to you, Your Highness." Bron's voice broke in hesitation as if he'd cried as well. Anger raced through her heart. How could a servant love her mother as much as she?

Bron blinked his red-rimmed eyes and gazed down at her with envy. "'Tis for Danika."

Chapter 13

Descending through Darkness

Bron awoke with Valorian's cloying songs ringing in his ears. He shook his head, ridding his mind of the flowery words.

As much as he cursed his longwinded ballads, they allowed him to rest and protected the campsite from harm. If anything with a brain was mad enough to venture this far into the dark mountains in the first place.

He sat up and scanned the camp. Mist rolled off the backs of the Darkenbite range, settling over the placid lake and concealing the entrance to the caverns below. Nip and Danika slept peacefully, and Valorian perched on a rock, plucking his lute in minimalist notes. The minstrel's head turned toward him. He acknowledged the warrior with weary eyes. "Good morrow, brute." Although the taunt danced in his words, a hint of a smile played across his lips.

"Good morrow, yourself." Bron stood, stretching his legs. The ground stiffened his back, making swordplay laborious. If Darkenbite lived up to its reputation, he'd need agility and strength for this day's quest. He unsheathed his claymore, swinging the blade, as silver as the lake behind him. The tip crested in an arc above his head, reflecting dawn's early light.

Valorian struck a sweet chord with one dissonant note. "From slumber to swordplay. Looks as though someone is trying to impress his company."

"I practice like this every day, whether in this campsite or outside the soldiers' barracks in Ebonvale." Bron sliced the air, gaining momentum with each swing. His sword danced like quicksilver in the air. "Best if you catch a few hours rest."

Valorian cast him a skeptical look.

Bron raised an eyebrow. Only a fool would cast off rest before venturing into Darkenbite. A fool with too much pride. "Suit yourself.

I'll be roasting the last of the hare within the hour. We leave when the morning mist clears."

Valorian strung one last chord and swung his lute over his back, strutting toward his tent as though sleep were his idea. "Wake me when the princess rises."

Bron stiffened. Now he wasn't trustworthy enough to spend time alone with her? He lunged, jabbing his claymore into a tree to release his anger. The bark split and flew around his blade, raining on his leather boots.

Valorian waited for a reply as Bron pulled the blade free, calming his raging heart. The warrior did not wish to sacrifice Danika's honor for his pride. "Of course."

After completing his ritual training session, Bron started a fire and hung the last scraps of hare over the flames. His stomach grumbled, and he poked at the tender meat with a stick, thinking of how he used to fight over the largest portions of meat with Hule. He wondered how his brother faired at the farm. After the queen had chosen Bron for the Royal Guard, Hule knew he had to stay home and look after their parents. His brother had married, expanded their family's land and had children, even a boy Nip's age. Now Hule had too much to lose to yearn for battle and a warrior's nomadic life.

Would he ever settle down? Bron glanced at Nip's tent. Have children?

"Do you ever sleep?"

Bron turned from the fire, his gaze resting on Danika wrapped in furs to stave off the morning chill. Desire filled his chest, and he pushed his yearnings away. "I slept all night. Valorian protected us with his song."

Danika glanced over at Valorian's tent with doubt crinkling the skin around her eyes.

"He took to his tent not long ago." Bron pulled a piece of meat from the fire and set the hearty ration upon a traveling plate. As much as he wanted time with Danika before they entered the caverns, he had to keep his word. "He said to wake him when you rose."

Danika sat beside him, poking the meat with one of Bron's cooking sticks. "Let us give the prince some time to rest, shall we? If he's played this whole night--as you've said--he deserves his sleep."

"I take orders from you first, my lady." Bron handed her the plate. "'Tis not our usual dining fare."

"'Tis sufficient." Danika wrapped her elegant long fingers around the edge of the plate.

Bron's gaze met hers. Hollowed, dark skin lined the bottom of her eyes. "Did you sleep well, Your Highness?"

Danika pulled the furs tighter as if fending off ill memories in the mist. Her gaze steeled, and he feared she'd closed her heart to him. She picked a piece of meat off the plate and studied the pink center as if her answer lay in the hare.

Bron made a plate each for Nip and Valorian before taking the last few pieces for himself. "My apologies. It's not my place to ask."

"No. It's not."

Embarrassment spread like fire in his cheeks. Bron's gaze shot up to hers and her face softened as a small smile curved her lips.

"However, I'm grateful for your concern." She placed the meat in her mouth, chewed and swallowed.

Bron thought she'd dropped the subject until she spoke again. "Seeing my mother again has brought back ghosts I didn't want to face."

His ghosts invaded his dreams each night. The dead army of Sill never let his mind rest, and in the center of the horde stood the king, the man he'd sworn to protect. Bron knew the pain of reliving the past over and over again until one questioned every decision he made on such a fateful day. "We all must face our ghosts in this life." He gestured toward the lake with playfulness in his eyes to lighten the mood. "Perhaps some of them lay in wait for us in the mist."

Danika made the sign of Helena's sword in the air. "Let's hope not. I've seen enough for a lifetime."

"As have I."

The mist rolled in, wispy tendrils playing around their feet. They sat in silence. Bron was content to share each moment with her, whether they spoke or not.

Danika turned. "Here comes a little ghost right now."

Nip's head peeked out from his tent. His mop of unruly hair stood up like an ill-tended thicket.

"He must have smelled the meat cooking." Bron smiled as Nip caught his gaze. The boy scurried from his furs. Rubbing his eyes, he joined them by the fire.

Danika handed a sleepy Nip his plate. "I trust you slept well?"

Nip nodded, accepting the plate. He walked to the lake and sat on the shore, nibbling on his piece of hare.

"Doesn't speak much in the morning," Bron sighed. "'Tis like squeezing water from stone."

Danika laughed, her eyes finally looking alive again. She tapped her finger on her chin. "I wonder whom that reminds me of?"

Was she teasing him? Bron opened his mouth to reply and closed it again, gritting his teeth together. He had sworn an oath to protect her, not provide pleasant company. Why would she make such an observation? Did she wish for him to say more?

Before Bron could inquire further, Valorian emerged from his tent, glaring.

"Looks as though I've angered him." Bron bit off a piece of meat. Amusement and guilt mingled in his heart. He should have woken the minstrel as he'd promised. Warriors did not fare well at kingdom relations.

"I'll make amends." Danika set her half-eaten plate aside on the grass. She rose and met him before he reached Bron.

Bron chewed his breakfast, trying not to watch them too closely, yet still keeping an eye on Danika. What could they possibly speak of for so long?

The royals' talk should not concern him. To occupy his time and his wandering mind, he started to pack their supplies, securing the rice to a wheeled platform the minstrels had given them. Their quest hung in the air like a foul stench, and he intended to focus on the plan and usher them through harm's way and back again unscathed.

* * * *

"'Tis black as death," Nip complained as Bron lit a torch, burning off tendrils of mist. They stood before a stone archway made from a crack in the mountain's base. Symbols from a strange language were whittled along the frame. A stone carving of Helena and Horred ushering a young child into the caves was carved on the right side.

"Who's that?" Nip pointed to the depiction of the boy his age carrying a sword longer than he was tall and a bulging sack.

"Halfast, Helena's and Horred's son." Danika traced the pictures with the tip of her finger. "During the rise of the dead, they hid him in these caves to live on in their name. He started his own underground society, and they lived apart from the people of the surface, developing different physical traits to combat life in darkness."

"Why have I never heard this tale?" Nip traced where Danika's fingers left off.

Danika looked to Bron. This boy was his apprentice, after all. The warrior nodded and stepped in. "Some temple monks don't tell his story because they consider any link with the cave dwellers sacrilege. Others say the traits were a curse for shunning fate."

Nip held his sword to mimic the boy's pose. "Why?"

Valorian spoke from behind them, surprising Bron with his openness. "They want you to think our race dominates this world. That our gods favor us over all others when, in fact, we're from the same flesh as the albinos. Every creature has a right to coexist: people, albinos and even wyverns."

Nip ran his fingers along his sword. Confusion saddened his eyes. "Is it right for us to kill them then?"

"The wyverns threaten the balance. They push their territory into ours when we've left their islands alone. Just like the dead army of Sill, they must be stopped." Bron placed a hand on his shoulder. "We must defend what is rightfully ours."

"Come." Danika took Bron's torch and led the way into the darkness. "We have no time for philosophical discussions. We must hurry."

Bron didn't know what was worse: leaving the boy with the carriage or taking him with them into the caverns below. Danika had insisted he stay with them, and Nip claimed his father had spoken of the tale so many times, he knew the way. At least he could watch the boy instead of wondering if he wandered into trouble.

Water dripped from a ceiling lined with furry bittle bats, their pale hides glowing faintly white in the shadows. Pink salamanders scurried underfoot, hiding in cracks between the rocks. The air stank of mold and the tang of wet earth. Bron dragged the small wagon with the rice behind him by a rope tied around his wrist. He felt like poor old Wafty, their family's mule back at the farm. Named for his wafting stench, he always struggled with the heavier loads. Bron used to help the old mule by carrying half of the bushels. Wafty wouldn't have liked this load one bit.

Soon the dim light from the entrance faded to a memory and the darkness enveloped them whole. Danika and Valorian carried torches, and the two blazing lights bobbed like fireflies at night.

The bobbing from Danika's and Valorian's torches stopped, and Bron increased his pace. When he caught up, they stood before a three-way fork in the tunnels. The right and left passages jutted down, while the middle passage remained level.

"What should we do?" Danika turned to Bron. The firelight brought out the high angles of her cheekbones, making her face strikingly beautiful.

Bron lifted a finger, testing the wind. Although he preferred the more level path, he knew fate would probably choose against him. "Nothing."

Valorian strummed his lute. He struck three vibrant chords, allowing the echoes to dissipate into the shadows. "Every passage rings the same."

Nip threw a stone at the ceiling and a bunch of bittle bats squeaked, dropping from the sky. Danika shrieked and shielded her head with her arm as they fell toward her. Bron thought he'd have to pick them out of her hair but the bats took flight, diving farther into the cavern.

Danika's gaze blazed as she turned back to Nip. "Why would you ever--"

Bron brought up his hand. He pointed to the cavern on the right. "That way."

"How do you know?" Valorian peered into the darkness.

"Because, that's where the bittle bats went." Nip sprung forward, strutting like the winner of a contest. "Come on."

"Excellent work, little one." Valorian patted the boy on the back as he followed him into the darkness.

Danika shot Bron an inscrutable look. "In Horred's name. Bittle bats telling us the course?"

Bron smiled. "You were wise to bring him along."

"Wise or foolish, which one, I'm not certain." Danika shook her head.

"All wise men were once fools," Bron muttered to himself as he picked up the rope, pulling the heap of rice forward. He hoped he'd passed the "fool" stage as a boy and that every day he grew wiser.

The passage sloped and Bron braced the wagon with all his weight, lest the wheels roll sprawling into the darkness. The ground grew uneven and their footsteps began to crunch.

"Stop." Danika raised her hand.

Bron shifted his feet to hold the weight of the rice from spilling on top of them. His muscles strained, but he'd hauled far heavier loads.

Arm shaking, Danika lowered her torch.

Valorian grabbed her arm before the light from the flames hit the floor. "Please, Princess, trust me. You don't want to see."

Bron stiffened as the minstrel touched her. Valorian's overprotectiveness showed how little the minstrel knew the princess. Danika yanked her arm back. "Nonsense. I need to know what we face."

Valorian held his hand to his chest as if her rejection had physically stung. "We must hurry on. There's no time for study."

While they argued, Nip brought up a piece of the floor. Silence fell as the boy held a giant man's femur to the firelight. "Bones."

Danika's eyes widened. "I thought the albinos ate rice."

"They do." Nip shook the bone in the air. "I saw him with my own eyes. My father did not speak of this."

"No one is questioning your story, lad." Valorian picked up a bone the size of a human arm and traced his finger along a gash of teeth marks stretching from top to bottom. "Perhaps your father didn't want to frighten you."

"I can handle it." Nip threw his bone to the ground and it clattered against the rest.

"Shhh." Bron whispered. "It's not the albinos we have to worry about." Hands still holding back the rice, he gestured with his chin to the slashes Valorian had found. "Those were made by something else."

Chapter 14

Sacrifice

"We cannot turn back." Danika shone her torch over the bones. The flames cast a reddish light on the ivory, making them look as though they sat in fires of hell. Skulls of all sizes littered the floor, from rats to kobolds, to men.

All these creatures had failed.

Fear rose up inside her. Would anyone in her party see the light of day again, or would this dark hole be their grave? The darkness pressed in, suffocating her under miles of hard-packed earth. She steeled her nerves, swallowing her fears. "We've come too far."

Bron nodded in agreement. "Perhaps we can sneak by undetected?"

Valorian plucked a few notes on his lute. "Or perhaps I can lull the beast to sleep?"

"That's if this one has ears." Danika didn't want a repeat of the encounter in the forest. "If it can understand the music's meaning."

"Like I said before, music is a universal language." Valorian plucked again, this time with a stronger force. The notes rang around them like an invisible shield. "My lute can quell any beast able to hear it."

Danika shot a questioning look to Bron. The warrior shrugged as if she'd asked him which gown looked better for Festival Day. She glanced at Nip. The boy's chest heaved as if he battled fear against courage. Danika was on her own and this was her decision to make. She could send them all back, saving their lives this day, but how many days would they have left before the wyverns came and breathed their world into ashes and dust? They needed that metal to launch their attack.

Danika blew on her torch, gauging the time she had left until the flames burned through the oily rags. Not long. Soon they'd travel past the point of no return, when they wouldn't have enough light for the trip back to the surface. "It's settled. We continue on while Valorian plays."

They shuffled through the bone, clearing a path for Bron's rice cart. Valorian's soothing tones echoed down the tunnel, and Danika thanked Helena every breath they took. The melody calmed her, transporting her from the dank hole in the ground to happier times--when she danced in the orchard with her mother or shot arrows with her father in Ebonvale's green woods.

The passageway opened to a large cavern with water dripping. A musky scent of fur and wet hide hit Danika's nose and she held up her torch, fearing the worst. Had they stumbled right into the beast's chamber?

Underneath their high perch, the floor moved everywhere with a steady rise and fall of hair. Danika covered her mouth with her hand to keep from screaming. She turned back just as Nip charged into her. "Shhh!"

Nip scratched his head and peered around her into the darkness as Valorian and Bron caught up. "What is it?"

"Something's alive down there. Something big."

"Let me see." Nip's hand shot up to take the torch.

Danika pulled the torch away, holding the flame out of his reach. "No. I'm not letting any of us go farther in."

Nip slipped by her, crept to the edge and sniffed. "Smells like peeper mice. Pa said there's a whole ton of 'um infesting the caverns. Enough to feed an army."

Pulling Nip back from the ledge, Danika shook her head. "We cannot be sure."

"Lower me down with the torch. I'll take a look."

Danika shot him a stern look. "Most definitely not."

Nip crossed his arms. "It's either that or we go back, and you said we cannot."

Valorian spoke softly over the tones of his lute. "Whatever the threat is, I assure you, I can keep it at bay."

Danika glanced at Bron. The warrior pursed his lips as though he didn't like the sound of Nip's plan. He sighed and untied a rope from his belt. "The boy is right. Someone has to look, and he's the lightest of all of us."

"Horred's Grave." Danika bit her lip and paced the tunnel. She stepped up to Bron and grabbed the rope. "Lower me down. I'm not much heavier than the boy."

Bron didn't let go. "Your Highness?"

"That's an order." She stared into Bron's gaze, challenging him.

"The kingdom needs your rule."

"And it shall have my rule after we succeed, correct?"

He lowered his gaze and pulled her close to him. She gasped as her hands fell on his stone hard chest. For a throbbing heartbeat she thought he'd kiss her. He threaded his hands behind her waist and the rope tightened around her.

Foolish girl. He was following orders. That's all.

"Tread lightly." Vulnerability softened Bron's voice, as if he'd told her he loved her.

Danika held her head down, pretending to check the knot to hide her blush. "Just lower me down."

Nip pouted but he agreed to help Bron with the rope. The sweet music kept Valorian's hands busy. He gave her a longing look as she passed. Admiration burned in his gaze.

Pride rose in Danika. He knew not to get in her way. She wasn't a dainty flower to shelter, but a strong woman with a mind of her own. If he didn't like it, then he didn't have to marry her. What a crisis that would be.

She needed a man to be queen. By law, as princess, she could only gain complete rule along with the title if she had a male counterpart.

Valorian strummed a triumphant chord. "Good luck, Princess."

Danika nodded to Valorian. She turned toward the darkness and stood on the edge. The rope pulled taut as she leaned into the cavern. Slowly, they lowered her down with the torch in her right hand.

Dangling above the musky mass made Danika feel like a fly on a horse's arse. She stuck her hand in her cloak grasping the hard hilt of Valorian's dagger. If the beast awoke, she'd stab out its eye. Wanting to get back up as soon as possible, Danika held the torch below her as far as her arm would reach. A hairy, brown mass covered the cavern floor in small mounds back to back.

No beast was this large.

Nip was right. Peeper mice slept across the entire floor. Relief flooded through her before she realized they'd have to pick their way around the herd without disturbing them. They weren't called peeper mice for no reason, and a mass that size would raise enough of a racket to wake her handmaidens back in Ebonvale.

Danika righted herself, her feet resting on a boulder a head's length from the mice. She untied the rope and tugged. Bron, Nip and Valorian peered over the rim at the circle of hides illuminated by her torch.

"Do you see a spot for the rice cart?" Bron whispered over the edge.

Danika held out her torch and scanned the mass. A pair of black eyes blinked, reflecting the flames of her torch. Danika held her breath as the mouse scratched its head and settled back into the swarm. Valorian's song held true.

She shook her head. "They're everywhere."

Above her, Bron spoke in a muffled murmur. "Nip, did your father speak of how he circumvented this obstacle?"

"No."

The air left Danika's lungs and she forced herself to focus. There must be a way.

As she stood above the horde, her torch sizzled, and a spark fell like a falling star. Danika held her breath, watching the arc of the golden ember as the spark landed on one of the furry hides. She covered her mouth with her hand and prayed to Helena, Horred and even their hidden son.

The mouse squirmed as if annoyed as the ember persisted, igniting the fur. The animal shrieked, cutting her ears in half and echoing throughout the cavern. The mouse ran into the pile of hides, beginning a cascading ripple of movement and screeches. Danika dropped her torch and covered her ears with her hands. The high-pitched conglomeration of peeps rang in her head until she could think of nothing else.

As the thousands of peeper mice scurried away, the sound trailed off into silence. Danika stood as still as a willow, waiting. A wheezing hiss, like the wind in a sea storm echoed from the tunnel behind them. Above her, Valorian's lute fell silent. Bron shouted: "Run!"

"Watch your head!" Nip shouted as Bron and Valorian threw the bags of rice along with the cart over the rim. They climbed down the rope and Danika helped Nip to the cavern floor.

Bron grabbed Danika's hand and squeezed. "Go!"

"What about the rice?" She gripped his hand, not letting go.

Bron peeled her fingers from his. "I'll catch up."

Valorian pulled Danika and Nip forward as Bron loaded the cart. "Come, we must make haste."

Danika stumbled. "Bron--"

"He's coming. Right behind us." Valorian urged her with a steely gaze as they took off. "Do not look back."

She couldn't resist. Danika whirled around. Bron had loaded the cart. The muscles in his arms bunched as he pulled the rice behind him, sprinting as fast as he could to catch up. Above him, the tunnel vomited an oily-white, scaly mass onto the ridge. The thick, tube-shaped body expanded and contracted like a giant muscle.

The beast slid to the cavern floor in a never-ending length of shimmery scales. A jaw with long, spindly teeth snapped forward, while a second head rose, black eyes leering. Stalagmites grew from its dual heads and back in a pointy ridge. Lichen crusted its upper back in patches of jade and ocher.

"A hydra!" Nip squealed, scurrying forward faster than Danika'd ever seen him run. Danika cursed, wondering how she hadn't thought of such a beast before. The white worm made perfect sense: an underground world mirroring hers with distant cousins of people living amongst distant cousins of wyverns.

Danika grabbed Valorian's velvety cloak and pulled him to her. "Can you hold the monster back with song?"

"No." Valorian's face paled as they ran side by side. "Not while it's awake. This beast is beyond my abilities."

Danika's stomach coiled. Never had Valorian claimed defeat. One look over her shoulder told her the hydra gained with each step.

"Over here." Nip had found a crack in the cavern wall wide enough for them to fit through and narrow enough to hold the hydra back. They'd be trapped, but at least they'd be alive. He slipped in, waving an arm. Danika and Valorian reached the crack, and Valorian pushed her forward.

"No." Danika struggled in his arms. "Bron!"

The warrior's torch rested on the cavern floor illuminating the cart without him. Danika's heart jumped to her throat and she choked on horror. Bron stood with his claymore raised against the beast, a single man shielding all of them from death.

Awe hushed Valorian's tone. "He's staying to fight."

"No!" Danika snagged the hydra's attention. The beast swiveled in their direction and Valorian pulled her back into the crack. She gripped the sides, refusing to leave Bron alone.

Bron swung his claymore, blocking the beast from slithering toward them.

"Can the worm breathe fire?" Nip whispered from behind her.

Danika couldn't move or speak from fear of losing Bron. Valorian answered for her. "No. The earth serpents lost that ability when they burrowed underground."

"That doesn't make them any less dangerous, only more sly." Danika bunched her fists together and watched helplessly.

"Can it be killed by one man?" Nip's voice quivered.

A quiet pensiveness fell over Valorian. "No one has single-handedly defeated one."

Danika glanced at him with fierce conviction and perhaps a little denial. "If any man can do it, Bron can."

The hydra hissed, extending a forked tongue in Bron's direction. The warrior ducked as the tongue licked the air above his head. He stabbed his sword up, but the hydra retracted its tongue too quickly. Meanwhile, the other head curved around, trying to take him by surprise.

"Watch your back!" Danika shouted.

Bron whirled around as the second head thrust toward him, jaw open to swallow him whole. He raised his arm and braced the jaw with his sword. The tip of the blade cut through the skull while the bottom hilt lodged in its pin-sharp teeth. The head swerved up, taking the sword with it.

The first head lunged, teeth snapping. Bron ducked and punched the muzzle sideways just as the tip of the tail curled around his boot.

Bron reached down to his leather boot and unsheathed a dagger. He swiped, slicing a gash in the tail. The hydra tightened its grip, winding around his lower leg like a vine. It yanked Bron to the ground as he swiped again, deepening the gash.

The hydra dragged Bron closer and yanked him up, dangling him upside-down in the air. Danika couldn't watch, yet her eyes remained fixated on the horror of Bron's precarious situation. She bit into her lower lip, tasting blood. He would defeat this beast.

The first head snapped and Bron swung away, arms flailing for control. He reached up and sliced his dagger through the tail. The appendage tore in two and he fell to the ground, landing on his back.

Bron rolled behind the beast as the stubby tail whipped through the air, spewing black blood. He stuck his dagger between his teeth and climbed its great neck, using the stalagmites on its back for handholds. The beast swung from side to side and bucked underneath him to dislodge him. Bron held on and reached the head. Bracing himself with one arm, he used the blade to blind both eyes. The hydra jerked in anger, slamming its head into the cavern ceiling, just as Bron slid down its neck.

A crack as loud as thunder erupted, echoing throughout the cavern as pebbles rained down, followed by larger chunks of rock.

"Cave in!" Valorian pulled Danika back into the crevice in the wall as rocks tumbled from the ceiling, stirring up a cloud of dust. She fell on top of him, and Nip buried himself in her arms as debris rumbled around them. Danika's teeth clamored in her skull, and her bones shook until she felt as if they'd shatter into a thousand pieces. Suffocated and trapped together, Valorian held her tightly, whispering a sweet, soothing song in her ear.

All she could think of was Bron.

Chapter 15

Song of Resurrection

The rumbling subsided like an earthquake lulled to sleep. The faint flickering of their last torch cast shadows on a pile of boulders blocking the entrance to their crevice. Coughing, Nip pulled away and staggered to his feet. Dust covered his small body from head to toe, camouflaging him against the sand and stone. He climbed the pile of rocks and pushed debris from the top. "There's a hole! We can squeeze through."

"Are you all right?" Valorian's hands ran up and down her arms.

Danika nodded, pulling away. How could she seek comfort in Valorian's arms while Bron's fate remained unknown? She gathered the torch and followed Nip's steps, climbing the pile of rubble. "Bron?"

"We'll check for him." Valorian's voice lacked hope, leaving Danika with a gaping hole in her heart.

Refusing to give up, she pulled herself through Nip's hole and slid down the other side.

Half the cavern, including the tunnel where they'd come from, had caved in. The hydra's head lay lifeless, protruding from a pile of stones with Bron's sword still stuck in the jaws. Black blood seeped from its mouth, coagulating on the cavern floor. Danika stuck the torch in between two rocks to keep the flame upright. She pulled Bron's claymore from the spindly teeth, the blade almost too heavy for her to lift, and dragged the tip behind her, looking for any trace of its owner. The rice cart lay unscathed, as if Bron had shoved the wheels to safety in a last attempt to further their cause.

She didn't care about the rice. What had she done? She'd ordered him to his death and he followed her dutifully.

"Bron?" Her voice rose as if she called him all the way from the throne room in Ebonvale. "Bron!"

She dropped the sword and started to dig, pulling large stones from the pile and shattering them on the cavern floor. Dirt, beetles, tree roots and worms fell on top of her and she brushed them off. Her fingers dug around a stone the size of a horse's belly. She yanked, tearing her nails and ripping the skin of her palms. Nip joined her, both of them using all their weight, but the stone wouldn't budge. A hundred more that size and larger had fallen on top of the heap.

Danika beat the rock with her fist. "Son of a wyvern hunter!" She collapsed to the ground, her body convulsing with sobs.

Valorian's gentle hand squeezed her shoulder. "Princess."

She looked away. "I'm not leaving him."

"Think of the others in Ebonvale. Of Nip. We have to continue on to trade."

"No." Danika whirled around and clutched his shirt with both hands. The fabric bunched in her fingers. "You have to do something."

Valorian shook his head, his eyes full of shame. He glanced at the pile of rocks behind them as if she'd asked him to move the whole world. "'Tis beyond my capabilities."

"Nonsense." She leaned in, her lips a breath away. She had no idea what he could do, if anything. Desperation drove her to the brink of madness. He was the only person she could turn to. "You're the Prince of the House of Song. Legends have been made of the resourcefulness of minstrels and the power of their song."

His gaze lowered to her chin. "I cannot."

She moved her head closer to lock eyes with him and wrapped her fingers around his upper arms. "I refuse to leave without knowing what happened. If there's any chance he's still... Please, Valorian. Do it for me."

His eyes were silver pools of hope. He relaxed into her touch. "I'll try."

She placed her head on his chest, finally finding comfort in his arms. "Thank you."

"Don't thank me yet." He pulled her against him, breathing in the scent of her hair as he nuzzled his nose against her cheek.

Danika backed away. This was hardly the time for romance. "Do your best."

"I always play my best." He slipped his lute from his back to his arms and strummed a harsh, dissonant chord sounding more like a random tangle of notes. "This has never been done before. Not by me or any other minstrel. Cover your ears."

Danika stood back, pulling Nip away from the minstrel. She placed Nip's hands over his ears, then blocked hers. Through her palms and the beating of her own heart, a low growling hum resonated deep within Valorian's throat. The primal drone stirred acid in her gut. His voice rang more like a warning than a song, and the rocks reverberated around them, struck like tuning forks to the vibrations of sound. He strummed so hard, drips of blood leaked down the wood of his lute to the cavern floor.

The rubble shook, and a few rocks shattered, flinging dust and pebbles at their faces. Danika turned her back, shielding Nip with her body. She shouted at his hand-covered ear. "Close your eyes."

More rocks shattered, pelting debris at her back. Danika huddled with Nip, still covering her ears and wondered just what she'd asked the minstrel to accomplish. Explosions erupted behind her, and she squeezed her eyes shut, afraid slivers of stone would embed in her pupils, blinding her. The onslaught lasted for several minutes, until she held her breath and released it again. Valorian's voice trailed off into a howl, and the blasts stopped.

Danika turned around and opened her eyes, squinting against the dust. Valorian lay on his back, unconscious. Slivers of stone had cut gashes in his face, and the tips of his fingers were red with blood. The strings on his lute had broken and curled. Beyond him, a hand protruded from a mound of dirt, thick fingers with calluses so large it could only be Bron's.

Danika ran to the mound and pushed the dirt off. Bron's face surfaced, his eyes closed. "Bron!" She slapped his cheek. No response. "Bron, wake up."

Nip took the warrior's hand and held the palm to his heart. Tears rolled down the boy's face, muddying the dust on his cheeks.

Had she lost them both? Too greedy to leave one behind?

"No!" Danika pounded on his chest. "No, you cannot leave me."

Bron sucked in a gasping breath and stared at her as if she'd lost her mind. "My lady?"

Danika laughed and cried at the same time, laying her head on his chest. "You're alive."

He sat up and brushed the dirt from his arms. "Why shouldn't I be?"

"The hydra." Nip pointed to the dead head. "It caved the ceiling in. You were covered in rubble."

"Yes. I seem to remember something of the sort." Bron rubbed his head. "It would explain the pain behind my eyes and the reason my throat is full of dirt."

Bron met the princess' gaze, as if seeing her for the first time in years. "How did you find me?"

"Valorian. He saved your life."

Nip tugged on her arm, and they turned to the minstrel, still lying unconscious in the dust.

"Helena's Heaven!" Danika ran to his side, pained with guilt. How quickly she'd forgotten him. He'd risked his life and his lute for her. She pressed her fingers to his neck. A faint pulse answered her pleas.

Danika dabbed at his bloodied cheeks. "Help me lift him."

Nip scurried behind and helped Danika prop him against a boulder. His eyelids flickered and his gaze rested beyond Danika, to Bron. "You're alive." His usually melodic voice was wispy and hoarse.

"Thanks to you." Bron offered his hand and pulled Valorian up. "My apologies, Minstrel. I've underestimated your power and your heart. I owe you a life debt."

"You don't owe me anything." Valorian bent and picked up his lute. He inspected the broken strings with skeptical eyes. "I did it because the princess asked me to."

Danika avoided Bron's gaze. What would he think of her now? Using another man's love to keep him alive? She'd had no choice.

"Which makes you a better man than I'd initially thought." Bron clapped him on the back as Danika bandaged Valorian's fingers. "Someone the princess can rely on and trust."

Danika listened to their conversation carefully as she tied the scraps of fabric in knots around Valorian's knuckles. Did this mean Bron would think Valorian worthy of her hand? She had no idea how to digest that thought.

"You saved our lives by fighting that beast." Valorian leveled his eyes with Bron's. "Which makes you a braver man than I'd initially thought."

"So we're even then?" Bron stepped forward, offering his hand once again, this time for a truce.

"Even as the horizon on a clear day." Valorian took Bron's hand and they shook, a gesture Danika never thought would happen. Unease stirred in her stomach. She'd become used to them fighting over her, and suddenly she felt outnumbered.

Chapter 16

An Honorable Name

Bron followed Danika, Valorian and Nip deeper into the mountain despite the weakening flame of their single torch. They could not go back from whence they came and their need for the metal drove them forward. Ironically, the only way out was delving further down. Hauling the rice behind him, he replayed the fight with the hydra over and over in his head.

How had he lost control?

Valorian's skill had saved him, and the significance of that life debt, whether Valorian swore it off or not, weighed on his soul. Any honorable man would stand by it. Which meant he could never have Danika.

Not that he'd had a chance with her anyway.

To steal the bride of the man he'd bonded to in life debt would curse the gods and spit on their graves, throwing away every ideal they'd given their lives for. Bron was not a lesser man.

"There's light up ahead." Nip's voice echoed down the tunnel, waking Bron from his musings. The warrior increased his pace.

The tunnel narrowed and the walls became hard granite, explaining why the hydra couldn't tunnel farther to plague the underground denizens of the mountain. The walls glowed up ahead with a faint white light, akin to moonshine. Nip ran back to him, holding up a wiggling glowworm he'd pulled from the ground. "Look!"

The worm curved its thick body in a ball in the palm of Nip's hand. Nip scrunched his nose. "What's it doing?"

"Self-defense." Bron picked the worm from Nip's hand and placed it on a ledge in the wall. The sections of its body spread out again and the worm crawled away. "We'll learn more about defense tactics later, when your training starts." Bron resumed his heave and the cart creaked forward.

"Hopefully you'll teach me better tactics than that." Nip followed him like a puppy.

"Simplicity is sometimes the better way." Bron smiled. Teaching him would prove satisfying. *If* they got out of this hellhole alive.

Danika and Valorian stopped up ahead. They no longer had the luxury of Valorian's lute to lull their enemies to sleep, so they had to tread cautiously. Bron caught up and dropped the rope tied to the cart by his feet, resting his arm. "What is it?"

Danika put her finger to her lips and whispered, "Voices."

Bron held his breath. Down the tunnel muffled voices spoke a language he'd only heard when the monks recited ancient text at temple. "It is indeed the albinos. They speak in the old tongue."

"Wonderful." Danika rolled her eyes. "Valorian, I don't suppose you speak it?"

"A small amount." His face was stoic, now slightly scarred by the flecks of stone. The markings gave him more character.

Danika furrowed her eyebrows. "Can you tell them we come in peace?"

Valorian absently stroked the place where the strings used to lay on his lute with his bandaged fingers. "I'll certainly try."

Danika shot a look to Bron and then his claymore. He nodded once. If it came to it, he'd unsheathe the blade before the pale faces could blink a half-blind eye. They continued forward, rounding a corner where several hunched, robed figures collected glowworms in baskets. The figures straightened.

Danika nudged Valorian. "If you can say anything, now would be the time."

Valorian cleared his throat and raised his hand, spreading his fingers. "*Dotheth cuman innan frio niman.*"

The figures whispered among themselves then scurried away, leaving their baskets. Bron let his hand hover over the hilt. His senses heightened, like on the eve of battle.

Danika clasped her hand on Valorian's arm. "What did you say?"

"What you told me to say." Valorian seemed overly defensive, like a husband blaming his wife.

Bron stepped forward. "Nip, stay back and guard the rice."

"Hold on." Danika placed a weighty hand on Bron's chest. "A fully-armed warrior is not the finest diplomat."

"I wasn't thinking of negotiations."

"My point exactly." Danika slipped by him, taking the lead. "I'm not afraid of these albinos. Follow me."

The tunnel widened to a ledge overlooking a city of small, earth-packed huts, streetlamps filled with squiggling glowworms, cobblestone walkways and hooded figures. A long, winding stairway led to the bottom of the valley, where a pool of water glowed. A semicircle of hooded figures waited at the bottom. Bron saw no weapons, but that didn't mean they didn't have them.

He resisted the urge to shout commands. He wasn't the one making decisions. "Shall we descend, Princess?"

Danika rested her hand in the crook of Valorian's arm. "Yes. Valorian will present me." She cast Bron a meaningful look. "Guard my back."

"As always, Princess."

Lugging the cart of rice down the narrow stairs was not easy. One misplaced step in the dim light would have him and the cart sprawling down the steps in an undignified heap, leaving the whole party vulnerable. Nip took up the rear and kept a solid hand on the top pack of rice. If they proved hostile, the cart could be used as a projectile, allowing them time to escape.

They reached the bottom landing, and the princess and Valorian stepped forward. Bron resisted the urge to hold the hilt of his sword. Mustn't look menacing or Danika would scold him.

One of the hooded figures stepped forward. As he held his head up, the hood fell back and a hairless, rodent-like face came into view. Blue veins laced through pale skin. His eyes were wide and oval shaped, with no pupils, only darkness. Thick whiskers twitched around his toothy mouth.

"Greetings, surface dwellers."

Valorian stepped forward. "You speak our language?"

"At times." The albino folded his hands in front of him, and Bron relaxed his tense stance. Threading one's hands was far from the gesture of any warrior.

Valorian gestured toward the bags of rice. "We come in peace, to trade in the name of..." He looked to Nip.

"Alhearn Blueborough," Nip announced, surprising Bron with such a sophisticated name. Then, Bron realized he shouldn't be surprised at all. He had an honorable name for an honorable man. Someday Nip would claim the family title and make his father, and Bron, proud.

"Indeed, no ignoble man, falsifier or thief could pass through the caverns above alive. Only a truly courageous heart can find its way once the darkness sets in and the reaper starts claiming souls."

Bron crossed his arms. It was old superstition to leave such judgments to fate. "If you are speaking of the hydra, 'tis dead. The tunnel has caved in."

The rodent-like man smiled. "The hydra is just one of many, as is the tunnel. Though, they all lead here."

Danika gave Bron a warning glance as if to say, "*Stay out of kingdom relations.*" Bron bowed his head, not wanting to cause trouble. This was why warriors weren't diplomats.

She offered the rat man her hand. "I'm Princess Danika of Ebonvale. This is Prince Valorian of the House of Song. Behind me stands my bodyguard and the Chief of Arms, Bron Thoridian, along with Alhearn Blueborough's son, Nip."

"Nathaniel," Nip spoke up. "My real name's Nathaniel."

Danika assessed Nip with a new respect. "May I correct myself: Nathaniel Blueborough. We seek a certain metal alloy to aid us in our campaign against the wyverns, for a massive She-Beast rises, as we speak, to blight our lands. We've brought rice to trade."

The rat-man placed long white fingers in her hand. "Oster Snipple at your service, Princess. I know Alhearn. I'm afraid to ask why he didn't join you."

Danika's voice grew strong as steel. "For the same reason we're here. The wyverns leveled Shaletown. Nip is all that's left."

Oster's whiskers drooped and he held his white hand over his heart. "I'm sorry to hear that. Alhearn saved one of our elders while the elder completed a crucial mission. He also visited our city, bringing us delicacies from the surface. Alhearn has gone down in our history books as a hero."

Bron placed a hand on Nip's shoulder and squeezed. He whispered, "You should be proud of your father."

Oster waved to the others around him to assist Bron with the rice. "Come, let me offer you some accommodations. It looks as though you've had a rough journey."

They followed the rat-man through town, passing fields where workers farmed glowing coral rising in giant fanlike shapes. Lizards the size of dogs slithered against the rails of fenced coops, and small children stopped and stared as if the travelers were the ones who looked strange. Nip gaped right back at them and Bron had to pull him away to keep pace with the others. "Don't stare. It brings attention to your fears."

"They're staring at me."

"Because they fear you. Walk tall, look forward and show them you have no fear."

Nip seemed placated by Bron's wisdom. He straightened and took his place at the warrior's side.

Oster lead them to an earth-packed hut, larger than the rest, in the center of town. "This is the meeting house, where we gather to make decisions concerning the entire community."

The inside had a ring of roughly woven pillows in the center, where Oster had them sit.

He gestured to Nip. "Your father joined us in this very place, telling us stories of the world above."

Nip nodded. His chin shook and he wiped his eyes.

The talk of his father must weigh heavily on his heart. Bron wanted to reach out to the boy. His fingers tingled and he fisted them by his side. He had to allow Nip time to grieve.

Two rat-women stood at the door with washcloths and clay bowls filled with water. Oster waved them in. "These healers will tend to your wounds."

One of the healers moved to Bron and he waved her back. "I'm fine."

Danika shot him a stern look and mouthed, "Do not refuse their offerings."

He sighed and nodded to the rat-woman. For Danika, he would do anything. "Okay. Do your worst."

The rat-woman wiped him down and spread a white, cooling gel on his wounds. Valorian had the same attention to his face and fingers. Danika and Nip were dusty but unharmed.

The rat-women left and returned with trays of tough-looking meat. Oster waved his hand over the food as if it were a delicacy. "Grilled glowworms and lizard. Eat."

With one look at Danika's stern eyes, Bron knew not to turn this away. He picked up a strip of lizard meat and stuffed it in his mouth, swallowing the portion whole. Danika nibbled on a worm and Nip pretended to eat by hiding the pieces in the cushion underneath his rump. Valorian pulled a small knife and fork from his coat as if he was dining in the throne room.

"Please enjoy our root cider." Oster handed them mugs of frothing liquid then took a seat at the head of the table. "The wyverns have been a concern of ours for almost a decade."

Surprise flashed in Danika's features. "Why? You live far removed from the surface."

"Everything is linked in this world. The rain that falls on your soil trickles down to nourish us, bringing minerals and vitamins gleaned from your fertile lands. The bats that feed on your insects outside the caves distribute droppings that feed the glowworms, giving them energy for our light. If the wyverns take over these lands, this city will die as well."

Oster took a long sip of his root cider. "That is why you need not have brought the rice. We will gladly give you the metal you desire to equip your army."

Bron threw his hands up in the air. "Well, I'm not carrying that rice all the way back."

Danika placed a calming hand on his arm. "No one said you were." She leaned to Valorian and they whispered between themselves.

Biting on a chewy piece of lizard tail, Bron tried not to seem annoyed. He'd have to get used to being the third carriage wheel if Danika decided to marry Valorian. Imagining her in the minstrel's arms sent a dagger to his gut.

Danika turned to Oster. "We will leave the rice with you for your stocks as a gesture of peace."

"That is very kind of you, Princess. We'd fight by your side if the sun's rays didn't scorch our skin." His eyes grew dark. "If the wyverns reach these mountains, we may not have a choice."

"They won't because my army"--she gestured toward Valorian--"and that of the House of Song will stop them. All we need is the alloy to strengthen our armor."

Valorian leaned forward. "We don't have much time."

"Very well." Oster signaled the women and they left in a hurry. We'll get your metal and help you carry it as far as we can go. That is the best we can do."

"'Tis enough." Danika stood, gesturing for them all to rise.

Bron resisted the urge to rest in the cushions and fall asleep. "Just when I'm getting comfortable." The root cider had given him a fuzzy serenity and made the lizard meat taste like chicken. He'd planned on finishing another plate and having a good nap before they left for the surface. Warriors had no time for the pleasantries of life.

Creaking came from the doorway. Three rat-men hauled their rice cart, now loaded with blocks of a silvery alloy. When Bron craned his neck the right way, the blocks shined in a pinkish hue, reminding him of the bellies of the fish he caught in the stream back at the farm.

Several more men stepped in, carrying bags of metal on their backs. Bron's arms ached just thinking about how much more that metal weighed than the rice. He straightened, knowing he had to set a good example for the boy. "I'll take the cart."

The three rat-men handed Bron the rope and he pulled the cart forward. Audible gasps rang out around him as the rat-men stepped back. Valorian gave him an admonishingly weary look. "Haven't you hauled enough today?"

Bron smiled, finally feeling as though he had a say in these discussions. "I can handle this." The load wasn't as heavy as he'd imagined. Besides, warriors never complained.

Chapter 17

Letters

The albinos knew the caverns and tunnels like Danika knew the secret corridors of her father's inner keep. Circumventing the cave in, the pale-faced men and women brought them to the surface in mere hours without waking a single peeper mouse or bittle bat.

As the light from the end of the tunnel came into view, the albinos stayed back in the shadows and set down the packs of metal at their feet.

Oster bowed, pulling his hood over his pale features. "This is as far as we can travel, Your Highness."

Danika bowed. "You've done so much to help us. I wish our people could overcome the differences separating us and establish trade venues."

Oster waved his pale fingers and soil-crusted nails. "Prejudice is a powerful evil and will take more than a mere load of metal to overcome."

Danika thought of the temple monks and their exclusion of Halfast's tale. "At least your peace offering opens the door to reason, if but a crack."

The sun's rays grew stronger behind them, and the line of shadows drew back.

"We'll see." The rat-man backed deeper into the darkness, and Danika knew their time together was at an end.

She raised her voice so Oster and all the others could hear. "We will return your kindness by protecting the borders of our shared lands."

Oster's voice echoed down the shaft. "So be it. May Halfast's light show you the way."

It took them an hour to haul the metal to the sunlight and load the carriage. The horses had dined on the fine, thin grasses by the lake in their absence, and they moved with restless grace.

Danika and Valorian took the lead, choosing the path for Bron and Nip as they carted their shipment behind them. The heavier load forced them to move at a slower pace, circumventing the deep forest in a southeasterly direction toward Ebonvale. Danika made use of the relaxed stride to lure more information from Valorian.

He'd sent piles of letters over the years. Letters she hadn't answered, many of them lying unread. Perhaps if she'd reached out, even once, they'd be companions rather than acquaintances. An uneasy current spread through her gut as she played with the idea of turning back time. She'd be a different person, a different leader, and she was proud of who she'd become.

Danika glanced over to Valorian as he rode with nimble ease, poised and proud in his saddle like a true prince. "Why did you send so many letters?" Her voice came out softer and more vulnerable than she would have liked. Valorian's hands fidgeted with the reins. His features grew guarded, as if he debated between telling her a sweet nothing or the stone, cold truth. "Because my father told me to."

Danika nodded solemnly. She'd suspected such an answer, but didn't think he'd give in to total honesty. Reality slapped her in the face, and a sliver of disappointment cut through her heart. She thought his advances of late had had some ring of truth, that he'd felt something for her. Hearing about his adherence to duty made him more real, someone she could relate to. Ironically, the truth drew her toward him even more.

Valorian pulled on his reins, turning his horse toward hers, stopping them both. "For many years I sought you out of duty. My father lectured me endlessly on how our two kingdoms would benefit from joining. I believed in his ideal of a strong union, so I wrote to you out of my love for my father, out of love for the House of Song and all the minstrel kingdom represents."

He grabbed her reins and pulled her closer toward him. Their horses sniffed in annoyance, then obeyed. "Now it's much, much more. I had no idea how beautiful and strong-minded you are, how your courage is inspired by a deep love for Ebonvale and how you fight for its security."

Danika's heart sped and every moment flew by too fast to grasp. She wanted to hold onto each word, studying these new, blossoming feelings. "Valorian--"

"Danika, you're everything I've sought without knowing it." He reached forward and grasped her hand, squeezing her palm as if he could hold her next to him forever. "I know now."

The wheels creaked as the carriage rounded the bend, spooking their horses apart. They broke contact. Danika regained control of her reins and pulled a safe distance away, not wanting Bron to see them so close. Valorian gave her one last longing look, then continued forward.

Danika sat on her steed, unmoving, processing what had just happened. Valorian had so much as professed his love for her in a matter of seconds, turning her entire world around. She could no longer ignore and delay their relationship and what their union meant for Ebonvale. Their quest was almost at an end.

"Something the matter, Princess?" Bron had caught up, waking her from her trance. Nip had fallen asleep in his arms and snored peacefully, leaving the two of them to speak freely.

"We're almost home." Danika looked away as a surge of melancholy hit her. "So much is going to change."

"Aye." Bron's face was stoic, his tender mouth solemn. "But, some things will never change."

Danika snapped to attention, studying the warrior's scarred face. What meaning did his words have? Their relationship would never change. His and her duties would never change. His feelings for her would never change. So many possibilities sat unspoken between them. If he wanted her to know, it would be better to say his feelings now than in the castle, full of listening ears and fluttering tongues.

She opened her mouth to ask but Bron had already snapped the reins, spurring the horses pulling the carriage forward. He spoke over his shoulder. "Ebonvale awaits."

The castle's ivory turrets poked through the tree line up ahead, decorated by Ebonvale's purple and green flags fluttering in the breeze. A wash of emotions came over Danika. It was the only home she'd ever known. First and foremost, she thought of her father and his big, gentle hands full of calluses and scars from battle, his scratchy beard and his emerald eyes--eyes she'd inherited from him. She remembered how he had gazed at her with fondness, as if she was the only thing in the world that brought him happiness.

Then she thought of her mother. Since seeing her in the forest, her emotions had morphed from confusion and hate to pity and maybe more. She still had to sort those feelings out, and she didn't know where she'd end up. Danika sighed, riding down a path into the valley of orchards where she and her mother used to walk. It didn't matter, because she'd probably never see her again.

As apple and pear trees surrounded them, Danika's thoughts turned to Bron and all the mornings he'd spent training her against her parents' wishes. If only they'd known she'd need that training more than ever when they were gone. He'd come to the castle when she was still a young girl, but he'd made a lasting impression from the first time she saw him fight so bravely on the tournament field. He'd given her so much by believing in her abilities, by teaching her that a girl—now a woman--could fight as well as any man. How could she look at Ebonvale and not think of Bron?

As they neared villagers collecting ripened fruit in baskets, she pulled her hood over her face. Her dusty, dirt-stained travel clothes provided the best disguise. She would appear as the princess' messenger and nothing more.

The orchards tapered off into a golden field of wheat. Up ahead, the stone walls of the palisade rose with archers positioned at even intervals throughout.

Valorian pulled back on his reins. "I can go no further."

Danika halted by his side, a warm breeze caressing her cheek. "You're not going to come in? At least for a day to rest?"

He smiled. "I wish I could." His gaze traveled to the busy gateway bustling with traders, villagers and castle dignitaries. "Let's just say minstrels are not highly regarded in Ebonvale at this time." His eyes grew mischievous. "Someday, I'd like to change that."

Bron's carriage caught up, and he and Nip jumped out. Valorian dismounted and walked to them, offering his hand. "My journey takes a different path. I will return to the House of Song and prepare our minstrel army, bringing my father news of our success and what is to come."

"Very well." Bron took his hand. "You have proved yourself a worthy ally, and I commend your abilities, as well as express my gratitude again for saving my life."

Valorian bowed his head. "You are a truly courageous and honorable man. Your respect is enough."

Bron nodded but frowned as if he didn't believe him. Danika wondered why the fact Valorian had saved his life irked him so.

Nip dug into his shirt and pulled out the pendant Valorian had given him in the forest. The boy bowed. "This belongs to you."

Valorian accepted it, placing the cord around his neck. "Thank you for guarding it, son. Someday you may have one of your own." He ruffled the boy's hair. "You're in good hands. Be good and we'll meet again."

Bron lifted Nip to the carriage and climbed in after him. He nodded to Danika. "We'd best be on our way to deliver this metal to the forge. Say your goodbye in peace."

The carriage hobbled away. Why did Bron leave her with the minstrel when just two days ago he was reluctant to wake him? Had he given up?

Surrendered himself and her to her rightful fate? No. She couldn't believe he'd abandon her or else she'd lost him as a confidant and friend. Perhaps he was concerned about bringing the metal to the forge. Aye, that's all it was.

She dismounted and approached Valorian. His silver eyes held a swirl of emotions: fondness, melancholy and a special sparkle reserved for her. She touched the new scars on his face. His skin was no longer flawless, but she thought him handsomer because of the scars. "Thank you for saving Bron."

He threaded his arms around her waist and pulled her close. "I have to admit, I didn't think he was alive. But, you were right. Your persistence saved his life, not I."

Danika paused. The next she'd see him they would be going into battle. There wouldn't be another moment like this. "I was wrong about you. I'm sorry I never returned your letters."

"It doesn't matter now." He leaned his head down and his nose brushed against hers. She opened her lips slightly. Doubt and a fierce loyalty to Bron kept her from leaning forward to kiss him.

"If you do not try, you'll never know," he whispered.

Danika rose on the tip of her toes and pressed her lips against his. So soft, so smooth, so gentle, so sweet. Valorian kissed her back with restraint and respect. She was a princess, and he a prince. A long, drawn-out courtship should have taken place before they even touched. Danika pulled away, still digesting her feelings. A life with Valorian meant many things, good and bad. She'd live in the House of Song and follow in her mother's footsteps by moving to a new kingdom through marriage and by choosing a minstrel lover. Most of all, choosing Valorian meant leaving Ebonvale and Bron.

Valorian smiled, but it was sad. "Farewell, Princess. A long journey awaits both of us. I hope to see you at the end."

She knew he hoped they'd be together, but she couldn't promise him anything. Danika had a lot to think about and very little time.

Chapter 18

Stewardess of Ebonvale

Emotions running rampant, Danika ascended the large, table-wide stone steps to her castle. A middle-aged woman carrying a basket of apples hobbled to her left, and two farm kids darted past her, weaving in and out of the crowd in a game of tag. A temple monk hummed as he marched to her right, his face and shaved head painted with ancient symbols. Silver offerings tied to the end of his staff clinked with each step. He smelled of smoke and incense, drawing Danika to turn toward him. The monk locked eyes and stared as if he could see the shape of her soul.

She pulled her hood further around her face and increased her pace, shuffling behind a young castle archer with a bow slung over his shoulder. The travelers formed a line, waiting for the guards to grant them entrance into the main keep.

A guard that had worked for her father for many years held out his hand. "Reason for business, or your pass, ma'am."

While hiding her face in her hood, Danika dug into the folds of her cloak and brought out a silver emblem of a horse and rider, the emblem of the royal messenger. The guard nodded once and moved to the older woman carrying apples.

Once through the main gate, Danika picked up her long cloak to free her legs and jogged through the courtyard. She passed the fountain and, like always, the airborne dolphins and mermaids brought memories of her mother and the minstrel on that fateful night. The familiar gurgle of water whispered to her and the scent of cherry blossoms rode the wind, bringing fond memories as well, mostly those of her father bringing her flowers from the training field or a sparkly rock from the upturned earth caused by battle. She was finally home.

After presenting the messenger symbol repeatedly, she climbed the spiral stairway to the main throne room. Familiar paintings of her relatives and ancestors greeted her as she passed. Her father's rigid features belied the kindness in his eyes as he stood in his prime with his sword perpetually raised, clad in shining armor. Her mother's soft, round face, ivory skin and velvet shawl showed a much earlier time before fate turned her into a scavenger of the woods.

If only Danika had known then what she knew now.

Danika paused by her mother's sweet picture. Would she have still left?

Between the paintings of her mother and father lay the former Queen of Ebonvale, Islador. Danika had never noticed how the first wife's painting was the largest and the only frame gilded in gold with rubies and emeralds clustered at every corner. Her face shone like an angel mixed with a temptress, with star-white hair and entrancing, sapphire eyes. She was gorgeous, and now the extent of the golden slippers her mom had been forced to fill was more evident. Sybil had failed because Danika's father had never moved Islador's painting. The dead queen still claimed her right by his side, as if she'd entranced him in a spell besting death.

Tapestries depicting her father's glory over the dead army of Sill covered the walls as she rounded the bend. On the right, he rode a black horse, leading Ebonvale's Royal Guard. On the left, he swung his sword, slicing a putrefied soldier of the dead in half. One battle after another in a long slew covered the extent of his campaign with precise detail down to the rotting faces and hollow eyes of the enemy and the gleaming silver of the guards' raised swords.

Her mother's words had skewed everything Danika knew about the past. Her father had disappeared often over the years, and she had only seen them together on formal occasions. Her mother *had* been a pet, confined in the castle like a bird in a cage. How could Danika have been so blind? Having no time for further ruminations, she took a right turn and reached the throne room, throwing open the massive oaken doors.

The tiles in the marble floor depicted the galaxy above, with swirling cosmic clouds and glinting stars of mica. The artist's work represented Ebonvale's never-ending reach throughout the world, stretching throughout the universe. At the center of the cosmos stood three thrones made from the pillars of Helena's and Horred's temple before the dead army stomped their palace to ruins. The ancient, cracked ivory was carved with stony ivy and large winged butterflies climbing the sides.

Only one throne, the smaller one between the king's and queen's, was occupied. Several handmaidens holding fans and trinkets stood or sat around it. One of them plunked on a harpsichord in the center of the room, singing in a high-pitched, child-like voice.

Danika entered, and the handmaidens parted, revealing a woman wearing a gown of golden silk trimmed with black lace. She rose abruptly and clicked her silver heels, sending all her handmaidens scurrying away.

She gestured toward Danika and invited her forward. "Come."

Cords were draped around the woman's neck, holding the pendants of Helena's sword and Horred's hammer. A veil punctured by pearls at even intervals covered her face. Her long blond hair was pinned and braided in a severe bun on top of her head.

Danika bowed, her face almost touching the floor. "My Highness."

"It's about time you've returned." The princess waited until every handmaiden and guard had left. When the doors closed, she pulled Danika to her feet and wrapped her arms around her. "I thought I'd lost you and I'd have to pose as Princess for the rest of my damned life."

"Sorry, Muriel." Danika hugged her, glad to have some female company after so many days with a boy and two men. "Much has happened."

Muriel ruffled her gown. "Come. Let us discuss this in your quarters where I can shed this awful monstrosity."

Danika wasn't looking forward to her old life or wearing the hideous gowns her mother had instated for the Ebonvale women royalty at court. The ensemble's only logical use was hiding her long absences when she rode off on her adventures. After such a long journey, britches and cloaks felt more comfortable.

They scampered behind the triple thrones to an alcove in the back, where pigeons flew into the rafters and golden sunlight trickled down from windows high above. Muriel pulled the dress over her head, exchanging clothes with Danika. Her handmaiden's features were blunter, her nose bigger, and her eyes smaller, but they had the same honey-colored hair and small stature. Their clothes fit nicely on one another, allowing Muriel to assume the throne when needed.

Danika pulled off her breeches, embarrassed by her dirt-stained leggings underneath. "What has happened at court?"

"A whole lot of nothing." Muriel rolled her eyes, pulling the pins from her hair. "Count Viscos wants to throw a party, the gardener cannot decide whether to plant more roses or petunias, and the Royal Guard grows restless without the army of Sill to keep them busy."

"Oh, they'll be busy soon enough." Danika told Muriel of her time in the House of Song and King Troubadir's story of the She-Beast.

Muriel slapped her hand over her mouth. She looked so vulnerable in her underdress and bare legs. "'Tis untrue!"

Danika tilted her head, weighing the same question. "There's only one way we'll know for sure."

"You're not taking the army to their lair, are you?"

"Aye." Danika pulled the dress over her head, feeling ten pounds heavier. "We've found a way to beat them, an alloy strengthening our armor enough to withstand their fire breath. Bron is at the smithy as we speak, instructing the blacksmiths on how to forge the armor and weapons."

"Oh, Danika! You've just come home. You cannot leave again."

Danika paused. She had unknowingly followed in her father's footsteps. Was she as monstrous as he had been? She tried to convince herself she left for the right reasons and faced Muriel. "Yes, but this time you won't have to pose as the princess. The kingdom will know."

Muriel wiped at her eyes. "Why?"

"My father is dead. The troops need a leader, an icon, a symbol of Ebonvale to guide them into battle." Danika put her hand on her handmaiden's shoulder. "Listen to me, Muriel. I'm appointing you as Stewardess of Ebonvale. If I do not return, you will be its queen."

Muriel snorted. "I'm no more a queen than a field mouse is a warrior."

"You've been doing it all along."

"I don't have royal blood."

"You do." Danika pulled Muriel to a mirror in the far side of the room. Her pulse quickened as she saw what had been on her mind ever since visiting her mother in the woods. "Do we not resemble one another?"

"Aye."

"And are you not one year my senior, which would place your birth between Islador's reign and my mother's?"

"Aye. But my father was lost at sea."

Danika widened her eyes as if she opened Muriel's eyes as well. "Since when do fishermen come this far north?"

Muriel covered her mouth again. Her words came out muffled against the palm of her hand. "You don't mean--"

Danika nodded. "Half-sisters. I have not the paperwork to prove it, but your claim, along with my signature, may be enough."

"Are you certain?" Muriel's eyes shone with unshed tears.

Danika nodded. "Aye."

Muriel threw her arms around her and pulled her close, squeezing so hard Danika thought her dress would pop open in the front. "It's what I've always wanted. Not to be queen, but to be tied to you. I always knew we had a connection, and now I can say we are bonded for life. To lose what I've only just now gained... Danika, I don't want you to leave."

Danika allowed herself to be held for a long time, finally giving in to her vulnerabilities. Tears rolled down her cheeks. "With any luck, I'll be back."

Muriel pulled back to meet her eyes. "You'd better come back. I don't want to marry a minstrel from the House of Song."

"If I don't come back, there may be no House of Song left. You're to move our people into the mountains and hide in the land of Sill."

Muriel scrunched her nose and pursed her lips. "That land stinks like rotten garbage. Crows circle the tainted earth to this day, picking at pieces of the bodies."

"Better to be smelly than to be dead."

Muriel slumped on an old cushion, now dressed in Danika's travel gear. She put her elbows on her knees and held her face in her hands.

Meanwhile, Danika pinned up her hair and cleaned the smudges from her face. She was in dire need of a bath, but to get to the wash basins, she'd need to look like herself, the princess.

Muriel's head snapped up. "How did you figure it out after all these years?"

Danika paused. This wasn't a subject she wanted to broach again. "I came across my mother in the forest."

"Your mother! I thought she went back to Jamal."

"So did we. In a way, I wish she had. At least she'd be happy." Danika slumped onto a stool. "Oh, Muriel. Fate has not been kind to her. She lives alone, deserted and exiled, with only her precious cherry blossoms to keep her company."

"How tremendously hideous."

Danika nodded, pushing away the rising current of emotion. "She said my father paid more attention to the handmaidens than to her. It took me a while to process. Sometime in the shadowy dank cave of Darkenbite, the truth came to me, and I knew if I ever saw you again, I had to tell you."

Muriel nodded, running her hands through her hair to twist out the waves caused by pinning her shiny locks up for so long. "Don't you think she stayed because of you?"

"What do you mean?"

"Your mother. She could have returned to Jamal with or without her minstrel lover. Her family would have taken her back. Why did she stay?"

Danika paused with a pin stuck between her lips. She hadn't thought about her mother's choice. Anger and hate had blinded her the entire time she visited the cottage. Danika covered her heart with her hand. Her mother had chosen the satiny fabric to complement her honey hair.

"Helena's Sword! I've been so cruel."

Chapter 19

Wish

The heat from the forge wafted down the walkway as Bron parked the carriage and brought the horses to a trough. Nip climbed out and Bron halted him with a steady arm. "I'll lead. I know the blacksmith well." The real reason he didn't want the boy wandering was the danger of the hot metal and flames. Nip had grown up in a blacksmith's forge, but not one like this.

"Aye." Nip took Bron's place by his side. Disappointment slumped his shoulders.

"I'll need you to speak of what you saw in your father's forge. Wait for my cue."

Nip nodded and Bron grabbed a block of pinkish silver. They walked through the door and into a cloud of smoke. Chains, breastplates of all shapes and sizes, claymores, daggers and long swords lined the walls. A large steel vent hung from the center of the room over a pit of searing flames. Beside the simmering bed of coals stood a wrought iron anvil taller than Nip and as wide as their carriage.

A hefty man with a black beard as thick as brambles stood before the anvil. He brought a hammer down on a metal sword with a clang. Sparks flew, raining on either side of the anvil. Only when the smoke cleared did he look at his visitors.

The blacksmith wiped his forehead with his arm. "Bron Thoridian." His face cracked into a crooked smile. "Where have you been, old friend?"

"Garish, you old devil." No matter how many times he saw him, the old man still brought a smile to Bron's lips, even when he was trying to maintain his tough façade.

Bron met the blacksmith and they clapped their hands together and pulled themselves forward into a one-armed hug. Bron pulled away and showed him the metal. "Finding the answer to our problems."

Garish turned the bar over in his hands with curiosity. "Didn't know we had problems."

Bron nodded solemnly. "Aye. You're going to be very busy."

Nip tugged on Bron's pants leg and the warrior gestured toward the boy. "Garish, may I introduce Nathaniel Blueborough, son of Alhearn Blueborough."

"Good 'ol Alhearn." Garish crouched beside the boy. "You look just like your father." He turned back to Bron. "What brings his boy here?"

"War," Nip croaked. "The wyverns attacked my village and killed my family before my father could forge the armor to defeat them."

Bron nodded, placing a hand on the boy's shoulder. He gestured toward the silver in Garish's hands. "Now the task falls upon you."

Garish placed a hand on Nip's shoulder. "I'm sorry for your loss, son." He stayed there, locked in place for a long moment before standing to inspect the metal. He held the silver block in his hands, hefting the metal to feel the weight. "By itself, this metal is far too weak. I can't believe it blocks the wyvern's fire."

"The combination of this new metal with our own strengthens the alloy." Bron put a hand on Nip's shoulder. "The boy has a breastplate his father made that has proven itself against the fire."

Garish shook his head. "I wouldn't know where to start. I'll have to make several models and test the mix."

"We don't have time for experiments." Bron hated hurrying his friend, but an entire swarm of wyverns headed by a massive myth of a beast might be on their way. He softened his tone. "Nip knows how much his father used. He can help you."

"All right." Garish clapped Nip on the back and gave Bron a wink. "Leave us to our work."

Bron nodded and rustled the overgrown hair on Nip's head. This was the first time they'd be apart, and the thought saddened him more than it should. An overprotective urge to look after him every second came upon him, but the boy needed his space if he was ever to grow. Bron's father had let him and his brother run free and, in doing so, they'd become capable men. "Do well. Make me proud."

Nip only nodded, then scurried over to where Garish stood above the melting pots. It was hard to believe the kingdom rested on the shoulders of such a young boy and his memory. Bron left, having faith Nip would recall the right balance. That boy was as smart as a ravencrock.

Bron took the horses to the stable. As he handed them over to a young boy a messenger galloped in to return his horse. Mud-covered and travel-weary, he fell, more than jumped, off, and waited in line behind the warrior while his horse guzzled from the trough. He was Bron's age, with the thin build the princess looked for in messengers to ride swiftly without burdening their charges.

Bron turned, knowing one weary man asked another to give an ounce more than either of them had left in store. "Can you do me a favor?"

"Of course, Chief." The man bowed, and Bron gestured for him to rise.

"Assemble my men in the center field of the barracks for a quick briefing." As a token of gratitude, he dropped a gold coin into his hand.

The messenger's face brightened with the tip. "Thank you, sir." He turned on his heel, took another horse from the stables, and rode off toward the barracks.

When Bron arrived, walking hard on his aching feet, the Royal Guard had begun to shuffle out of hiding, bellies fat and round and beards overgrown. Without an enemy to kill, they'd fallen into laziness.

This ought to coax them into shape.

Bron's wearied muscles longed for the softness of his bed in the barracks, but with an enemy at their doorsteps, he needed his men to start preparing. Brushing travel dirt off his shoulders, he stood before them as their Chief of Arms and gave the order to assemble in rows.

"Men, I have journeyed far these past days and seen sights few men see. I have witnessed a wyvern attack on a village firsthand and spoken with the leader of the House of Song. I traveled to the bowels of Darkenbite in search of an alloy to fend off the wyverns' fire attacks and come back with a cartload of metal to equip all of you in battle."

His men straightened and sobered as he talked. Some of them held fear in their eyes, while others licked their lips with hunger for battle. Bron allowed them their own personal emotions. They needed both fear and bravery to instill diligence and keep their edge.

"In a fortnight we are to journey along with the minstrels of the House of Song to Brimmore's Bay, where we'll take carracks to Scalehaven. There we'll combat the growing horde of hatchlings produced by a legendary She-Beast with scales as big as festival tables. The minstrels will distract the horde with their song while we track down the She-Beast and put an end to her fiery reign."

Silence fell as the soldiers digested his words. For some, it would be their last battle. For others, their way to prove themselves to further their rank. Everything he loved lay on the line: his kingdom and the woman he secretly adored. The solemnity of the mission hung heavy in the air.

"What are the odds this mission will succeed, sir?"

Bron turned to a man the same age he was when he joined the Royal Guard. Anticipation brightened his features and twitched in his lips.

With no scout ships, Bron had no idea of the extent of the She-Beast's horde. Any scout sent would be sent to their lonely death. He only knew one thing: if they didn't go, the battle would be fought on their lands, and more people would die. Stepping to the man, Bron put a hand on his shoulder. "What does your heart tell you?"

The young man straightened under Bron's heavy hand, as if by touching him, the warrior had lent his strength. "That we can succeed." A tremor cut through his voice.

"Good." Bron turned to address the whole army. "We cannot fail, or the wyverns will overrun the southern coast then continue north to overpower Ebonvale's ramparts with their sheer numbers. I need you rested and trained to the best of your ability. Go now and prepare."

As the army disassembled, most of them jogged to the training fields, already overgrown from disuse. Their boots stomped the blossoms of wildflowers as they pulled their weapons off the dusty racks.

Task completed, Bron retired to his chambers on the top floor of the men's barracks. He pulled off his boots and rocks the size of marbles rolled across the floor. Tomorrow, he'd work on that field with them, but for now he could rest his wearied muscles. He tossed his clothes in a heap and collapsed onto his bed. His last thought before sleep took him was a wish.

If only King Artemus still breathed to raise his sword.

Chapter 20

Dying Words

Clanging metal reverberated through the valley, cutting through the northern mountains of Sill. Heavy mist rolled off the foothills, covering the grasslands in an ethereal fog and spreading insidious chill throughout the men's bones. If Bron's armor hadn't pulled down on his shoulders and across his chest, he might have thought himself part of a dead army as well, ghosts forever roaming their last battle, searching for fallen brethren.

The weight of his armor fell on his body in a reassuring shield between him and the rows of un-dead spreading out like a plague upon the valley. The creatures teased them by clanging together their ill-forged weapons in a crude, staggering, rhythmic heartbeat. The smell of death, rot and mold hung heavy in the air, choking Bron's throat until he couldn't remember the sweet scent of the cherry blossoms in the courtyard or the newly cut hay in his father's fields.

"Helena, take me into your forgiving arms." He made the sign of her sword across his chest, at peace with the path of his destiny. Bron did not fear death.

"Hold steady." King Artemus' deep voice resonated above the troops. "Wait for them to come to us."

The king had positioned the Royal Guard on a hillside overlooking the valley. If they waited, they had the advantage of a higher position and the momentum of a thousand horses plunging hooves into the enemies' chests. Only necromancers rode horses. The rest of the dead crawled up from the filth ridden swamps of Sill festering between the two mountains.

King Artemus' decision was wise. They were outnumbered by twofold and had to seize any advantage the terrain had to offer. Even when the soulless monstrosities hissed and clanked their crude weapons in derision, the Royal Guard held its ground. The dead army would have to fight their way past them to soil Ebonvale's ramparts with their disease.

The Necromancer King broke through the front lines, riding on a blood-smeared dead horse. He wore a crown of nails and thorns. He was too tall and thin to be a human, as if someone had stretched him out or his body kept growing despite the lack of sustenance. Bron pulled a telescope made from rolled leather and two spyglasses from his travel bag. Another rider rode behind the necromancer, arms draped around his neck with hands tied.

Something was not as it should be. Necromancers rode alone. Bron studied the pinkness of the hands. Those hands still had blood running through them, contrasting with the pale, black-blotched skin of the necromancer. A member of the living amongst the army of the dead?

The necromancer dismounted, black cape flowing, and pulled the living man to the ground with his metal-lined fingernails. The clanging ceased in one great crash reverberating into tense silence.

Bron recognized his prisoner and dread stirred in his gut. Fiobald Rosenditch, a member of their army two ranks below him, collapsed to the earth. Up to this day, they'd thought Fiobald a deserter. Now Bron wasn't so sure. There were stories of wraiths taking people in the night to feed the army of Sill. Either way, to be held at the hands of a necromancer was a fate no man deserved.

"It's Fiobald," a man beside Bron exclaimed in horror. "What will they do to him?"

King Artemus raised a hand to silence him. "We will not respond to their threats." Under the stoic mask of his face, a bead of sweat trickled into the collar of his golden armor.

Fiobald cried out, pleading with anyone who would listen as the necromancer began to chant an incantation, evil words twisting their way up to the Royal Guards' ears.

Two members of the legion stumbled forward on their cracked knees and torn limbs and knelt beside Fiobald. The necromancer took a handful of Fiobald's hair and pulled his head up, exposing his neck.

"Don't watch. Move your eyes away," Bron instructed his troops as he glanced at his horse's leather reins. He allowed his gaze to wander up again, as if he couldn't give up on Fiobald, even though the sick feeling in his gut told him it was too late.

The necromancer's words stopped and the dead leaned in. Fiobald screamed as they plunged their ragged teeth into his skin. The members of the Royal Guard murmured uneasily and shifted on their horses. Bron looked to the king to give them wisdom, yet Artemus tightened his grip on the reins.

No. He couldn't fall into their trap. Bron wanted to shout at him but it was not his place. Fiobald's screams died away to low moans, curdling Bron's blood even more than the cries of pain as the blood flowed down Fiobald's chest and his face paled. Bron wondered if the man had a family, a wife. Would she wonder what his last moments were like for the rest of her life? Bron might not live through this day, but if he did, he vowed to find her.

The necromancer waved his arm above the man's head and Fiobald rose, taking staggering steps, and joined their army.

"Blasphemy!" someone called out behind Bron.

"Murder!"

"Kill the bastard!"

The front lines of the dead army parted again, and three more healthy men stumbled forward, ropes attached to their necks. They wore civilian clothes. These weren't members of the Royal Guard, but farmers.

Bron spit bile in front of his horse, feeling the urge to shed some black blood.

No. Not more. Would the necromancers force them to watch their friends turn all day, increasing their army before their eyes? Nothing could be more horrible than to see an ally turn into an adversary and know you would have to deliver their death blow.

As the men lined up and the necromancer began his chant once again, King Artemus growled deep within his throat and took off, sprinting on his black battle horse. "In honor of Fiobald!" he shouted. The men echoed him until Fiobald's name became a war cry. Bron scrambled to stay with the king in the charge. Artemus had let anger and revenge fuel his mind and his deeds and, in doing so, he'd become reckless, squandering their position. The king's loosening grasp of control sent panic through Bron's usual calm.

They raced down the hill and across the long grasses, meeting the enemy in the mud-caked sludge seeping from Sill's festering swamps. The dead were quick, despite their handicaps, fueled by black magic. They charged, blinking in and out of existence like ghosts visiting from another realm.

Some of them blinked in just as the horses reached them and were trampled underneath the hooves. Others dodged the initial onslaught and darted between the soldiers, biting their legs where their armor didn't cover.

Bron plowed through five walking dead, slashing more with his claymore on either side. He kept Artemus in view and a sword's width away. He'd sworn an oath to protect the king at all times and for all costs. The men with the ropes tied around their necks cowered in the confusion. Although their plight called to Bron, he couldn't save them because he could not leave the king.

"Bronford Thoridian," Artemus beckoned.

A white-eyed ghoulish remnant of an old man jumped in front of Bron's horse, black lips drooling froth. Bron speared the man and threw his body to trampling hooves. He reached the king within a heartbeat. "Yes, Your Highness."

"Rescue those men. They aren't soldiers. They don't deserve this fate."

The dead had swarmed, cutting their army into small groups, and even now they whittled away the clusters of the living. If they stayed together, they had a chance. If they broke into even smaller groups, they were done for.

Bron had never talked back to the king. He sucked the sides of his mouth in indecision. "Your Highness?"

"Go." Artemus slapped Bron's horse and the beast turned away. Bron took the reins and turned its head back to the king. "I cannot leave you."

"This is an order, Bronford." Artemus' eyes were filled with desperation, as though he couldn't see another innocent person die. "I can take care of myself."

Every nerve in Bron's body screamed for him to stay. The clusters of the Royal Guard were separating farther and farther apart and the ring surrounding the king thinned. But King Artemus was too proud to let the necromancers have another soul. Was Bron supposed to protect the king from even himself?

Artemus swung his sword, cutting down two charging dead men, and looked back to Bron. "You have shielded me long enough, my son."

The Necromancer King approached the three tied men, weaving through the Royal Guard. A foul cloud tainted every soldier he touched, bringing down his horse.

"You can take him." King Artemus encouraged as he moved toward the brunt of the dead army. "I will hold his minions back. Taste the sweetness of victory on the tip of your sword."

Bron's blood boiled with the thought of the necromancer pulling Fiobald's face to the sky. This was his chance to put a stop to the army once and for all. The king had given the opportunity to him rather than taking it for himself. "I'll be back soon, Your Highness."

Bron ripped through the dead between himself and the three men, pounding them to the sludge with his battle horse. He positioned himself between the necromancer and the cowering men. The fear in their eyes was too familiar, stirring anger in his gut.

He cut their bindings with his sword and shouted over the clamor. "Run to safety in the hills."

The men nodded and scurried uphill just as the necromancer approached, hovering over the ground. Bron had never seen one so close. He marveled at the hollowness of the man's face, with skin pulled taut over angular bones and eyes as black as midnight with no whites. How could this atrocity once have been human? His headpiece of thorns and nails cut into his skull, tearing his flesh to seep black blood down his face where flies feasted in swarms, their oily bodies like emeralds on his skin. Pain seemed to fuel his magic.

"You have stolen my prisoners, young warrior. Now you must offer your flesh and blood in return."

"Never." Bron growled, raising his claymore. "You have taken your last soul."

The necromancer held his palm out, and his metal fingernails clicked together. A black mist emanated from his fingertips, growing ever larger.

Even though he'd grown up a farm boy, his mother read to him at night, pointing to letters, teaching him the sounds and the meaning of the symbols in the flickering candlelight. When his father dismissed reading as a waste of time, she used to whisper, "Knowledge is the greatest form of power."

Later, when he trained with the Royal Guard, he walked to the temples in the inner keep and read the long scripts scrawled by the monks, not so much for the content, but to feel close to his mother again. On one of those dark, lonely nights, a night where he missed the bleat of the goats and his mother's apple pie, he snuck into the temple and read a passage about the necromancers, a passage about a simple farm husband who defeated a young black-blooded creature to save his wife and children. This peasant claimed the necromancers needed a body for their dark magic. They were weak when they were in-between physical manifestations.

Bron took a chance and threw his sword. His claymore sprawled through the air, hilt over blade over and over again in a blur of silver. It sliced the necromancer's arm, severing the appendage from his body. The necromancer screamed, and black moths flew from his mouth.

Bron wasn't finished. As the necromancer blinked out in a puff of smoke, Bron reached for his dagger. The creature would reappear beside him--of this he was certain. He had four directions to choose from, and only one choice to make.

Necromancers were evil. They didn't fight fair. Bron turned in the last second and threw the dagger behind him, thinking the foul creature would attack from behind.

Even though the dagger tip sailed through thin air, the blade stuck in mid-arc. The necromancer materialized with the dagger through his heart. He fell, lifeless, to the ground. When his body hit, his skin and bones fractured into ashes.

Panic edged up Bron's spine. He'd left the king for too long. He scanned the battlefield for the gilded lion's helmet and the golden armor atop the black charger. The king had fought his way across the battlefield, banding the groups together in one last front. They charged at the brunt of the undead, cutting a wedge through the army.

Bron shouted, "No!" He wished he rode by the king's side. He retrieved his claymore and spurred his horse into action, galloping to meet them.

Dead swarmed the Royal Guard until each soldier squirmed with three or four attackers on top of him. Bron tightened his grip on the reins, pushing his horse to its utmost speed. So many places to be bitten. Every second they lost another beating heart to dark magic.

He fought his way to the king, slashing four attackers into halves. King Artemus had been pulled from his saddle and he panted, falling against a lichen-crusted boulder. Eerily, the gold in the rusty growth mirrored the gold in his armor.

"You defeated him, Bron. Well done."

Bron knelt beside the king, inspecting his wounds. A bloody slash to his upper arm would heal. At first he thought mud crusted the king's hand, but then he realized the skin had turned as black as the blotches on the necromancer's face. An icy hand clutched Bron's heart and refused to let go.

"Your Highness! You've been bitten."

The king shrugged as if it were old news. "You've done well, my son." He put his healthy hand to Bron's face and touched his cheek. "I'm proud of you."

"I have to carry you back. The healers can try--"

"You know how this must end. Even now I feel the evil in my veins. I'd rather not return to my kingdom as a raging, soulless devil, but a king who gave his life for Ebonvale. You must give me this last dignity before the healers find me."

Bron scanned the battlefield for an answer that wasn't there. His gaze returned to the king with tears brimming. "You're like my second father. I could no more raise a hand to my own flesh and blood."

The king's emerald eyes grew misty. "Look after Danika for me. Tell her I love her."

Bron nodded, overwhelmed by emotion. "I will. Always."

King Artemus took his hand and squeezed. Bron had never seen him appreciate a moment such as this. For a heartbeat the battle was only a memory, and they stood together in heaven with the gods. "You and she are the only good I can claim in this world."

His eyes closed, and when they opened again, they'd turned black. In moments, the king's body would become the thing he abhorred, and Bron couldn't let that happen. The troops would never leave him. They'd take him home in a cart, chain him up and let the healers try all manner of concoctions. He'd turn into a circus freak, and Bron couldn't have Danika see the monster her father would become.

He raised his claymore. With tears running down his cheeks, he screamed a war shout, and King Artemus was king no more.

Bron awoke with a heave of breath and a face hot with tears and sweat. The dream had rattled him to the core, and he kicked off his sweaty sheets as if the dead had bled their poison upon them. His memory remained as clear as the day the battle happened. His fate for killing the one man who meant everything to him would be to relive that horrifying day until his death.

He stood and leaned on the washbasin. When he'd gathered enough strength, he filled the ivory bathtub with buckets of water the maid had left the night before. He'd clean, shave and find a bunch of cherry blossoms to place on King Artemus' grave.

Maybe his visit would ease his heart. Maybe not.

Chapter 21

Forgiveness

Danika slipped into cool bath waters, the muck and filth from her journey washing away. As arduous as the quest had been, she reflected on her time with Nip, Bron and Valorian with fondness. The four of them had formed a bond, albeit strange, and she'd always remember those days of freedom from the court's prying eyes.

She dipped her leg into the water and bent her knee back out again. The bath house was an open platform, shielded by covered porches on every side, with the center open to the rays of sun. Golden light played upon her wet skin, illuminating the effects of the journey on her body. Her muscles had hardened, turning from rounded fat in her arms and legs to smooth, sleek curves. Her skin had tanned from porcelain to a healthy gold. Overall, she looked more like a warrior than a princess and that thought made her proud.

Thank goodness Muriel had sent all of her handmaidens away for the day. Her changed body would be hard to hide in court. She'd have to claim a pastime of walking in the orchards like her mother.

Her mother. Danika's heart had softened the more she thought about her. If she could relive those fleeting moments at her mother's cottage, she would have been kinder. She would have asked her if she needed anything. With anger blinding her, she'd left her mother in the woods alone, with no promise of ever coming back.

She'd find a way to see her again. Danika promised the soap bubbles drifting from her hair on the breeze. If they won the battle, and if she could keep Ebonvale safe, she'd find a way to contact Sybil.

Staggering odds piled against her. No one had challenged the wyverns in battles as they swarmed from the deserts in the south. Instead, the Royal Guard had fallen back, leaving the beasts to inhabit the southern islands.

Looking back, their negligence had been a dire mistake. The worms only grew stronger, breeding their army to expand their territory. Danika had been tutored in the art of war, and it was hard for her to believe a reptile could outsmart her father.

If it wasn't for the army of Sill, he would have seen their attack coming. As bad a husband as he was to her mother, no one could question his battle tactics. She wished she could speak with him now to gain wisdom for the conflict at hand. She wished he could see her dressed in silver armor, riding her horse upon the shores of Scalehaven. Of course, if he was alive, he'd never let her go.

Finished with her bath, Danika stood and dried her weary body. A sudden urge to visit her father's grave came over her, even knowing her questions would ride on the wind unanswered.

She slid on a clean underdress and a glistening, silken moonlight-hued gown and made her way through the bath house to the hill of daisies marking her father's last resting place.

What she didn't expect was Bron Thoridian, standing in prayer with his hands folded over his fresh tunic, cleanly washed and shaven at the foot of the hill.

Although she stepped silently, he turned. She could never sneak up on this warrior. Redness rimmed his eyes as if he'd been mourning.

"My lady."

Suddenly she was aware of the sleekness of her gown over her body and how the silk hugged her curves. She'd chosen the garment for comfort, not thinking of how much of her body lay exposed. He'd think of her as a seductress. Danika crossed her arms over her low neckline, then quickly uncrossed them. She hadn't meant to make her breasts look bigger. "I didn't expect to see you here."

"Or I you." His neck reddened with embarrassment, as if she'd caught him in a rare vulnerable moment. Seeing him reduced to his emotions made her want to throw her arms around him and bury her head in his burly chest.

"I miss him." Danika plucked a daisy and tossed the flower before the headstone reading *Ebonvale's most valiant king*. "I wish I had his council now."

"My thoughts exactly." A cool breeze blew through the courtyard and Bron invited her closer.

As she took her place by his side, he put an arm around her shoulders. He would have never touched her anywhere other than beside the grave. While sharing their grief, this gesture made perfect sense.

Danika nuzzled against him, giving in to her cravings. She thought they'd stay like this in silence, but Bron breathed in and spoke.

"There's something I must tell you."

Danika's heart skipped. Would he denounce her affections? She swallowed a lump in her throat. Rejection was the price she had to pay for making a move. "Go on."

"Your father was a brave, headstrong man. He commanded me to separate from him in battle, as you know. But I've never told you exactly what happened that day after we broke apart."

Nervous jitters ran through her. She tightened her grip on his arm. All this time he'd left her in the dark, dodging questions whenever she asked. Now she'd know the truth. "I'm listening."

He caressed her arm with his rough fingers. "This will be hard for you to hear."

"I'm ready." She'd been ready the day he returned without the king.

"Your father commanded me to kill the necromancer king. I'm not certain why. Perhaps he wanted me to come into my own, to follow in his footsteps. Maybe he was aware of my personal connection with the man the necromancer had killed in front of us in cold blood. Whatever the King's reasons, he'd have it no other way. I have to admit, I wanted to slice open the necromancer as much as he wanted me to have him. The king commanded me, yes, but I was also blinded by my own sense of justice and revenge. I'm sorry."

Danika smoothed her hand down Bron's arm. Her anger at him for leaving her father sizzled to a burnt ember. His apology wiped the anger away. "'Tis understandable considering the circumstances."

He ran a hand over her hair, smoothing it over the back of her head. "I wished a thousand times I'd stayed with him."

"We cannot look back. If we do, we lose sight of our future."

Bron nodded. "But, I must look back one last time to tell you the truth. I killed the necromancer king. I know the stories say your father did. In a way, he did by sending me. I made sure to give him that last victory."

"Bron, you shouldn't have. You should have taken the glory for yourself."

"After what happened, I could not in all conscience take any glory from that day."

Danika steeled her voice. "Tell me what happened."

"When I found the king, he'd been bitten. He asked me to end his life before he became one of those creatures." Bron's voice cracked. "I thought of how the healers would take him back anyway and how they'd torture his body to get him to regain some semblance of consciousness. Either way, even if they found an ounce of who he had been, he'd never be the same."

Bron turned to face her, a tear running down his cheek. "I thought of you. I couldn't allow you to suffer seeing him as a monster."

He pulled away from her as if he expected her to slap him across the face. "I ended his life with my blade, making sure he died with his dignity. I should have been imprisoned for a traitor. No one knows how he died except for you."

Danika froze as his words sank in. Walls came crashing down inside her as everything she'd once believed turned on its head. She'd known from the first night when they brought her father home, she didn't have the entire story. Bron would never leave the king's side and someone as great a warrior as the king would never allow a dead creature to cut his throat. That sense of not knowing had plagued her for the past year, like a book with the end ripped out.

"Why did you tell the historians my father killed the necromancer king?"

"I only defeated him because your father gave me time. I wanted him to be remembered as a hero."

"I would have never allowed such a thing to happen." She stepped toward him, finally feeling a sense of closure, knowing her father's last moments were with someone he loved, knowing he'd thought of her. As horrible as his end was, her father knew he'd be taken care of, his last wishes carried out. Bron's story comforted her. "You helped him, Bron. You showed enormous courage and for that, I thank you."

She took his hand and held his palm to her heart. His skin warmed the sleek fabric between them. "I thought you'd failed, and yet you gave him the greatest form of protection: that of his honor, his pride. Now they think of him as a war hero, when you are the true hero. You saved the kingdom by defeating the necromancer king. Yet, you gave my father the credit and the glory."

Bron shook his head, not speaking, but he didn't have to. Danika wrapped her arms around his neck and stood on her tiptoes, pressing her lips fiercely against his. This was not the gentle kiss she'd given to Valorian, but a passionate embrace, giving her whole self.

Bron stiffened, but Danika continued undeterred. She smoothed her hands behind his neck to his strong jaw and pulled his head down to hers. She sucked on his lower lip before opening her mouth, inviting him to kiss her back.

Bron cupped her waist, pulling her body against his as he opened his lips against hers and kissed her like she'd never been kissed before.

She moved her hands to his chest, trailing over his muscles, and down his arms over where his hands held her. She wove her fingers through his and tightened her grip as though she never wanted to be parted again.

Danika lost all sense of propriety. She released his hand and wandered her fingertips up his chest, pulling the ties of his tunic open and feeling his bare skin. So many times she'd thought about what he would feel like under her touch. Her dreams could not compare.

Bron pulled away, chest heaving, his muscles taut with restriction. "We cannot."

"I don't care anymore about duty."

He pressed a finger to her lips. "Princess, you are not yourself. Be true to your title. Remember who you are."

In all the pain, the sorrow, the anticipation of battle, she'd allowed herself one blissful moment to forget. Bron had made her into a swooning puddle by opening up to her, by being himself. But, his caresses offered a false comfort. If she ran away with him, she'd be the same as her mother. Many people depended on her and Bron to run the kingdom.

He spoke again, his voice now soothing. "This is not the time."

He was right. Their kingdom lay at siege, and the only hope they had was allying with the House of Song. What if word of this traveled to Valorian? Their indiscretion could bring down two kingdoms at the very time they needed to be joined. Many would die because she couldn't contain her heart.

Shame heated Danika's cheeks and stilled her heart. She pulled back, tears brimming. She was stronger than this love lust. She turned away, unable to meet his gaze.

"Princess, wait. I didn't mean--"

"Leave me." She crossed her arms, back turned to the one person she cared the most about. Many times she'd chided her mother for running away with her own inclinations, and now she realized just how hard it was to avoid temptation. She'd been a judgmental fool.

Her muffled sobs covered Bron's steps. When she turned back, he was gone.

Chapter 22

Bargain

"About face!" Bron stared at the rows of troops clad in their sleek new armor, gleaming in the noonday sun. War loomed, and all he could think of was how he'd sabotaged his chances with Danika just a few weeks ago. Not every soldier on that field would come back, and he hoped they all left with no regrets. He could die without telling Danika how he felt about her. All because of duty, obligation and responsibility. Why did everything he'd ever stood for conflict with the one woman he wanted?

Fate tempted him, but he knew where his true destiny lay: on that lava rock, holding a sword, slaying the She-Beast, even if the mission took his life. He only wished Danika could know how he burned inside for her touch, how she was the only woman for him even if she wasn't his, how he'd never love anyone else half as much as he loved her.

"Weapons raised." He shouted the command as much for himself to snap out of his haze as for the troops to adjust to the new, lighter armor.

A unison metallic hiss sounded over the field as every soldier unsheathed his sword. The armor reflected Garish's superb craftsmanship. He'd styled each sword in the tradition of Ebonvale's Royal Guard, with insignias on each hilt and small jewels embedded in the wide part of the blade. Even though the finishing touches didn't make the swords any more deadly, the ornaments inspired courage and pride in the troops. They'd fight for a kingdom that valued their service.

Hooves galloped in the distance, and Bron whirled around, wondering which fool had the guts to interrupt his training practice by bringing a charger onto the field. The rider was small, clad in the same pinkish armor, but with a filigreed pattern along the helmet. His arms and legs were slender, too slender for any man that could have made the Royal Guard. The armor protruded in the chest in two rounded curves--breasts.

Aubrie Dionne

Bron's stomach leaped. That was no man, and he knew of only one woman who would have the gall.

The horse reared in front of the army, and the rider pulled off her helmet, exposing a rippling wave of blond hair, as golden as the hay in his father's fields. Audible gasps came from the troops as they stared at her with awe.

Danika jumped from her horse and unsheathed her long sword, taking her place beside the army. She didn't challenge his position, and he couldn't refuse her in front of the troops. She was the reigning leader of Ebonvale. She could do as she pleased.

"Choose a partner." Bron walked over to Danika. Every soldier stepped up to the next one in line.

Danika's row was uneven by one, and she stood before Bron and extended her sword. The tip touched his armored chest. "I choose you."

"Very well." Bron's eyes widened in skepticism. He didn't want to fight her. Was this her way of getting revenge? To make him look like an ass if he beat her or a fool if he let her win? Either way, he had no choice but to fight her. He shouted across the battlefield. "Engage."

Weapons clashed around them as Bron and Danika circled each other. Danika tried a lunge and he moved easily out of the way.

He tried reasoning first. "If you join us, there will be no one to rule Ebonvale."

"I've appointed a Regent Queen." Her emerald eyes flashed with another lunge.

Again, he moved out of the way as if their skirmish was child's play. "We have enough soldiers."

"But do you have a symbol of Ebonvale to give them hope when darkness draws near, when all hope is lost but that of their memories in their deepest hearts?"

She moved quicker this time, and the tip of her blade caught his upper arm with a clang before he turned out of the way.

He gave her an appraising look. She'd improved since their last training session. "We may not make it back."

"Please. I've had my fair share of tragic destiny."

He lowered his sword. "Princess, don't do this."

She slid her sword under his and brought the blade back up again with a ringing clang. "I thought you wanted me to be a warrior."

"I wanted you to be able to defend yourself if need be, not to place yourself in harm's way." All the days he'd spent training her came back to him. Should he have done it? She'd asked him to, and he could no more give up two more seconds with her than all that time they'd spent together.

Danika gave him a fierce stare. "I'll fight you for it. If I win, I come. If you win, I'll stay behind."

He considered her offer. Could he beat her without feeling guilty? *Yes.* Bron's determination hardened. If his triumph saved her life.

Bron swung their swords apart and stepped into duel stance. "I accept."

Before he could react, Danika sparred to the left, faking a lunge to lure him into leaving his right side undefended. He picked up on the move before she could complete it, meeting her with a clash of metal. "Very nice."

"Do not patronize me." She danced with excellent footwork, jabbing right and left to find a spot he missed. Bron stayed on the defensive, driving the tip of her sword away as if it were a fly. He could have struck her down any number of times, but his heart wouldn't let him. He loved her too much and, by her actions, she knew he wouldn't defeat her.

She swung again, this time coming in for a full frontal attack. He'd trained her better than that. She dipped, aiming for his lower leg.

He picked his leg up in time, but the slight delay threw him off balance. They both fell to the grass. Danika had speed on him. She scrambled on top of him, brandishing Valorian's dagger at his throat. Seeing the other man's dagger sent pain through him as if she'd plunged it into his heart. He lost his will to fight.

Her green eyes flared. "I win."

"You have too much of your father in you."

Danika leaned in and her breath fell on his lips. "I'll take that as a compliment."

She rose and brushed dirt off the front of her armor. "See you at the next full moon."

* * * *

The day of departure rushed at Danika like a vulture from the peaks of Sill. She awoke at dawn the morning before the full moon, unable to wrap herself back into the elusive tendrils of sleep. Walking through the empty corridors of the inner keep, she ran through all of the preparations she'd made in her mind.

She'd strategically placed sentries all over Ebonvale, ready to spur their horses at the first sign of ribbons in the sky. Muriel had the necessary paperwork if a stray aunt or uncle, nephew or niece decided to usurp the throne. The Regent Queen would wait exactly one month until the next full moon. If no one came back, she would usher the citizens to the shelter of the mountains. Half of the archers would stay to defend the people in the event of a counter attack and the other half would travel with them to Scalehaven. Would her father be pleased? Had she set her pieces on the battlefield auspiciously?

Only time would tell.

She returned to her room and brought out a blank sheet of parchment. Dipping her quill, she thought of the right words to say farewell to Muriel. Now she knew why her father had snuck off without saying good-bye for many of his quests in his campaign against Sill. Leaving hurt too much. It would be easier for both of them if she departed without seeing her half-sister.

As she walked down the corridors to the main entranceway, Danika stopped at the glass case protecting her father's golden armor. The healers had taken the armor off him and bandaged his body, burying him in the robes of Ebonvale. Knowing her father, he would have wanted to be buried in the armor with the stains of battle still splattered across him.

Danika liked this better.

With a small key, she opened the case and took the metal hand in hers, the armor clinking against one another. This gave her a physical representation of her father. It was the closest she'd get to fighting at his side.

Bron had said she had too much of her father in her. Was she truly like him more than her mother? She thought of Sybil standing on the porch of her cottage. She'd given in to her heart. She was too ashamed to return, yet too afraid to leave what she loved most. *No.* Danika was more like her father, for she sacrificed what she loved most for the good of the kingdom. Was her father's sense of undying duty good or bad?

Placing the armored hand back in its spot, she closed the case and kept the key on a chain around her neck. Enough of this melancholy reflection. She was ready.

Shuffling down the steps, she passed the paintings of her family dating back to the first people ruling Ebonvale after Helena and Horrid. She would make them all proud.

The training fields were bare, except for one man. Bron stood at the center, watching the ravens dip in the sky and feast on the swarming black flies. He, too, already wore his armor.

Seeing the warrior brought a new wave of emotion. All this time, while they were back at the castle, she'd stayed away from him despite the yearnings in her heart. Now she wished she'd followed her feelings at least one more time. For this might be their ultimate end.

"Are you sure you want to come with us?" He didn't turn around. How did he know she walked behind him? Could they have such a bond that grew warmer as they stood together and cooler as they pulled apart?

"Certain as the seasons, as the rise and set of the sun."

Bron shrugged, and his armor clinked. He turned toward her with longing in his eyes. "I had to ask you one more time."

"I know. At least I'll be by your side."

"'Til the end." Bron held her armored hand. Would their end come too soon?

They needed no more words. She took her place by his side, and they watched the sunrise turn from a crimson-pink flush to amber gold.

Chapter 23

Blockade

Riding a white charger, with Bron by her side, Danika led the Royal Guard as they marched in proud lines. Even though her heart pounded in rhythm with their steps, she couldn't deny she followed her destiny. A sense of finality came over her as she gazed back to the large numbers rippling behind her as the army fell into step. Ebonvale's pennants whipped in the breeze, carried at even intervals by consecutive soldiers on the edges of the formation.

She turned her gaze back to the horizon, watching with keen eyes like a mother hen protecting her brood. For half a day, the road had remained empty. By her edict, all of the trade routes had closed. At least her people followed her orders. Still, the emptiness reminded her of the end of the world.

A black speck winked on the road up ahead. Was it her imagination or did the heat waves bounce off the cobblestone? An unseasonably hot and dry wind had blown in from the south. Did the swarm of wyverns belch enough hot air to raise the temperature forever?

She put up her hand and the army halted behind her. Shielding her eyes from the sun, she spotted the speck again, this time bigger. Her heart quickened.

Danika turned to Bron. "There's a disturbance ahead."

Bron reached into his travel bag and rolled his telescope, snapping the two lenses in place carefully with his large hands. "On the ground or in the air?"

"On the ground."

Bron peered through the lenses. "It's a scout rider. One of ours."

Danika's heart raced. The scout reported too early. Danger was afoot. More dots sprang up on the horizon, turning into an army.

Danika tightened her grip on her reigns and cast a look upon her sheathed sword. "Tell me what we face."

"Carriages, wagons, people on foot." Bron handed her his telescope.

Had they gone against her orders? Danika peered through the dual lenses. A man and woman led a goat with sacks strapped to its back. Mules hauled a carriage with rows of feet dangling from either side. A little girl dragged her belongings in the dirt behind her, followed by a burly man pulling an old woman in a wheelbarrow. These weren't tradesmen.

"It's an exodus."

Bron nodded solemnly. "Aye."

The scout rider pulled up in front of them and bowed in his saddle. "Chief of Arms, Princess." He huffed and wiped sweat from his ashen brow.

Danika rode up beside him. "Why are these people leaving?"

"They seek entrance to Ebonvale's protective gates." He dismounted and opened his leather water bag. "Forgive me, Your Highness. I must tend to my horse."

"Do what you must." Danika dug in her travel bag and gave him the messenger's seal, a gold medal on a leather strap. "Take them back to Ebonvale and give this to the Regent Queen. Tell her I approved their entry."

He nodded, smoothing his fingers over the gold as if he'd never touched any item so important in his life. "Yes, Your Highness."

The first few travelers had reached them. They ambled past the army with weary, fear-filled eyes. Burns covered the entire right side of one man's face, his skin melted over his right eye. A small girl held his hand. Tears streaked her cheeks through a layer of soot covering her skin.

Danika jumped off her horse and pulled the nearest man out of line. Were they too late? "Where are you from?"

"Innisborough, just west of Shaletown." His eyes widened. He dropped to his knees. "Forgive me, Princess. I did not know it was you."

"That's no matter." She dug in her travel bag and pulled out a wad of dried beef. "Take this. Share the rations among the others. You will be welcomed in Ebonvale."

He stood with more confidence. "Thank you, Princess."

The others had caught on and they started to surround her, chanting, "Save us." "Save our village." "Save my children."

They pulled on her arms and grasped at her hands. Danika grew smothered and panic rose in her throat. "I'm trying. You will be welcomed in Ebonvale. I have no more food. I can do no more."

"Leave her alone." Bron's horse cut through the growing crowd. "Go." He offered his hand and pulled her up on his horse with him. "You are too kind, Princess."

"I wish I could help all of them." She held onto him as he cut through the crowd. He was her rock, her driftwood at sea, her compass. He'd always pull her up.

"You will." He rode up to her horse and she dismounted. "Believe in our quest."

"I do." Danika climbed onto her charger then met his gaze, and they froze, locked on one another. His belief in her solidified her resolve. Together they could rule the world. If only Bron had a kingdom to justify their union. Danika sighed. A farm in Oaten's Dell was hardly a kingdom, and his brother, Hule, was to inherit it. Bron had nothing except his courage and reputation to his name.

That was enough for her. But was he enough for Ebonvale?

Bron broke their stare. "Onward, march."

The army began moving and the tide of travelers kept their distance, pushing to the sides of the road. Danika could bear to look no longer; instead, she focused on the path ahead. Only when the sun rose high in the sky did her shaking subside.

The countryside turned from green fields to brown wasteland with blackened patches. The brook that had followed them along the way dried into a muddy hole, and the sky was empty of birds. No insects buzzed on the wind. The unnatural silence rang in Danika's ears and she focused on the rhythmic clomp of the army's feet.

They crested a hill, looking down upon the bridge linking Ebonvale with the southern districts, the same bridge the wyverns had kept them from crossing before their journey to the House of Song. Although the lake had dried, the muck would still slow them down, and the higher ground of the bridge provided a superior advantage in battle. They had to cross the bridge instead of trekking through the dry lake.

"Do the wyverns still guard it?" Danika already knew the answer. The dark clouds moved unnaturally, shady tendrils weaving in and out.

Bron peered through his telescope. "Five, maybe ten."

Danika checked the position of the sun and a sinking feeling sucked at the bottom of her stomach. "None of the scouts have returned besides the one."

"I know." Bron stuffed the telescope back in his travel bag. "We could go around."

"And tramp the whole army though the forest?" Danika thought back to the kobolds. "Not only would the diversion take us more time, time we don't seem to have, but, the kobolds are just as dangerous as the wyverns, and our armor will not protect us against their attack. Besides, I'm not comfortable leaving these beasts in my kingdom to wreak havoc while we sail south. What if they press north to the castle?"

Bron held her eyes with a courageous stare. "Move on, then?"

"It will be a good test of Garish's design and practice for what is to come. I'm sure many more than ten hover over Scalehaven. If we cannot defeat this swarm, then we are doomed to fail."

"We will not fail." Bron secured his travel bag and unsheathed his sword. "'Tis best to take them by surprise." He spurred his charger into action with his sword pointed in front of him. His voice boomed across the army. "To battle!"

Danika paused, blinking in shock as Bron took the lead. The time of reckoning had come. A current of panic shot into her legs and she spurred her horse after the front lines. Bron wasn't charging into battle by himself.

The thick mass in the sky spread into spiraling tendrils. Danika shouted, "Faster! They've spotted us!"

Archers released a volley of arrows. The first three beasts dove toward them in fiery balls. Danika forgot how to breathe as she watched their path with disbelief.

"Keep firing," Bron shouted to the archers. He turned to the rest of the army. "Give way!"

The archers held their ground as the wyverns descended, pricking their bodies like pin cushions and shredding their wings. Unable to control its landing, the first wyvern plummeted to the ground, breaking the cobblestone to shards. Bron rode to the fire worm in an instant, slicing its scaly throat with his sword.

One slayed. Four to go. The air burned like Garish's smithy, and Danika wiped sweat from her cheeks, steering her horse to the right as the second worm fell from the sky.

Too many soldiers had clumped together, avoiding the first wyvern's descent. They scrambled to escape the next fiery wyvern's wake as the beast hit, rolling in a two-ton mass toward the front line. Its tail alone took three men with it.

Danika shielded her eyes as grief wracked her body in shudders. She didn't have time to honor them because a sharp cry echoed over her head. She gazed at the sky in horror. The third wyvern had redirected its course to the other side of the army. As the worm fell the beast turned its snout and set its own wings on fire.

"Dirty bastard." Danika whipped the reigns. "Everyone, move!"

The army spread, fragmenting the core, and Danika lost Bron in the commotion. She ducked as one of the leathery wings scraped over her helmet. The reek of sulfur, spicy incense, and the whiff of fish flared in her nostrils. Danika coughed and rode down an incline as the beast hit the ground behind her.

A rolling wave of heat followed, and Danika threw herself on top of her horse to cover the beast as much as she could, burying her face in its mane. Garish had also equipped the horses with armor, but their bodies were much harder to cover. Smoke clouded everything around her. Her eyes burned as her throat itched raw.

Danika coughed and heaved. Would she perish with her horse into one large lump of charred flesh? Somehow, the animal's presence comforted her. Her fingers dug into the beast's mane and she held on with all her strength as it staggered forward.

The smoke cleared and Danika straightened in her saddle and gazed down at her still-shining armor. Her horse whinnied in response.

She was still alive, thanks to Garish and Nip. Her heart fluttered. Where was Bron?

A sizzling hiss brought Danika's attention back to the sky. Two more wyverns blazed fiery lines above her with their wrath. She directed her horse toward the incline and crested the ridge, scanning her fragmented army.

Bron led a battalion of soldiers to the bridge. They rode directly under the wyvern's path.

What a brave-hearted fool. "Horred's Grave!" She spurred forward, knowing she couldn't reach him in time to drive him off course.

The two wyverns positioned themselves facing Bron and his men. They breathed their fire in one stream, strengthening the blaze by tenfold. Bron and the others ducked behind their shields in their saddles and Danika held her breath as the flames engulfed them.

For a moment, fiery red and orange covered the troops. The flames surged then evaporated, disappearing into crackling sparks in the air. The soldiers straightened in their saddles, holding up their swords.

A roar of triumph erupted from the troops and Danika joined in, pumping her sword in the air. Garish's armor proved worthy.

As the wyverns dove and whirled, forming a counter attack, archers took the opportunity to release a wave of arrows. A few shots blessed by

Helena's breath struck one wyvern in the neck. The beast shrieked like a giant bird of prey as it went down beyond the hill.

The second wyvern landed on its clawed feet, blocking the entrance to the bridge and rumbling the bile in Danika's stomach. While most of the hatchlings were no bigger than cows, this fully grown wyvern had matured into a gigantic beast that would have towered over Ebonvale's ramparts, picking off archers with its teeth. Arrows stuck from its wings and back and smoke oozed from its nostrils. The beast brought its head down, horns spiraling backward like ill-grown roots on the crown of its head. It hissed, and steam puffed from its toothy jaws as its claws scratched the cobblestones.

Bron raised his sword and the other men followed. He shouted a war cry and they charged, the sound of their feet rumbling like thunder.

On all fours, the behemoth barreled straight for the army.

A dead wyvern carcass oozing lava-like blood on the broken cobblestones separated Danika from the battalion. She could only watch and pray as the two enemies collided.

The wyvern opened its jaws as it neared the front lines. Bron's horse broke from the front lines and took the lead. Danika clamped her arm against her chest, trying to keep her wildly beating heart from breaking through her armor.

Horred's Grave, the beast would swallow him whole.

Bron brought up his sword as the beast's head came down upon him. Like before, in the cavern with the white worm, he jabbed the tip into its top jaw. The wyvern reared back, bringing its snout up with the sword still stuck through it. Soldiers raced around the beast, slashing at its wings, as Bron held onto the hilt.

Danika's heart stopped as he jumped into its mouth, using the bottom jaw as a foothold. Bron shoved the hilt against the beast's lower jaw. He leaped to the ground as the wyvern shrieked, shaking its head trying to free the sword like a man would do to a toothpick stuck in one of his teeth.

Bron used the distraction to rally some of the archers. He pointed to the beast's exposed neck.

They fired as Bron dug into his boot and pulled out a dagger. He threw the blade in an arc and the tip wedged just below the beast's jaw. Lava-like blood oozed as the beast took its last wheezing breaths.

"Back away!" Bron shouted as the snout came down in a steaming heap.

A dust cloud rose, obscuring the scene. Danika dismounted and climbed the steaming carcass of the wyvern separating her from the one

Bron had just killed. The soles of her feet heated to near burning as she slid down the scales on the other side. The stink of sweltering seaweed filled the air. Danika coughed and covered her mouth. She'd never been fond of seared fish.

The dust cleared slowly to reveal the carnage. The peaceful cobblestone street was now a wasteland. Chunks of road lay between the stinking scaly bodies. Danika scrambled around the debris.

Soldiers called for their friends and leaned on each other, while healers raced around tending to wounds.

Danika had dealt with the tragedy of battle since her father began his campaign against the dead army of Sill. She'd witnessed soldiers carrying wounded men missing arms and legs and mourners crowding Ebonvale's gates shrouded in black, throwing white flowers at the rider-less horses' hooves.

But, she'd never experienced the rush of battle and the moment where a person's fate changed in an instant all because of where he or she stood in the ranks. As much as she believed in destiny, the hand of the gods dealt random blows, and any one of those fallen soldiers could have stood in her place, or she in theirs.

"Princess, fair you well?" A medic rushed to inspect her.

She waved him off. "I'm unharmed, thank you. Tend to the others."

Bron emerged from the dust like a hero rising from conquering the underworld. Soot covered his body, blackening his armor. But he stood in one piece with no visible wounds. Danika melted into a puddle of relief. She couldn't run to him in front of the troops, so she stood as still as Helena's statue and saluted his bravery with a raised hand to her forehead.

Everyone else on the battlefield, along with the carnage, the horror and the debris, vanished for a moment as Danika locked eyes with Bron.

He bowed to her. "Princess."

Her soul yearned to touch him, to wipe the soot from his brow and bring her parched lips to his, proclaiming her feelings. But he would only push her away.

Bron knelt before her like a knight before his king. The formality of the gesture iced Danika's heart.

"Well done, Bronford Thoridian. You are a true warrior with the heart of a lion and you are an asset to Ebonvale. You served your kingdom valiantly this day."

Bron straightened. "My thanks to you, Princess. It was a wise choice to lead us into battle. We have learned much about our failings, tested our armor and discovered their weaknesses, coming out victorious."

Danika stepped toward him and lowered her voice. "If five wyverns could do this much damage to our forces, imagine what a horde of them will do."

Bron's face soured and he looked away to the west, to the House of Song, where Valorian rallied his army. "Let's hope the minstrels will remedy our shortcomings."

The unspoken mention of Valorian built a wall between them.

Danika stepped away. "This will delay us for some time. We must hurry to bury our wounded and move on."

Bron's voice turned melancholy. "Aye."

For a moment she thought he'd forsake all inhibitions and reach out to comfort her, even with just a brush of his fingertips on her cheek.

He blinked, and his stoic composure returned. "I must rally the army. Although this is a victory, we have lost many, and their comrades' deaths will shake the morale of the men."

Disappointment weighed on Danika as she assumed her professional demeanor. Bron was too noble for such a temptation. His sense of honor drew her to him even more. "Do what you must. I'll aid with the fallen."

He approached the jaw of the fallen wyvern, dug inside the steamy teeth and yanked out his sword. Using the horns to hoist himself, Bron climbed the wyvern's head. Murmurs in the army lulled as Bron positioned himself between the wyvern's dead eyes and raised his sword to the sky. "Our triumph is due to those who have fallen this day. May the temple priests note their bravery in Ebonvale's historical archives."

A smattering of shouts and applause rose from the dust cloud.

Bron brought his sword across his chest. "Helena and Horrid lived in a time such as this, a crossroads where man had to take a stand or forever go down as a blink in history to the evils imperiling this land. They gave their lives for our freedom, and we must offer ours for those of our children, nieces, nephews and cousins, and their children's children. If we succeed this day, the people of our future will thrive and Ebonvale will live on."

Bron extended his arm to the soldiers crowding around the wyvern's head. "Follow me, and together we can bring hope back to a time of darkness. I swear, as Bronford Thoridian the First, I will bring you all to glory whether in this life, or the next."

The soldiers cheered, some of them chanting Bron's name. Danika walked away, consumed with her thoughts. She'd almost lost Bron, and the thought of him being gone tore her apart. Could she stomach yet another battle where her lifelong friend, ally, bodyguard and possible lover could disappear in an instant, leaving her life so empty she didn't want to carry on?

If the wyvern corpse hadn't blocked her way, Danika would have charged headlong into danger, putting the kingdom at risk in a time of flux. Would her people truly follow Muriel upon her death?

Danika feared losing Bron, but more than that, she feared what she'd risk to intervene on his behalf.

Chapter 24

Rogue

A haze of mist covered Brimmore as Ebonvale's army marched through streets winding down an incline to the bay. Three-story houses and brightly painted storefronts cluttered the thoroughfare of the continent's busiest port city. Usually, the congestion of carriages, horses, street performers and peddlers clogged the main artery so thickly it took half the day to carve a path to sea level. Today, the cobblestones lay silent, the windows boarded, and the inhabitants, if they were still there, were huddled inside.

To Bron, Brimmore seemed like a different city altogether than the one he'd visited six fortnights ago to encourage able-bodied men to compete for Ebonvale's ranks. Some of the men he'd recruited returned with him now, only to come back to a ghost town. Bron hoped this would give them more reason to fight.

Danika reined her horse beside him. She'd kept her distance since the battle, and he wondered if he'd done something wrong by performing his duty to the kingdom. She *must* know his true feelings, even if he couldn't show them.

She clicked her visor back, and he caught a glimpse of honey blond hair framing eyes more cold and emerald today than the warm, meadow-green irises that had peeled his layers away to reveal his heart at her father's grave. "This does not bode well for our escorts."

She talked of Valorian, of course. He was a constant thorn in Bron's heart.

"They made it." Bron nodded to her and steered his own charger away. He refused to believe Valorian and his men dead. If that were true, they'd be next to follow. "Wait and see."

They turned a corner and the azure waters of the bay sparkled between the tall buildings on either side of the street. Two carracks bobbed at anchor, each with three masts and a high rounded stern made from giant blackwoods. White sails draped over the rigging, fluttering in the ocean breeze.

Bron pointed and turned to his men. "Harbingers of our triumph." Valorian had made good on his word.

The army cheered behind him. He turned to Danika, expecting the good news to bring a smile to her lips.

Danika nodded grimly and spurred her horse forward. "Let's be done with this once and for all."

Bron couldn't fathom what she referred to: the voyage, the battle or meeting Valorian again. He rode in step behind her. How would he feel to see the man who had saved his life again?

The pier rose up in a giant slab of blackwood, punctuated at even intervals by moorings made of wood posts decorated in seashells and draped in old lobster nets. The ships stood as tall as Ebonvale's ramparts, dwarfing the men and women in the signature velvet robes of the minstrels who scurried in preparation. Some of them halted mid-step, watching the army with gazes filled with awe and relief as they drew near.

"Attention. Halt!" Bron shouted, and the army stilled in the next step, falling into rest position.

The onlookers parted and Valorian came forward. His eyes rested on Danika alone, and his lips stretched into a smile as if she were the only ray of sunshine in a dark, dire time. He wore a reddish leather tunic and a black satin cape trimmed in a matching rose.

Bron sighed, not impressed. Only minstrels dressed in finery for occasions such as these.

Valorian stepped from the pier and walked straight to Danika's horse, his long brown hair and cape fluttering in the breeze off the sea. Bron swallowed hard as the minstrel offered his hand. Danika accepted his gesture graciously. She dismounted and Bron, ever the bodyguard, followed suit. He stood behind her with enough room to protect her should wyverns spring from the sky, but with enough space to allow her to speak with Valorian.

"I am most relieved to have you and your army with us, Princess." Valorian kissed the back of her hand. "Although, I am surprised you decided to come."

"I appointed a regent queen to the throne." Danika sounded defensive. "I intend to see this through."

"Of course you do. Ever the brave-hearted woman, willing to sacrifice heart and soul for her kingdom. I admire your adherence to duty beyond measure." Valorian's gaze traveled from her engraved helmet to her curved breastplate and then her armored legs. "I see you have made your armor."

"Yes." Danika gestured for a soldier to bring her a carriage from the back of the army. "And, like we discussed, I brought a shipment of only the finest armor for you and your men."

"How very generous." He leaned forward and Bron had to strain to hear his words. "But no kiss?"

Bron tightened his grip on his hilt. The princess was not his. Would repeating the thought make it stick? She was not his. Duty bound her to Valorian just as deeply as it bound him to Ebonvale.

Danika paused. Bron wished he could read the expression on her face.

"Of course, my mind drifts to battle too soon." She rose on her tiptoes and placed a light kiss on his cheek, over one of his healing scars.

One of the scars he earned by saving Bron's life.

Valorian's gaze strayed to Bron as if sensing an increase of heat radiating from his armor. "Bronford, my friend. I am pleased to see you again."

"May the wind bring us swiftly to victory. My greetings, Valorian." Bron bowed. His neck itched under Valorian's silvery gaze. Could the minstrel see what had happened between him and Danika? What a rogue he'd been to have allowed Danika's advances and have reacted in the passionate way he had. They could have brought down both kingdoms with their indiscretions. Yet, he did not regret it.

Valorian smiled easily, as if whatever had happened in the last month didn't matter--which it probably did not. Danika would marry Valorian, and Bron would save his memory of one kiss as a secret sustenance for his beleaguered heart. Could he live with that? He'd have to try.

The minstrel took her arm. "Come. Let us make preparations together."

Danika finally turned back to Bron. Her eyes were cold, hard emeralds with no passion. "Bron, find a place to rest the army."

Bron bowed as his father had trained him to do in front of royalty, no matter how close they'd been in the past. "As you wish, Princess."

Valorian escorted her down the pier, and in an instant, she was gone.

Collecting himself, he turned to his men. They needed him, and he wasn't about to let his heart sickness weaken this campaign. "Attention!"

They stomped into place and shouted in unison. "Yes, sir."

"Follow me to the boardwalk. Let's find an inn that isn't boarded up to rest our feet."

Leading the troops away from the pier, Bron took comfort in one thought.

She hadn't kissed Valorian with a fraction of the passion she'd kissed him with.

* * * *

Danika allowed Valorian to lead her to the two majestic blackwood carracks bobbing with the tide. He looked dashing in his finery, with his thigh-high riding boots and long hair loose in the wind. He was beautiful in every aspect that Bron was plain. Yet, she couldn't get over that stolen kiss by her father's grave. The memory of Bron's lips on hers still burned fiery madness in her heart.

Kissing Valorian in front of Bron had made her stomach squirm like a thousand wyverns in the sky. However, after the battle at the bridge, she needed the minstrels more than ever if Ebonvale's army were to succeed. A simple kiss was the only way to keep Bron and her army alive.

"Behold, the *Destiny* and the *Fortune*. Made by Brimmore's finest artisans and craftsmen with the strongest lumber from the Blackwood forest." Valorian beamed with pride. The glossy wood shone ebony in the sunlight. Each plank had a slightly varying hue, some as black as night, and others a deep purple, reminding Danika of overripe plums. A wooden carving of a minstrel strumming a handheld harp stood with his back to the bow of the *Destiny*, while a warrior with his blade outstretched to the ocean decorated the bow of the *Fortune*. Ebonvale's flag, along with the crest of the House of Song whipped from the masts in the ocean breeze.

"They must have been costly, indeed." Danika laid her hand on the railing, the wood under her fingertips smooth.

"We spared no expense." Valorian placed his hand over hers, interlacing their fingers. "You and your army deserve only the best."

"My thanks to you and those who worked hard to build these wonderful, seagoing vessels." Danika made certain to group Valorian with the others. She danced a fine line between leading him on and remaining cordial enough for him to ride with them to a likely doom. Would he do it for love? Probably, but would he do it for someone with whom he had no future? She had no idea.

She was as vile as a black widow or, worse yet, a tavern wench.

Danika reminded herself the wyverns would come after the House of Song eventually. The minstrel's music might not be enough to keep the worms at bay. Valorian fought for his people as well as hers. She shouldn't owe him anything more than battlefield loyalty.

So, why did she continue with this charade?

Valorian squeezed her arm. This close, his silvery eyes reminded her of the moon's reflection on the lake. "Come, I have something to show you in our cabin."

"Our cabin?" Danika's stomach leaped to her throat.

"Yes, I assume you'll ride with me and the minstrels on the *Destiny*, while Bronford takes Ebonvale's army on the *Fortune*."

Danika paused. Bron would not favor this in the least. "I hadn't considered it."

"Well, I had." He opened the cabin door and gestured for her to enter first.

A lantern hung from a rafter in the ceiling, illuminating a table draped in red satin set with porcelain dinnerware. In the back, two windows framed with a velvet-cushioned lover's seat opened to the sea. The air smelled of salt and brine, along with roasted pheasant and sweet potatoes.

Any hope of meeting Bron for dinner disappeared. "For us?"

"Why, of course." Valorian pulled back an elegant, high-backed chair. "Will you join me, Princess?"

Danika didn't move.

"Ah…" He opened one of the window seats and laid out a low-chested velvet gown with golden brocade. "Perhaps you'd like to change into something more comfortable?"

Shielding her breasts all night didn't seem comfortable. Danika sat down in a final declaration of armor clinks. Anything to keep the night from turning romantic. "No. I prefer to keep my battle gear. One never knows when a wyvern will dive from the sky."

Valorian pursed his lips. "Very well. You are ever vigilant, my lady." He took a seat across from her, unlatching the clasp on his cape. The fabric fell to the floor, revealing his hard-edged shoulders and smooth river-stone chest rippling underneath his thin white shirt. "I trust your journey was pleasant."

"It was nothing of the sort." Danika pulled off her helmet and set it against the chair. Her hair fell around her shoulders, catching Valorian's gaze.

Drat. She should have pinned it up.

"Pray tell what happened, my dear." He lifted the lids of the china pots, revealing steaming heaps of poultry and vegetables.

Despite not eating all day, Danika had lost her appetite. Would this be what life would be like if she married him? Polite conversation over fine china? Danika cringed. She preferred sparring with Bron on the fields. "Five wyverns attacked us. We lost seventeen men as well as three horses."

"Horred's Gambit. How terrible!" He stabbed a potato and brought the food to his plate.

How could he eat at a time like this? "Yes, and that's not all. The wyverns are craftier than I thought. After we felled them, they dove straight for our front lines. One lit its own wings on fire to take us down."

"Interesting. And also encouraging." Valorian tasted a bite of pheasant, chewing slowly.

Danika placed her fork on the table with a clink. "Encouraging?" Was he not listening?

Valorian swallowed. "Minstrels always consider intelligence and intentions so we can turn their thoughts in our songs. Perhaps I can craft a melody that will convince them their lives are too valuable to spare."

"I thought you said you cannot change a person's mind, only draw out what is inside them."

"Very true, Princess. I cannot. Yet, a beast intelligent enough to sacrifice itself for vengeance may have other, deeper emotions belying its motives. Perhaps the beast has younglings or fights alongside its comrades. Songs can play upon those emotional ties and bring them to the foreground, until all the beast can think about is returning home."

As much as minstrels bending other creatures' intentions sounded like a rogue-ish way to get what you wanted, Valorian had one point. Danika stabbed a potato. She might as well look like she was eating. "'Tis a peaceful way to end a battle."

Valorian nodded. "Sadly, sometimes the underlying motives, the ones with true heart to them, are not enough to sway the beast."

Danika swallowed a bite of potato hard. This rang too true to her inner battle between Bron and Valorian. She feared her heart's wishes wouldn't be enough to sway the outcome. "What do you do then?"

"Let us hope these fiery worms have hearts bigger than their stomachs. If not, we find smaller battles to fight within them, convincing them of weariness or blindness."

What would choosing the smaller battles mean for her? Being able to visit Ebonvale on occasion? Seeing Bron as a stranger once a year? She couldn't lie to herself any longer. That life of small battles wouldn't be enough.

Danika shifted in her seat, her armor feeling heavy on her shoulders. "Surely I cannot stay here with you if I'm to protect my honor."

Valorian smiled and his eyes traveled down to the sword at her side. "A woman of your capabilities hardly has to worry about protecting her honor? However, safeguards are in place. There are two separate rooms branching from this cabin, and I can station a minstrel bodyguard at each one to protect us both." He winked and sipped a glass of wine.

A minstrel bodyguard? What about Bron?

Danika knew she'd only accept one man as her true bodyguard.

"Leave them be. You're right. I can take care of myself."

"Excellent." Valorian's cheeks flushed. Obviously he'd taken her request as an invitation.

Danika choked on a buttery bite of pheasant, feeling like a bird trapped in a cage.

Valorian stood. "Are you well, Princess?"

"Yes." She gulped down her glass of wine and stood. "I'm weary from travel. Allow me to retire and we'll talk more in the morning."

"Of course." He walked around the table and snaked his arm through hers, leading her to the room on the right. "Tomorrow we set sail. With the direction of the wind, it will take three days to reach Scalehaven, so we'll have a lot of time to catch up."

He opened the door. Her room was richly furnished with a four poster canopy bed. A redwood chest sat open at the footstool, filled with silken nightdresses and velvet gowns, and an oaken desk lay before a window with a four foot view of the sea.

"I trust the room is to your liking?" Valorian gazed with a worried look etched on his scarred, yet gorgeous face.

"Of course. Thank you." Danika turned, then a current of guilt spread through her as she remembered Bron. She whirled around. "You must send a messenger to find Bron and the army. "Tell them to return to the dock at sunrise at the latest."

"Certainly." Valorian kissed her on the cheek. "I look forward to our time together." With a suggestive smile, he left, closing the door behind.

Danika collapsed on the flowery bedspread. How would she deflect Valorian's advances for three full days?

Chapter 25

Only One Woman

There was no sense in marching Ebonvale's army down a deserted street when their feet already chafed in their boots and they'd squeezed the last few drops from their sheepskins. Instead, Bron led them to a small park where they could watch the ocean waves lap across a sandy beach. Travel-worn and heart-sore, he took off on his own to find shelter and food.

Wind gushed across the usually bustling boardwalk with no vendor stalls to block the gales from the ocean or the salty spray of the sea. Hastily nailed boards covered every window and door to all the inns. Bron walked the length of the bay. Would he find any provisions, or would they have to sustain themselves on Ebonvale's dried jerky and whatever they could fish out of the sea? Surely, one would have to be mad to stay open in a no man's land.

Bron turned back. How would he brace his men for the ill news? A gust of wind blew and hinges creaked. He whirled around, hand over hilt, and spotted a sign with yellow painted letters reading *The Broken Oar.*

One more. He owed it to his weary men to check.

Gazing down an alley to make sure he wasn't being followed by looters, or something worse, Bron jogged the remaining steps to the sign. The old wooden door stood slightly ajar and a warm fire glowed from inside painted glass windows depicting sailors lost at sea.

Seemed like a trap.

Bron tensed his fingers over his hilt, ready to draw at any time, and walked in. His armor clinked as he stepped, stealing any sense of surprise. Wooden booths with linen pillows lined the inside walls, and a series of bottles of all shapes and sizes stood on a glossy oaken bar.

"Good afternoon, soldier. May I tempt you with a draught of our famous, or shall I say infamous, blackwood brew?" An older man with a leathery brown patch over one eye and a head full of silvery hair standing up on end stared at him. Two blue bottles filled with a bubbly substance stood before him.

"No thank you, kind sir." Bron stepped toward the bar, acutely aware of any motion on all sides. Bron didn't want to give away the position of his army, or of Danika and the ships, until he knew more about the situation and this man. "What brings such a dutiful bartender to open his tavern in times such as these?"

"Kingdoms rise and fall, rulers come and go, but one truth remains." He paused, examining a bottle of dark, amber liquid. "If the sun continues to set and the moon dances in her shadow, there will always be a need for drink for the likes of any man."

Bron didn't like the idea of kingdoms falling. "What have you heard of the wyverns?"

"Rumors, mostly. Yula's son found a scale as big as that door washed up on the beach. Old Wolly upstairs saw a cloud of worms amassing over the eastern seaboard. City folks have abandoned their dwellings for fear the beasts will pay a visit to Brimmore's Bay. Pah!" He waved his hand. "If they come, then so be it. I'm not gonna let some fish-headed worms ruin my life's work. They've already driven away all my business, but they're not running old Tarle Bluebottom outta town!"

Bron smiled. He was beginning to like this man. "You have the bravery of a soldier."

"Nah. I was never one for battle and bloodshed. Give me a bucket, though, and I'll brew mead that will knock your helmet to the starry sky."

Bron stepped to the bar and dug into his travel bag. He pulled out a velvet sack and dropped it onto the countertop. A few golden coins leaked out, glinting in the hearth's light as they rolled and spun on the oaken tabletop. "I believe I can drum up some business for you."

Tarle Bluebottom leaned forward with a glint in his good eye. "Just say the word."

* * * *

As the first round of the Royal Guard filed into the booths with four men squeezing onto each bench, Bron took a seat at a one-man table in the back. Seeing Danika with Valorian again brought out the brooding side of him, and conversation wasn't a dance he wanted to engage in.

"More water, soldier?" A chubby-faced barmaid no older than Bron leaned over the table with a metal pitcher, condensation forming on the sides. She gave him a quizzical look, probably wondering why he hadn't tried Tarle Bluebottom's famous blackwood mead.

Bron never consumed mead on a quest. "Certainly. Thank you, ma'am." He pushed his mug forward.

Her black curls fell over the table as she filled his mug. Dark eyes studied the scar trailing along his jaw. "What'll it be tonight?"

Bron absently rubbed his chin where the scar ended. The image of a man with blackened skin and white-blue eyes, thick with cataracts, flashed through his mind. A leather rope hung around his neck, a golden ring dangling around his Adam's apple. He'd been human once. It had only taken that millisecond of pause for the undead to awkwardly swing a knife at Bron's face. It was good fortune the morning chill had frozen the dead man's limbs, and the reanimated had imperfect aim at best.

Bron blinked to clear his thoughts. "The pork and mutton dumplings sound tasty."

"An excellent choice for such a fine man." She appraised him with a smile. "Name's Lisha if you need anything."

Bron nodded without comment. Her interest in his scar unnerved him. He was a fractured man made tough by battle and silent by duty. Only such a woman as Danika would truly understand.

The barmaid twisted on her heels. Her hips swayed as she walked to the next table.

He'd killed the undead man in one fatal swing. A lull had fallen over the battle, and he had had enough time to bend over the corpse and break the leather strap around his neck. Holding the ring between his forefinger and thumb, he'd read the inscription.

Bound by love, Ursula and Claric.

Bron had searched for Ursula when King Artemus brought the men home. He'd found her in the farmer's village beside his, and it took him more courage than heading into battle to return the ring. She'd cursed him, saying he'd killed her one true love and his scar would never completely heal. True to her word, the scar burned in the sun and chilled in the evening air.

Another battle with more carnage, more death, loomed.

"Here you are." The barmaid Lisha pushed a plate of steaming pork and mutton dumplings with brown gravy in front of him. "Enjoy."

"My thanks to you." Bron picked up his fork.

"Oh, and one more thing." She dug into her apron and pulled out a small silver flask etched with a filigreed pattern on the front. "Courtesy of Tarle." She placed the flask on the table beside him.

Bron studied the glinting silver, running his hands along the grooves in the pattern. He admired the beauty and craftsmanship. "I have no need for this. I do not drink."

"It's a gift. Take it. You'll find a use for it." The barmaid leaned on his table, exposing her neckline and robust chest. "Is there anything else I can fetch for you?"

"No, ma'am." Bron cut a piece of meat with the side of his fork. He expected her to tend to the other tables, but she leaned on his as if she planned to stay. Bron wished for the company of his soldiers. Eating alone wasn't such a good idea anymore.

Her fingers trailed along his arm. "Tell me, do you have a sweetheart pining away for you back in Ebonvale?"

Bron couldn't lie to this young woman. "I do not."

She inched up closer and her fingertips left small halos of heat on the shoulder of his armor. "A man strong and honest-gazed as you should have women in droves surrounding him."

Bron pulled away and took a draught from his mug. "Duty keeps me from love."

Her chubby face scrunched up in sadness. She could be pretty when she dropped her seductress façade. "Pray tell, why ever is that so?"

Bron paused. If he gave her a shadow of a reply, she'd hound him all night long. He took a bite of bread, thinking upon his words.

The barmaid chewed on her bottom lip.

The bread had no flavor. Nothing could compare to Danika's kisses. He breathed in. "There is only one woman for me, and I cannot have her."

Lisha gasped and put slender fingers over her pouty mouth. "Parted by death?"

"Nay." Bron turned toward her. He'd never opened up to a stranger before. "Bound by duty."

The barmaid pursed her lips and gave him a scolding look. "Not a valid excuse, soldier." She placed her hands on her wide hips. "Love transcends all worldly trappings. If you truly loved her, you'd find a way."

She turned around and tended to the next table, her sly eyes and seductive facade returning.

Bron waited for her to come back to his table to explain further, for she'd made him out to be a fool. His empty plate sat on his table and his mug sat dry until the last soldiers had made their way back to the docks.

A saying his father used to mutter on occasions when his mother threw him out to sleep with the pigs came back to him:

Wise advice comes when you least expect it, but when you need it most.

Chapter 26

Voyage

Hazy sunlight trickled through the gossamer canopy surrounding Danika's bed. She reached to the light. Was she back in Ebonvale? Her heart surged with hope, soaring lighter than it had in months. Bron would be calling out orders on the training fields and Muriel would be waiting to serve her breakfast with all the latest gossip from the last courtroom ball.

She pulled the window fabric back, revealing a never-ending glittering sea. Seagulls cawed, riding white-crested waves, and the tang of salty brine hung in the humid air. The floor swayed underneath her feet as a wave hit the bow, spraying her nightgown with icy droplets. Danika placed her hand over her heart.

Valorian's boat.

Last night's dinner.

She had to tell Bron she was safe.

Bron wouldn't approve of her riding in Valorian's boat. To throw away the minstrel's offer would tempt the demons of fate, though. They needed their protection.

Danika washed herself in a small porcelain basin, then turned to the chest of gowns. Each one had been fitted to hang perfectly over her slender frame. Lace, velvet, pearls and intricate brocade were only some of the many adornments. Valorian had exquisite taste and had spared no expense.

She picked up an amber gown with a tight bodice wrapped in satin ribbons. What would Bron think of her, strutting around like a harlot in Valorian's dresses aboard *his* ship?

No, one slap in the face was quite enough. Danika folded the garment and stashed the gown back in the chest. As much as the metal weighed her down and the sun beat down in waves of heat, she chose her armor. Perhaps the heavy metal would hold in her wild heart.

Danika emerged from the dark cabin into bright morning light. Around her, the crew untied the rigging and minstrels sang songs to bless their voyage and raise morale. They nodded as she passed, never missing a beat.

Valorian stood on the helm with a dark-haired older man with a thick beard wearing a blue captain's hat with a feather through the side. Valorian waved to her, and Danika nodded in return. At least the captain busied him for now.

She walked across the boat and scanned the dock. Soldiers loaded their equipment, along with weapons, from the pier to the second boat, the *Fortune*. Bron stood surveying the operations with his usual straight-backed stance. He'd polished his armor since the attack, and the metal gleamed like a nobleman's silverware in the morning sun.

If he saw her on the deck of Valorian's ship, he did nothing to solicit her company.

It was now or never.

Would he realize her true intentions? Or would her betrayal tear them apart? Ebonvale hung on a harried thread. She had to take the risk. Danika walked the plank to the pier, passing by minstrels carrying bushels of fruits and vegetables and cages of poultry on deck. She marched down the dock, saluting the soldiers she passed.

Bron bowed as she approached, hiding any expression that may have crossed his face. "Princess."

Too many soldiers hovered to speak with him on any personal level. "Chief of Arms."

He straightened, and his eyes softened. "Did you sleep well?"

"Well enough."

"The decks of the *Destiny* provide safe refuge then?"

Danika stiffened. Of course he knew which boat she'd slept on. He was her bodyguard, after all. "A refuge, no."

Bron quirked an eyebrow, and she tried to be careful not to overstep Valorian's generous gifts. "How can one find refuge with such a momentous battle looming? As for safety, the ship is secure. In fact, I dismissed the minstrel bodyguards Valorian offered."

A smile curled on Bron's lips. "Chances are, if a wyvern dove from the sky, you'd be saving them."

Danika matched his sly grin. "We'll see about that. Did you find adequate accommodations last night for you and the men?"

"More than adequate." Bron put a hand on the armor plate covering his hard abs. "My stomach is still full."

She shifted, wishing she could have joined him. Due to her dinner companion, she hadn't eaten much last night, and her stomach gurgled with the thought of food.

His features grew somber as he nodded to Valorian's boat. "So, you've made your choice then?"

The question caught her off guard. Of what exactly did he inquire? Did she choose the boat or the man? She sucked in her lips, thinking of an appropriate answer with so many soldiers and minstrels around.

"For now, this arrangement is most beneficial to the kingdom."

Bron's brow raised and his eyes bore into hers. Did she see a flash of hope? "For now?"

"Aye." She nodded and leaned toward him. "No one knows what this battle will bring. We must make amends if we are ever to stand united."

A minstrel walked in front of them, trailing a cart of extra instruments filled with flutes, fiddles and a tambourine.

"A wise choice, Princess." Bron's gaze returned to surveying his troops. Along the dock, Valorian parted with the captain and waved to her.

She bowed to Bron. "Duty calls."

Bron's face showed no emotion as he scanned the dock. He didn't even look back to her to say goodbye.

This may be the last time she spoke to him before Scalehaven. Flustered, anger brimming, she turned to walk back to Valorian's ship. Fine. Pretend nothing had happened between them. Was she that easy to forget?

Bron's velvety voice followed her on the wind. "I hope it won't keep you forever."

She gasped and her heart sputtered before beating wildly. Every muscle in her neck itched to whirl around and study Bron's face.

Valorian watched her approach from the stern with a pleasant smile stretched across his lips. Under Valorian's gaze she could do nothing of the sort.

She tensed her fingers into fists and kept walking.

Had her imagination run away?

* * * *

They rode white waves out to sea. The wind blew in their favor, filling their masts with violent gusts ushering them to their destiny. Danika stood on the railing wearing the least revealing gown from Valorian's chest. With all the minstrels around, she felt like a statue amongst villagers in her gleaming metal. Better to fit in for the time being. When they reached Scalehaven she'd don her armor once again.

Her gaze wandered to Bron's boat as the wooden warrior carved into the bow cut through the waters beside them. The distance between them was so close, yet uncrossable. Her castle had suffocated her from time to time, but the deck of a ship imprisoned her. Already, the sides pressed in with sea-filled horizons all around.

There was no sign of the armored Chief of Arms. Danika smiled to herself, remembering how he avoided all quests beyond the boundaries of land. He never did like boats.

"A brilliant day for a journey, is it not?" Valorian placed both hands on the railing beside her. Instead of gazing at their sister ship, his eyes strayed to Danika.

She stepped away from the rail. Better not to let Bron see her mingling with Valorian. "It would be, if we weren't heading into battle." And if she stood on the other ship. The cramped quarters made it almost impossible to avoid the minstrel.

Valorian followed her around the deck to the other side where the wind whipped fiercely. "You doubt our victory?"

"I fear what I must sacrifice to win." Danika looked away. Had she spoken out loud? She hadn't meant to open up so deeply.

"My dear." Valorian spread his hand across the deck. Minstrels sang an old ballad of a battle long past and triumphantly won, and the captain stood at the helm, searching the sea. "Every man on this boat will meet their end, either in battle, by sickness, or in the deathly grip of old age."

He placed his arm around her and pulled her close, blocking the wind. "Nothing is forever. We must enjoy the days we have together and content ourselves, knowing our sacrifice is for both our kingdoms."

Danika allowed Valorian to hold her, even though his arms provided small comfort. If he spoke the truth, her time with Bron had come and gone, and she'd squandered it.

"Are you a realist then?" She had trouble believing a man who created words from thin air would plant his feet firmly in reality. In a way, Valorian was a shrewd, courageous man. Danika longed for Bron's idealistic bravery.

"I don't imagine what's not there, if that's your meaning." Valorian's voice was steady, almost stern.

Danika froze against him. Could he feel her cool disposition like a dead fish in his arms? She danced around the subject. "Do you see our victory?"

"I see the possibility, aye."

Danika eased back in his arms. "That bodes well."

Valorian buried his face in her hair. His voice turned wistful. "If we both survive this battle and emerge victorious, what will the future bring?"

A minstrel's voice from the lower deck wafted up on the wind. He sang of a great and mighty love transcending the conventions of court. Interesting choice.

Danika knew he'd broach this topic eventually, and she had an answer ready to give. "An alliance between our kingdoms, strengthened by the fact warriors and minstrels fought side by side."

"Is that all?" He took her hand. His voice deepened as his thumb traced circles on the back of her hand. "I can think of another way to strengthen our ties."

Men shouted from the sister ship. Queasiness overtook Danika, and her knees weakened as distress spread throughout her gut. She turned to the captain of the ship who pointed to the sea off the bow. "Call to arms!"

Minstrels raced around them, and Danika clutched Valorian's arm. "What's the matter?"

Valorian placed his hands on her shoulders. "Go back to your room. Allow me to handle this."

Before she could respond, a tentacle burst from the surface just feet away from the sister ship. Suction cups as wide as her arm spread as the tentacle unfurled and moved toward the bow.

Valorian pushed her toward the cabin. "Go!"

Danika stumbled forward in shock. Then she remembered her armor. Helena's Sword! The one day she didn't wear it! She followed Valorian's order to return to her cabin, but with the intention to reemerge.

Around her, the minstrels began a deep, low hum, vibrating deep in her gut. They were preparing for battle.

Danika burst through the doors to her cabin with her dress already half untied. She tore the back open and leaped from the fine fabric. The tentacle had been heading straight for Bron's boat. Could she reach him in time?

Chapter 27

A Heroine's Rise

A loud horn wailed, like the cry of an ancient beast after predators stole its young. Bron woke from a hazy dream, and the remnants clouded his mind. He'd played *Knights and Wizards* with Hule, whittling away each piece until only six remained. On his side stood his queen, his king and one knight. On Hule's side stood his queen, his king and a bishop. They danced upon the board like figures sliding across the ballroom in court. Every move locked them in a duel that could not be won without Bron sacrificing his queen. He could not part with her.

Bron cleared his head of game pieces. His battle horn. He'd given the alarm to the man with watch duty, ordering him to blow the call if under attack.

He stood and grabbed his helmet, slipping it over his clean-shaven head. His sword was already sheathed at his side. He never slept without it.

Shouts rang out above him, sending adrenaline flowing through his veins. Bron leaped up the steps to the deck and emerged into chaos.

Men ran across the deck, shouting orders while a cannon fired at a shiny lump the size of a hillock protruding from the sea. The man beside him screamed as he rose off his feet and over Bron's head. A giant tentacle wrapped around the soldier's torso, squeezing slowly as the fishy flesh wound around him.

Bron climbed the steps to the upper deck and leaped into the air, slicing his sword over his head and through the meaty flesh. The tentacle and the man fell to the deck in a wet lump. Bron ran to his side, recognizing Eli Wilkins, second regiment of the Royal Guard. He'd recruited him only a year ago from Oaten's Dell. Pulling the dead end of the tentacle off him, Bron checked his pulse.

Eli moaned and his eyelids fluttered.

"Are you all right, soldier?"

"Yes." Eli coughed, wrapping his arms around his stomach. Around them, three more tentacles sprang from the sea, probing the rigging. Bron needed to get back to the battle.

"Do you think you can stand?"

"Yes, sir." Fear welled in the man's eyes and Bron wondered where his training had failed. If these men were afraid of a sea beast, how would they react to a swarming horde of fire-breathing worms?

He helped the man stand. "Get to the infirmary below."

Bron released Eli and brought up his sword. Soldiers swiped at the tentacles, cutting some in half. For every one they felled, three more sprang up. The air hummed with the minstrel's song as the sound changed pitch from a low growl to a high shriek. Had they gone mad? Whatever the minstrel's were doing, Bron wasn't going to wait until their song worked.

The captain stood at the wheel, turning the ship away as tentacles reached toward him.

Bron sprinted toward the helm. If he lost the captain, he'd have to steer the boat to Scalehaven. The warrior had as much experience steering ships as he had wearing women's gowns.

A tentacle closed on his arm, and he swiped the wet flesh in half with his sword. More wiggled on the deck at his feet and he jumped over them as the tendrils tangled in the netting, pulling at their supplies. One soldier, a cityman from Brimmore named Ale Cleary, writhed on his back, a tentacle wrapped around his neck. Bron's first instinct was to help him, but the captain was more important.

Three tentacles wrapped around the captain's left arm and both ankles. He held onto the steering wheel with white knuckles, his grip slipping.

"Hold on, Captain!" Bron threw his dagger as he took the stairs two at a time. The dagger sliced through the tentacle on the Captain's arm as the ones around his ankles slowly climbed his legs. He lost his grip and fell, slipping along the deck toward the railing. Bron dove forward on his stomach and skidded across the deck. He grabbed the man's hands with both of his and gave him a stare so strong, it should have held him in place all by itself. "Hold on."

The captain winked in relief. "I'm not letting go."

"You'd better not." Bron gritted his teeth as he heaved. They locked in place, just like the *Knights and Wizards* game in his dream. Only this time there could be no stalemate. He could not overpower the pull of the sea beast. He'd have to find another way.

"Hurry!" The captain kicked at the tentacles as they traveled up his back to his neck.

Bron transferred all of the captain's weight to one hand. As his muscles bunched with the strain, he sat up slowly and drew his sword. "Duck!"

The captain shoved his face against the deck and Bron swung, slicing one of the two tentacles. The appendage released its hold and slithered back into the foamy waters.

Bron cut at the second tentacle, careful not to injure the captain's leg. The fishy flesh slithered away, half torn.

"I thought I was going under." The captain panted on the deck as he lay on his back.

Relief and shock flowed over Bron as he forced himself up. "Did you not know? The captain must stay with his ship." He pulled the captain with him. "Can you steer us out of here?"

The captain eyed the deck, half tangled in tentacles as the men loaded cannons and shot into the water blindly. "I'll try."

"I'll guard you." Bron cemented his feet in front of the helm. He chanced a glance at their sister ship, thinking of Danika. The *Destiny* bobbed closer to them, dropping anchor instead of sailing away.

The minstrels must have lost their minds. Their music failed to have any effect on the sea beast, and their fighting skills were less than desirable. What did they mean to accomplish?

Perhaps they knew destiny tied their fate to the *Fortune's*. Without the steel of the Royal Guard, Danika would have no triumph at Scalehaven. Her life, the minstrels' lives and the safety of Ebonvale depended on him and his army and they on them. Both sides were duty bound.

Pressure tightened around his ankle as a tentacle coiled up his calf. Bron raised his sword to slice the appendage, and another one stuck to his arm with suction cups, holding his sword in place. Before he could react, a tentacle thick as an aging blackwood shot from the railing and knocked him off his feet. He hit the deck hard, air stolen from his lungs. As he struggled to rise, the thick tentacle wrapped around his chest, bending his armor as the leviathan pulled him to sea.

Bron breathed in, his chest pushing against his armor as he filled his lungs. Metal armor sank like boulders in water. The beast dragged him to his death.

He wished he could have told her how he truly felt.

Bron tightened his grip on his sword even as the tentacle cut off circulation to his fingers. He'd fight to the death before he lay in such an abysmal, watery grave. He may still have time.

A silver blade arced above him, glinting brightly in the sun. The blade hacked the smaller tentacles first, then cut through the large one, hitting the deck with a thunk. The force of the lunge embedded the blade deep into the wood, splintering the plank. Stunned, Bron shielded his eyes from the sun as a slight figure knelt beside him. Two bright green eyes shone from the helmet's visor.

It could not be.

"Are you all right?" Danika's voice spoke to his heart.

Had he died in the beast's grasp and awakened in heaven?

"Are you hurt? For Helena's Sword, speak!"

"I am unharmed." Bron's voice came out wispy with awe and disbelief. How dare she risk her life to save his? "How did you travel to this ship?"

"Rope." Danika raised her visor and a smile stretched. "I convinced Valorian to steer closer. Though, I must say, I will not be auditioning for the festival acrobats when we return. Now get up! There is a battle to fight."

Bron took her hand and they stood. Danika yanked her sword from the deck and swung the blade in front of her, testing the arc of the edge. Her eyes were fierce emeralds. "This blade will still fight true."

Tentacles slithered toward them, and the starboard side of the ship looked more like an overgrown weed garden than a deck. "Come, let us clean this mess." Bron lunged forward. They fought side by side, clearing a path through the tangle.

The boat groaned and started to tip as the tentacles pulled the masts toward the water. Bron leaned backward, trying not to slip. "Find something to hold onto!" He snaked his arm through the railing of the stairway leading to the helm. Danika skidded, and he grabbed her hand as boxes, netting, and other supplies slipped into the sea.

Beneath them, the oily hump emerged, water raining off the slimy surface as the neck rose and uncoiled. A massive headdress of leathery fins framed a long toothy jaw and white eyes with no pupils. The beast towered over them, seawater and slime dripping on their armor in goopy streaks. Bron licked salt from his lips. Was it from the spray of the sea or his sweat?

"It's a leviathan." Danika whispered as she dangled from Bron's hand. "A distant cousin of the wyverns. I thought them to be myths."

"Unfortunately, they are not." Bron tightened his grip on her hand as if his courage alone could save them.

The leviathan hissed and opened its jaws, dipping its head toward them. Its scales were paler than the wyverns', reflecting an oily blue, which turned to silver in the angle of the sun. Danika raised her sword, arm shaking.

Would she be safer dangling from his arm under the leviathan's jaws or dropped into the sea? She'd never forgive him, but at least then she'd have the slim chance of swimming back to the minstrel's ship.

She shouldn't have deserted Valorian and risked her life to save Bron. He and Danika had grown too close, developing feelings running too deep, risking everything he'd sworn to protect.

He must abandon this dream before it was too late.

The leviathan smacked its jaws above them. It might already be too late. Bron had to release her, but his hand wouldn't let go.

Around them, the low, droning hum separated into harmony. The sound resonated in perfect chords, harmonies building upon each other, to create a cathedral of sound. The notes changed, growing farther apart, and the collective song wailed with dissonance. The sound reminded Bron of a thousand cries of suffering. Were the minstrels truly mad? Or did they sing their own funeral ballad?

The beast shrieked and whipped its head back and forth as if the tones shot daggers through the membranes covering the earholes. The tentacles loosened, retreating across the deck as the beast released the ship. The deck pitched backward and Bron slammed into the stairway as the *Fortune* rocked upright once again.

The leviathan disappeared into the dark waters, leaving a trail of sea foam in its wake. A fountain of water and bubbles shot up from the surface as it expelled its breath. A mournful cry, deeper than a whale's call, echoed over the sea.

"They did it." Danika lay on the deck beside him, propping herself up with an elbow as Bron released her hand.

"Did what?" Fog covered Bron's mind. All he could think of was pure, comforting silence in the dissonance still pinging in his head.

"Found a chord ugly enough to drive the beast away." Danika shouted above the din and stood.

Bron felt as though a storm had battered his body and soul. His breastplate was bent in where the tentacle had gripped, cutting into the sides of his chest. Disappointment outweighed his relief. He wanted to be the victor, not the one saved. He'd underestimated the minstrels' power. Once again, Valorian had saved his life.

Bron sat up, leaning on the railing for support. "We should return you to your ship, my lady." Perhaps she was safer there than he'd thought.

"Not a chance." Danika wiped slime from her armor and threw the sludge overboard like poison.

Bron blinked in confusion. Had she lost reason?

Danika winked. "I told you, no more acrobatics. You know how I despise ropes." She walked away, helping the healers tend to the soldiers.

Bron sat back with his legs sprawled before him. He knew her better. She'd never mentioned a fear of ropes before. In fact, he'd caught her sneaking out at night to swing across the chasm between her tower and the main building, hanging on the laundry ropes.

She wanted to be close to him. Bron had allowed his feelings to reach too far, endangering the very kingdom they sought to protect. The barmaid was wrong. He could not sacrifice duty for love.

Bron stood, swearing to himself he'd adhere to his sworn oaths and do whatever he could to gain victory. With the minstrels' magic song, they'd won this battle, but another, far greater clash loomed. Black volcanoes topped with smoke, oozing lava red as blood claimed the horizon. Scalehaven tempted him. Bron stared at his destiny with determination and acceptance.

"Thank goodness you've alive, sir." His first in command, Recktus Fairhaven, bowed before him. His long, black hair dripped as though he'd taken a plunge into the sea and someone had fished him out.

"Yes, it appears luck is on both our sides." He placed a hand on the man's shoulder. "Good to see you, my friend."

"There are many casualties, sir. The soldiers are wondering if we are to go back."

Go back? Returning home empty-handed wasn't an option. Bron took a deep breath. "Rally the troops we have left. We go to battle tomorrow at dawn."

"Yes, sir." The solider saluted him with a grim expression. He jogged toward shouts of triumph coming from the main deck.

As Bron's father liked to say, someone had beaten him to the mead barrel.

Danika stood at the helm, addressing the survivors. She'd taken off her helmet, and her golden hair glowed in the noonday sun. In her battle armor, she looked more beautiful and glorious than in any courtly gown. His heart sped.

As much as he feared for her safety he knew there was no escaping the wyverns either here or back in Ebonvale. If they failed, there'd be no kingdom to return to. Danika had been right to come. She embodied everything good and true in Ebonvale, and today she gave his troops hope. She'd trained like any soldier and had the courage of a true warrior. Why not have her fight for her kingdom if she wished it? But, he couldn't have her risking her life for his, or leaving Valorian unguarded.

Bron would do everything in his power to keep her safe, even if it meant sacrificing his life, his love.

At least he'd have her beside him one last time.

Chapter 28

Song of Power

The minstrels took no chances. They sang their foul song throughout the night and Danika tossed and turned in the spare bed in the captain's chambers, wishing she could clog her ears with seaweed. She'd left all of her elegant nightgowns on Valorian's ship, and she sweated in her undergarments, kicking the thick sheets to her ankles.

Ironically, she preferred to sweat on the *Fortune's* hay-strewn mattress than sleep in luxury on Valorian's ship. Bron lay only two rooms away and the beat of his heart came through the walls, calling to her.

Danika thought back to their quest to Darkenbite, when she'd slept an arm's length away. Why hadn't she reached out to him at least once? Why had it taken her this long to realize the shape of her heart?

Valorian.

He was why. Even if they succeeded in this quest and returned home victorious, Valorian would be waiting. Only a fool would tempt fate by rejecting the House of Song's union and leave her kingdom vulnerable and alone. First, the army of Sill plagued Ebonvale and now the wyverns of Scalehaven. What would rise up next to fight them? Could she handle a new threat with Ebonvale's army alone?

Her legs kicked at the sheets anxiously. She longed to ramble through her mother's grove of cherrywoods in Ebonvale's orchards outside the castle. A night like this needed a long walk to tire the useless wanderings of her mind.

Danika shot up and wrapped the sheets around her in a robe. The salty, wet decks of the *Fortune* would have to do.

The night air singed her eyes as she emerged under the stars. A foul, sulfurous stench blew from Scalehaven. The volcanoes' hulking shadows claimed the horizon, their fiery wrath lighting the southern sky in a reddish haze. Thunderous cracks echoed around her. The volcanoes stirred as if sensing their presence.

The captain stood as lookout, staring toward Scalehaven with determination set in his shoulders. He chewed on the end of a pipe, sending puffs of smoke into the air. Danika passed him unnoticed. She climbed the slick steps to the lower deck. All the rigging lay abandoned and the boat creaked with the pull of the current. The minstrels' song from their sister ship gave the night a haunted air.

One figure stood on the stern, watching the distant horizon from whence they came. The tall proud stance and the square shoulders were a permanent fixture in her memory.

Bron.

She should know by now he never slept on the eve of battle.

She longed to go to him and have him hold her in his strong arms. She could use his comfort at such a dark time, but her logical mind screamed for her to sneak back to the cabin. He could not give her what she sought. Or should not. Yet Danika stayed, her feet firmly planted on the deck as if a force beyond her control held her still.

"A foreboding night, is it not, Princess?" Bron's voice wafted back to her and she stiffened.

How could he know? She'd walked as silent as a ghost.

Bron turned, and the glow of the lava from the horizon behind her illuminated his square features and wide lips in an evocative glow. "I can smell your perfume on the wind." His lips curled. "Never spray strawberry mist before sneaking up on a foe."

Danika grinned and teased him with a narrowing of her eyes. "Are you a foe?"

"Only to my own inclinations." He shifted his gaze to the wake of their boat.

"Of what do you speak?" Danika stepped toward him, aware of her thin sheet covering her bare breasts. She pulled the fabric tighter against her body so the wind didn't steal it away, leaving her naked. She wouldn't want that.

"I would see Ebonvale live on in health and prosperity. Yet, I would sacrifice anything to ensure your safety, Princess."

"You are my bodyguard. You swore to my father to protect me. What harm is there in that?"

"That is not all." Bron's hands tightened on the rail. "I also swore my undying loyalty to Ebonvale."

"There's no harm in that either." Danika touched his arm. The armor felt cold to her fingers and she longed to feel the warmth of his skin.

"If I had to choose between the two, I'd choose you, Princess."

"You won't have to choose. Protecting me is protecting Ebonvale, for I am the only direct heir to the throne."

"In all this, there is one thing I failed to protect you and Ebonvale against."

"What threatens us both? The wyverns?"

"No." He placed his hand on his breastplate where filigreed patterns of roses bloomed. "My heart."

Danika's heart sped and her tongue felt heavy in her mouth. She'd been waiting for this moment for so long. A dizzying joy spread throughout her. She took his hand, hoping for some reaction. His fingers lay unmoving in her grasp.

"I had to tell you before the battle. I could not die without you knowing."

She squeezed his hand and held his palm to her heart, his fingers grazing her left breast, alighting fire inside her. "You are not going to die. I will not let them harm you."

With his other hand, he trailed a finger along her cheek, and she melted at his fleeting touch. Bron took both hands away and stepped back. "This is where I have failed, Princess. You must let me go. You and Valorian must live to see Ebonvale rebuild."

Danika breathed in to object and Bron brought his finger to her lips, silencing her. "I know what rests on your lips, and I urge you not to say it. I failed to protect both our hearts."

Hot tears rolled down her cheeks. "You failed at nothing."

"If you are lost in battle, or if you are not united with Valorian, I have failed at everything I've sworn to do. You must keep both yourself and Valorian alive at all costs."

Danika crossed her arms and looked away, her eyes stinging with more tears. "No. I cannot. If something happens to you…I fear I cannot live without you."

Bron put both hands on her shoulders. His gaze implored. "You will and you must. I cannot have another day like today, where you desert the House of Song for your bodyguard. I beg you. If you do nothing for me ever again, do this one thing." He bent his head, pressing his forehead against hers. He opened his mouth as if to kiss her, then drew back.

Danika shook her head, unable to speak. Everything she wanted stood before her. Bron's feelings were true and matched hers. Yet, she could not have him. The truth tore her apart.

He released her. "I expect no less, Princess."

Before she could form a response he turned away, leaving her alone on the stern with Scalehaven's hot breath breathing down her throat, threatening to take away the one man she loved.

* * * *

Dawn came swiftly and Danika rushed back to her cabin to change before the other soldiers spotted her roaming the decks in her sheet. Some icon of hope she'd represent looking like a wreck of a woman who'd just lost her only love. She doubted Helena ever looked so worn and despairing.

As she reached for her armor, something in the air changed. Danika froze, listening.

Silence.

The minstrels had ended their song, which could mean only one thing. They were too close to Scalehaven to risk the wyverns overhearing. She doubted the same vile chord would stall the fiery beasts. Unlike their distant leviathan cousins, the wyverns were too clever for a single sound to hearten their retreat. No doubt, the minstrels plotted which new tune to employ as she donned her armor.

Suddenly, she missed their twisted song. Without the sour turns of sound, she felt unprotected, naked to the wyverns' threat. Danika washed the tears from her face and secured her helmet. Hopefully, they'd come up with something soon.

The deck bustled with activity when she reemerged in her armor. Soldiers packed travel bags and unloaded crates full of swords and spears. Some sharpened their weapons on a gray whetstone brought up from the belly of the ship. The first volcano in a chain of smaller islands towered over them, casting an ominous shadow on their ship. The air reeked of sulfur and exotic incense, making her nostrils itch. Some soldiers and many members of the crew had handkerchiefs tied around their mouths.

She dug into her travel bag and pulled out one of her mother's old silken scarves. She'd brought the fabric for good luck, and as a reminder to contact Sybil when she returned. She tied the delicate, pink fabric around the lower half of her face. Would she return?

The captain pulled the ship into an alcove, hidden by the northern volcano's ridge. They'd risk too much to travel straight to the lair of the She-Beast. Instead, they had to cross three islands and a desolate wasteland using the volcano's treacherous ridges for cover.

The ship dropped anchor beside a slab of lava rock, as black as coal and as sharp as a blade where a chunk had broken off and fallen into the sea. The crew dropped rope ladders to the outcropping and the captain gave the gesture to disembark.

Scalehaven had come too soon, like a slap in the face after a long dream. Danika had busied herself with thoughts of Valorian and Bron. She hadn't mentally prepared for the trek and subsequent battle to come. Now she had no time for pondering her fate.

The crew of both ships stayed behind as the soldiers and minstrels climbed to shore. They'd wait five days for their return. If no sign of either army showed, they'd sail to Brimmore's Bay empty-handed and hide in the corners of Ebonvale when the wyverns' heat bathed the land. The thought sent shivers down Danika's back.

She took one last look at the stern, where Bron had opened his heart to her, then asked her to give it back. Could she follow his demand and stay with Valorian? Her father would beckon her to follow Bron's wisdom. Her mother, on the other hand, would plea for her to follow her own wild heart.

Who did Danika take after most? Only time would tell.

She descended the ladder, following the troops as they carved a path through the molten-backed rocks. Bron kept his distance, leading the way. The minstrels followed behind the last of the army. They'd exchanged their finery for the armor she'd brought from Ebonvale's smithy, and if it wasn't for the instruments on their backs, she wouldn't be able to tell them apart.

"Have you stayed behind to walk with me and the minstrels, my lady?" Dressed in full armor, Valorian stood before her in a vision of gorgeous knightliness. The armor brought out his willowy arms and legs and the smooth curves of the breastplate complimented his river stone muscles underneath. Where Bron was lumbering, Valorian was swift.

She'd do as Bron asked. Stay with Valorian.

"I have." She swallowed hard. "I will see that our union adheres during battle."

Valorian smiled and bowed. "You are most welcome."

Danika nodded and walked beside him. The lava rock felt hard and uneven under her feet. After walking on a boat three days, the firmness and solidity made her legs feel like ribbons. "I trust your minstrels have composed a song to enable our victory."

Valorian followed her, offering his hand whenever the terrain allowed. "Yes. We have studied the chordal patterns affecting the leviathan and drawn a new, more insidious drone for the wyverns." His voice grew deeply menacing. "We call it the Song of Power."

The title inspired awe. "What will this song accomplish?"

"Hopefully, our song will calm the fire in their bellies and send them into a comatose sleep."

"And how do you manage such a thing?"

"We deduced a great many things from the mind of the leviathan as we tried our array of songs. Restlessness governed the beast's movements. It had just woken from a long sleep and needed to feed. We believe, from the worm in the cave and from this recent meeting, these beasts have a hibernation cycle. Our song will instill in them the need to complete the cycle, the need for sleep."

The ways of the minstrels made Danika's mind dizzy, like one of her father's wood puzzles she could not solve. "Is that what you told the leviathan?"

"No. The leviathan had primal inner fears of the oceans drying up and the world turning to barren soil. We simply showed her our vision."

A thunderous clap silenced their conversation, and every soldier and minstrel turned his head to the sky. A flaming piece of the mountain sailed through the air above them like a meteorite. The burning ball of rock hit the sea, sizzling. A trail of white smoke rose up from the waters. Thank Helena and Horred their ships had already passed.

The troops resumed their walk, entering a canyon formed from a cataclysm cracking the earth in half. Danika followed. The soles of her feet burned and they'd just started their trek. "How could you fabricate such a lie?"

"We didn't." His scarred face turned sad. "We illuminated what the future may hold if our campaign isn't successful."

An icy chill shot across Danika's shoulders and seized her heart. "You said you can see our victory."

"I see many possibilities. Our victory is only one of countless paths."

Danika yearned for Bron's steadfast optimism. He'd tell her he knew in his heart they'd win. She drew her courage from his hope.

Movement distracted Danika from replying. A scout waved a yellow flag up ahead.

Bron's voice echoed down the canyon. "Seek cover! Wyverns dive from the southern ridge."

Panic shot through Danika's limbs. The canyon was too narrow for them to backtrack in time. They were sitting ducks in a trap.

"Quickly." Valorian pulled her to the rocky wall. They flattened in the canyon's shadow. The rest of the army followed suit, stretching into a thin line. Every clink of armor echoed against the close walls, making Danika wince.

Shrieks came from the sky and Danika held her breath. She twisted her neck to gaze through the canyon crack above her head. Black shapes darted in the air, circling. Danika held onto the rock, pushing her back against the hard surface until it dug her armor into her skin. She hoped the crew had hidden the ships a safe distance away.

"Please, Helena, do not let them spot our transports." Otherwise, this would be a one-way trip whether they triumphed or not. Only scraggly excuses for trees grew on Scalehaven. Nothing rose tall or wide enough to fashion into planks. Unless they sprouted wings from their backs, they were stranded without the carracks.

A soldier slipped, and his silver boot skidded into the light. Rocks tumbled down the canyon past Danika and Valorian. Danika squeezed her eyes shut.

Bron's intense whisper rode the wind. "Do not move."

If he moved, the glint of the silver would catch their eye for certain. As it was, his leg could pass for a large chunk of mica.

Movement in the canyon caused Danika to open her eyes. Bron slid down the incline in front of the line of soldiers, a hair's breadth from the light. He carried a leather blanket the same hue as the lava rock.

Bron threw the blanket on the soldier's leg, and the bright metal gleam disappeared. They waited until the last cries rang out in the sky above, then the soldier slowly moved his leg back into the shadow.

"That was close." Danika breathed in relief. Valorian's words came back to her. *Our victory is only one of countless paths.*

Doubt clouded her mind. Their quest dangled by spider strands over an endless hole of oblivion.

How could they hide their progress all the way to the highest island peak?

Chapter 29

Hope

By twilight, they'd reached the end of the first island. A thin peninsula of hardened lava jutted across the ocean's expanse, almost reaching the second island, and the largest in the chain. Bron stood at the edge, contemplating the depth of the ocean between the two lands. Could they swim across?

His first in command approached him, standing beside him at the water's edge, while the army rested under an overhanging cliff, dipping into their rations. "May I have a word, sir?"

Bron took off his helmet and ran a hand over the stubble on his head. "You are always welcome to speak freely, Mr. Fairhaven."

Recktus nodded and followed Bron's gaze off to the sea separating them from the next island. "The men are weary from the day's trek."

"I know." Bron narrowed his eyes, searching the crested waves for any signs of sea creatures. Did leviathans swim this close to shore?

"Sir?"

Bron blinked. The heat had baked his mind. He was just as weary as they were, if not more so from leading, then doubling back to show them the easiest path. "The peninsula offers no cover. If we cross by the moon's faint light, we can use the shadow as a cloak. If we wait until morning, we'll be fully exposed to any flying patrols."

"I see the conundrum, but it will be difficult to convince the men to walk past sunset. The heat grates on all our nerves." Recktus wiped a hand over his face. He was younger than Bron by five years, yet he had two little ones at home. Bron weighed his service heavily. He would not take any chances with his men, even if it meant pushing them past their limits.

Bron knelt by the edge and picked up a dried clump of seaweed. "The tide has been moving out all day. If we wait too long, it will return, covering the peninsula in twenty feet of sea." Bron threw the seaweed into the water, anxious to move. "Summon the men. We're going across." His first in command nodded with weariness and doubt in his eyes. "What if there are vermin in the water? Or if the distance is too far?"

"There's only one way to test it." Bron clapped him on the back and started toward the peninsula before Recktus could stop him. "I'll go first."

He had to gain a head start before Danika guessed his intentions and created a scandalous scene. The last thing Ebonvale needed was a princess who slighted her predestined union with a stronger faction for her lowly bodyguard, the son of a pitchfork-wielding farmer from Oaten's Dell's poorest region, no less.

Sea spray slickened the hardened lava of the peninsula. Some waves surged tall enough to cover the entire surface up to Bron's knees as he crossed. Warm as bath water, the tide seeped into the cracks in his armor, weighing him down. He hoped the salt wouldn't corrode Garish's metal alloy, rendering it useless against the wyverns' fire.

At least Danika had done as he asked. She'd stayed with the minstrels and, if anything came to pass at the front of the army, the trailing minstrels in the back would have plenty of time to retreat.

His army followed his progress across the peninsula. Halfway to the other side, Bron froze, studying the horizon. One tidal wave could wash them all away. He scanned the waves rolling in from the sea. Each crest swelled with the promise of power as the tide rolled slowly in. They'd have to hurry to beat the odds.

Bron reached the last ledge leading down into the dark waters. He searched for any sign of a sandy bottom but could discern nothing in the faint moonlight.

"Can you swim across?" Fairhaven joined him at the edge.

Bron judged the distance. It was a little longer than the lake in Oaten's Dell where he used to race Hule to exhaustion. Then again, he was taller now and stronger. He wouldn't let the distance intimidate him as a grown man. "I believe so, but only without my armor."

"We have no way of lugging the armor to the other side?"

"Maybe one suit, but an entire army?" Bron shook his head. He could not lose hope. If they returned to the first island now, this whole channel would be covered by morning. There had to be another way.

He unsheathed his sword and stuck the blade in the water, feeling the drop off of the ledge. Behind him, the army started to gather as they caught up. Soon the lines would back up. The tail end of the troops, along with Danika, would be stuck on the middle of the peninsula.

Bron lowered himself to his stomach and dipped his entire arm in the water, along with his sword. The tip grazed the ledge, feeling the dark abyss stretched before them.

He dared not look back. The troops must have thought he'd lost his mind.

Bron knew better than to accept their defeat at face value. He'd learned from the temple scrolls that lava flowed in swirling patterns, and volcanos spewed large chunks of rock like the one they'd seen hit the water earlier that day. The sea floor was not flat.

He pulled himself slowly across the curve of the ledge, reaching out with his sword in all directions until the water rose up his arm to his shoulder and then to his chin. Half his body underwater, the tip of his sword scraped something beyond the ledge.

Thank Helena and Horred. For Bron, it was enough of a sign that the gods were on his side.

He probed, feeling the circumference of the underwater rock. The surface was big enough to stand on.

Bron's muscles ached as he stood. Just a little longer, then they could rest. By now, the army had flooded the ledge to watch his progress, and he had to order them back. "At ease."

Fairhaven turned to the men. "Give the Chief of Arms more room." He nodded to Bron, then whispered in confidence, "What do you mean to do, sir?"

"Carve my own path." Bron took a running leap and landed with a splash on the next rock. Cheers erupted behind him. He turned to Fairhaven with a grin stretching across his face. "Lead them in my footsteps. Don't let anyone stray from the path."

"Yes, sir." Fairhaven smiled and saluted him with a wave. "Lead on."

Bron felt the edge of the rock a few feet away. He probed with his sword until he found another standing stone, then another. Some footholds were several feet underwater and Bron had to wade up to his knees, and others were narrow enough to barely fit both his feet. Bron made sure to stay ahead enough to backtrack if he found a dead end. It took over an hour, but after discovering enough standing stones, he jumped in up to his chest and waded to shore.

As the army followed, he heard a few splashes as men fell into the sea.

"Quickly, get them out!" Bron called, wishing he could sprint across the water.

Fairhaven had stayed behind and helped fish them out with rope. He waved to Bron. "All accounted for."

"Good." As the army came ashore, Bron realized the same rock where he'd jumped off into water up to his chest now had water up to the chins of men the same height. The incoming tide deepened the channel. He looked across to the peninsula. Half the minstrel army still awaited their turn.

"Faster." Bron called as he helped a man to shore. "We must cross faster."

As Danika stood on the last rock, Bron realized the water would flow over her head. Valorian stood beside her, offering his hand to lower her into the sea.

"Princess, wait!" Bron waded in toward the ledge. "The water is too deep."

Danika's head shot up and she froze. Bron positioned himself in the water below her. The waves now rose to the tip of his nose, and he struggled to keep his head afloat high enough to breath. "Jump to me."

Valorian's lips pursed as though he did not favor the idea.

Bron ignored him and beckoned Danika. This was no time for jealousy. "The tide is coming in. We must hurry!"

The princess nodded and lowered herself into Bron's arms, wrapping her arms around the back of his neck. Blood rushed to his face and his heart quickened. The solider who didn't balk at war trembled. Why did holding her feel so right? "Hold on."

Danika's green eyes flashed in the moonlight. She whispered, "I will."

He carried her to shore. Soldiers jumped into the sea around them, racing the tide, but Bron focused on Danika. "How are you faring, Princess?"

She looked away toward the island looming above them. "Fair enough."

Her answer didn't satisfy him. "You cast your gaze beyond me to the island. What do you fear?"

"I fear my own resolve wavering. Hope is difficult to hold in such a barren, unforgiving land. Valorian has seen many futures. In one of them a dried, barren earth plagues the land if we don't succeed."

Bron's chest tightened. "Valorian thinks too much with his head and not with his heart." Water dripped from their armor as he reached the shore and placed her gently on her feet. In Danika's presence, all of his worries had disappeared. He'd found the strength to believe. "We have found a path across the channel and our army is healthy and our weapons sharp. We have armor that will withstand our enemies' fire. There is still much reason to hope."

"Such a brave man you are." Danika's hand trailed along his armor as she released her hold. "You have always taught me to hope in the darkest of times."

"And I will continue to." Bron wanted to reach to her and pull her near. He did nothing, remembering they stood at the end of their known world, battling a foe who threatened all they held dear. Plus, she was not his.

"I see you have found your way to shore safely, my lady." Valorian's voice echoed behind him, reminding Bron to return to his post.

He nodded to Valorian. "We make camp here, by the water's edge in the mountain's shadow."

"Go back to your men, Chief." Valorian gestured to the shore, where soldiers sat and emptied sea water from their boots. "They need you."

Valorian dismissed him with a nod. "I'll tend to the princess' needs from here on out."

Bron's fists tightened as he swallowed his retort. The minstrel prince was right. His men did need him, and by staying with Danika when she was in no harm, he'd deserted his duty as Chief of Arms. "Yes, Your Highness."

It took all of his determination to walk away.

Chapter 30

Leap of Faith

Danika awoke to gray morning dawn with an arm stretched across her breastplate. Valorian slept beside her. He must have moved closer during the night.

No wonder she'd dreamed of leviathan tentacles.

Danika slowly removed his arm and sat up. Her legs ached from yesterday's trek, and a muscle in her back twitched from lying on the hard lava rock. She smelled like seaweed and smoke, and her hair stuck to the side of her face with sweat.

No one told her battle was glamorous.

Yet, she wouldn't wish herself anywhere else but here, at the end of the world or the beginning of a new chapter in Ebonvale's history, depending on who she asked. The question was: who did she believe?

Talking with Bron last night gave sustenance to her undernourished soul. He'd summoned the courage to believe in their triumph and given some to her in return. But was he an optimistic fool?

She dug in her travel bag and retrieved her pack of dried meat. They could coax no fires on the lava rock. The wyverns had already turned every living thing to ash. Regardless, they couldn't risk the wyverns spotting a stack of smoke not of their own making.

If she ate sparingly, she had enough rations for her return to the ship, but her sheepskin was dangerously low. She allowed herself one sip, licking her parched lips, and surveyed the army.

Where was Bron?

Danika scrambled up the ridge. Climbing over the ledge, she lay on her stomach and scanned the lava rock on the horizon. Miles of black terrain streaked with flowing magma stretched before them. A glint of silver caught her eye. Danika watched the rock where it had shone only moments before.

Nothing.

Then another glint shone farther down before disappearing into a crevice.

She lay for several moments, watching and waiting. Had the shimmer been her imagination? It was hard to believe anything in such a dark and barren land could shine.

Below her ridge, a soldier emerged, climbing the incline back to camp. He stood tall with broad shoulders and a wide gait.

Bron!

Danika rushed to meet him, careful not to wake Valorian or the other soldiers. They needed their rest and Danika needed her privacy. Sliding down a ledge, Danika intercepted the Chief of Arms before he entered camp. Black ash streaked his armor and soot covered his face.

A smile broke. "You rise early, Princess."

She helped him to the rock landing leading to a crack in the ridge where the army slept. "And you even earlier."

"I wanted to scout ahead before I led us into a trap."

"Indeed. But every soldier must rest, even the bravest, strongest ones."

Bron's lips curled before his expression turned serious. "You should be with Valorian."

Valorian. Why did they always speak of him when they were together? Danika sighed. "He's sleeping soundly and shouldn't miss me." She put a hand on his arm, stalling him from entering the camp. "What did you see?"

Bron's face turned grim as his wide lips set in a thick line. "Battle is upon us." He pointed behind him. "Wyverns bathe in the sun just beyond that western ridge. I stayed as still as a boulder and watched as they stretched over the lava, soaking up the heat from the rock. At dawn, a massive form, unlike any wyvern I've ever seen, broke from the mouth of the volcano. The flap of the beast's wings pushed hot air over her brood and into my face several hundred feet away like the gust from a storm, almost blowing me backward into the ravine."

Adrenaline flowed through Danika's legs. "Do you think it's the She-Beast?"

"I'm sure of it." Bron scanned the far ridge as if mentioning the beast would summon her before them. "She dove into the ocean. Moments later, she emerged with a white-backed whale, holding the massive catch from her jaw as if the whale were but a worm. She dropped the whale down the volcano then dove behind it, back to the fiery hell from whence she came.

"Helena's Sword! She must be feeding a whole new batch of fry."

Bron nodded, rubbing his chin. "That was my thought, aye."

Danika covered her mouth with her hand. "How will we beat such a monstrosity?"

"A plan formed as I watched the She-Beast spew fire into the twilight sky. We travel deep into the mountain, where her fry writhe in their horde. We throw the She-Beast deep into the lava core, combusting her belly of fumes to awaken the mountain's wrath, eliminating the fry and every other wyvern on this god-forsaken island."

"How will we reach the mountain with all the sunbathing wyverns?"

"Let us hope the minstrels' song of power works." Bron bowed and walked past her. "There is much to do. I must rally the troops."

Danika was speechless. Even if they managed to kill the She-Beast and conjure the mountain's might, how would they return to their boats with an active volcano at their backs? Her body tensed until the muscles in her legs quivered.

He wasn't planning on coming back.

* * * *

They made their way to the mountain, picking through a crevice in the lava rock. They followed the path with the most cover, the path Bron had chosen from his solo journey that morning. Fear for Bron grew with each step as Danika followed the line. Perhaps he thought himself disposable now that Valorian had claimed her as his, but Danika needed Bron as much as Ebonvale did.

The closer they got, the more she wanted to break her word and leave Valorian to watch over Bron and make sure he didn't do anything too brave.

Incense, like a hundred candles of different smells melted together, mingled with a thick fishy tang, tickling her nose. When she listened carefully, she heard the wyverns' breathing above them in great puffs of heated, sulfuric air.

The atmosphere grew so dry her eyes hurt, and sweat rolled down the sides of her forehead. The soles of her feet burned, and anywhere she touched, lava rock smoldered. Danika didn't think she'd ever be cold again, even when the mid-winter snow came down in blankets on her balcony. She couldn't remember what it felt like to catch a snowflake on her tongue or hold an icicle as a lance until her hands turned blue.

The army stopped before her and Danika almost bumped into Valorian, too entangled in her musings. She caught herself on a rock, while her other hand gently touched the minstrel's back. He turned to her and smiled as if she'd planned it.

"Time for my army to do what it's come to do." Finality weighed in Valorian's voice. He leaned toward her and placed a kiss on her cheek.

Suddenly, after wishing him away for so many nights, Danika couldn't let him go. She reached out and took his arm as he turned to walk up the line to the front. "What do you mean to do?"

"Keep us safe." Valorian placed a hand on her shoulder plate. "Do not worry. I intend to come back. I mean for us to be together in a kingdom safe and free."

He bent down again and his lips met hers more fiercely than the kiss at Ebonvale's gates. He tasted of salt and sweat and a sweet balm he'd spread upon his lips. Too shaken, Danika could only stand and accept the kiss as he moistened her dry, cracked lips with his.

Valorian pulled away and walked to the front of the line, leaving her emotions swirling. Behind him, the other minstrels followed as if they'd planned this move all along and need not speak for direction.

Danika touched her lips. What did Valorian have planned? Her heart pounded. She couldn't stand around and wait. She had to see his plan for herself.

Making sure no one saw her, Danika snuck to an alcove behind the army and climbed to the ledge. She took off her helmet to hide the glare of the metal and peeked over the ridge. A blanket of wyverns basked in the sun, stretched from one's jaw to another's tail. No patch of lava rock went uncovered. Their scales glistened oily green, red and blue in the sun.

If she squinted, she could imagine a treasure trove of thousands of jewels. Too bad the scales lost their luster once they fell off the heated body, or Ebonvale could be the richest kingdom in the world.

If they succeeded. Danika was dreaming again. The heat had sizzled her mind like a scrambled duck egg, dulling her senses.

A soft and low hum vibrated from the front lines. Danika held her breath. Either the song would work its magic, or the wyverns would know they were here and begin their onslaught. She should have scrambled back to the crevice and unsheathed her sword, but she lay mesmerized by the fatality of the moment. Would a sword do any good against so many?

Nothing changed as the song swelled, chords building upon chords as the minstrels spun their magic spell. The song inspired awe, humbling

Danika by making her feel how small she was in such a large, turbulent world.

The wyverns' breathing slowed. Their bodies grew limp and their glassy eyes glazed over as a thin membrane of leathery skin fluttered over the pupils.

Danika clutched the rock, her chest swelling. It was working!

Below her, the army began to move forward. She scrambled down the ridge and took her place in line. They marched up an incline into the bright sunlight. Wyverns rose around them in hills of flesh, their sleeping forms rising and falling with deep, sulfuric breaths. Danika had never been this close to a live one and her fingers itched to reach out and touch the oily scales. Each claw ran as big as her arm and some toothy jaws extended the length of two men.

How big was this She-Beast?

Each minstrel took his place, staying behind in a corridor of song for the army's protection as they passed. Were there enough minstrels to carve a path all the way to the mountain, or would the distance stretch their voices too thin?

Danika couldn't help but feel as if they walked a one-way path.

The army pressed on in single file with careful steps, picking their way through the bodies. Danika followed the line, afraid to breathe too loudly or misstep. A tail lay across their path up ahead. Each solider had to jump or step over it, depending on the reach of their legs. The tail rose to Danika's waist as she approached it, moving slowly back and forth as the wyvern dreamed. Small, tattered fins decorated the ridge, reminding her of a mermaid's tail.

How would she ever step across?

"My lady." The soldier who had just leapt over the tail offered his hand, wiggling his fingers. "You can make it."

She'd better, or they'd leave her behind with the singing minstrel to wait for their return. Only Helena knew what Bron and Valorian would do without her.

Over her dead body.

Danika steeled her nerves and backed up to gain a running head start. The soldiers behind her waited, and she could feel their eyes watching her back. She could not fail. Thank the gods Garish had designed the armor light.

Danika took a deep breath and dug her heels into the lava rock. The width reminded her of the ravine between the orchard and the courtyard. Whenever she was late, she ran and jumped over the ravine to take the shortcut back. This was no different. Except a steaming heap of wyverns slumbered an arm's width away.

She sprinted then jumped, spreading her legs to clear the tail. She soared in the air, praying to the gods as her legs brushed the fins, but left the scaly skin untouched. Danika landed and flailed her arms for balance. The soldier on the other side caught her and steadied her before she tipped too far to the right.

He grinned, not looking a year older than a stable hand. "Now that's the first time I've seen a lady leap like a man."

"You need to open your eyes then, lad." She released her hold of him and winked. "There are many strong women in Ebonvale."

Before the soldier could respond, she took her place in line with confident steps. Pride beamed inside her for the first time since they'd set out from the ships.

Chapter 31

The She-Beast's Lair

As Bron walked among the sleeping beasts, he thought of Malveric Baron's freckled face, Breathan Florin's crooked mouthed grin and Darious Clutterbow's collection of sailors' tales. So many brave soldiers had died at the hands of these vile creatures. Bron felt like a thief, sneaking around their sleeping bodies. If circumstances allowed, he'd much rather battle them here and now and gain vengeance. But a greater task waited with a foe that could not be left forgotten.

Cut off the head and the army is leaderless. King Artemus had advised his troops before battle and raced across the front line, clanging his sword against theirs. *Purge the evil at the source or you will only ever treat the symptoms and not the disease.*

Although these were beasts, they had a clear hierarchy, and the She-Beast ruled over all. Not only that, she was the only wyvern who could produce fry. Plus, her belly of sulfurous gases provided the ultimate weapon.

No, the minstrels were right to sing them in unharmed. Even though stealth and trickery wasn't Bron's way, he accepted their wisdom.

The volcano rose up before them with smoke-filled dark tunnels funneling toward the core.

Valorian broke through the front line. "I have enough minstrels to cover our escape, but if I divert too many inside the mountain, their absence will diminish the intensity of the song."

"I'll go without song, then." Bron gestured toward the troops below. "It's more important they have return passage home through the sleeping beasts. Keep this horde in deep slumber until the mountain erupts, and I'll take care of the She-Beast."

"I'll go with you. My voice will provide some cover along the way." Valorian gestured to his minstrels. Another man with a lute took his place as the leader of the song.

"I'm coming as well." Danika's voice wafted up to him from behind the front lines. She broke through, standing tall and proud, like the ruler she was born to be.

Bron's chest tightened and he wished he could keep her safe forever. "We may not make it back, Princess."

"I'm coming to see that you do." Danika took three long strides to his side. "I won't accept anything less."

Bron sighed, recognizing his words coming from her mouth. "So be it." He could no more stop her than wish this all away. Ebonvale was her kingdom, and she had a right to defend it, woman or not. Besides, she commanded him, not the other way around.

"So it is the three of us again, then." Valorian smiled. "Though I do miss Nip." He put a hand on Bron's shoulder and one on Danika's, uniting them. "What an excellent trio we will be."

But not without some discord. Only one of them could have Danika, and it wasn't him. Bron turned to his army. "Regiments one through three stay behind to guard our passage. The rest of you get ready to climb."

Walking beside Bron, Danika muttered under her breath as she tied the scarf around her mouth. "You told me to stay with Valorian."

Bron gave her his grimmest look. "Aye, but I did not mean for this."

He lassoed a rope around a ridge and threw the length down to the army. "Do not climb without it."

He tied the rope around his waist and scaled the lava rock to a plateau leading to the nearest entrance. Gray smoke bled from the tunnel.

Valorian threw Bron a fine satin scarf.

Bron took the fabric and blinked in question. This was not a time to look their best.

"It will filter the worst of the smoke." Valorian brought a wad of them from his travel bag and threw them to the army.

Once again, Valorian appeared the better man. Chastised, Bron tied the fabric around his mouth, and the rest of his army followed. He felt like a belly dancer at the mid-summer festival, but he swallowed his smart whip retorts. Better to look ridiculous and breathe than to look brave and die.

He gazed at Danika. She was the only one of them who wore her scarf well, the satiny fabric framing her sparkling eyes, making them peer at him seductively. Or so he imagined.

Danika didn't wear one of Valorian's scarves. Bron recognized that fabric from her mother's wardrobe. Despite her disdain for Sybil, Danika must have felt something to bring the scarf with her. He'd promised Sybil to keep her daughter safe and he meant to even if it meant his fiery end.

Bron gestured toward the cave and gave Danika a rise of his eyebrows. "Shall we?"

She unsheathed her sword with a clang. The resolution in her eyes cemented Bron's determination. "Let's end this."

They lit torches, and Bron and Danika took the lead. The tips of their swords pointed into the darkness. Valorian echoed the song of power from below, projecting his voice ahead. The tunnel magnified his volume with an echo. As the minstrels' voices from outside died away, Valorian's voice held strong.

Beneath them, the mountain rumbled as if stirring in its sleep. The ground shook, and they stumbled, using the walls to steady themselves until the quake subsided. Doubt flashed in Danika's eyes and the troops behind them whispered with uneasiness.

"'Tis a good omen." Bron spoke loud enough for everyone to hear, but not so loud as to interrupt Valorian's song. "All we need is the She-Beast's unspent breath to push this volcano over the edge."

The deeper they traveled, the more Bron roasted like a boar on a spit. He dreamed of summers where he and Hule jumped in the icy creek behind their farm, and winters where he chopped wood until his hands turned blue--anything to get his mind off the heat.

The tunnel curved inward, boring straight to the volcano's core. A deep intake, then exhale, resounded from the darkness as if the primeval world breathed through the molten lava. A heartbeat, weighted and steady as a giant leather drum thundered in Bron's gut. The air grew thick with sulfur and the reek of seaweed. Bron slowed his pace and held his hands for those behind him to pause. He dared not speak. They were close.

Up ahead, a glowing reddish light illuminated an opening where the tunnel widened. Bron placed his torch on the lava rock to light their way back. Even if he didn't make it out, Danika would. He snuck forward with both hands on his hilt.

A pool of lava illuminated a high-ceilinged cavern. At the far end, a skeleton of a large whale, with the flesh picked to the bone, cast striped shadows on the back wall. Beyond the skeleton lay a wide, smoking crevice leading down into the volcano's core.

Speckled eggs lay in clusters around the lava pool, as if they needed the heat to hatch. A few broken cases were strewn on the cavern floor.

Bron stepped on one and brought his boot up. A slimy, greenish white substance stuck the eggshell to the bottom of his boot.

He whispered, "Be aware. Hatchlings lurk in the shadows."

Although the hatchlings were no bigger than dogs, they could still rip an ox open with one swipe of their claw. Bron gestured for Danika and Valorian to come forward. Behind them, the army slowly filed in. Valorian's voice echoed in a haunting melody throughout the cave. He'd been singing ever since they found the wyverns. Bron wondered how the minstrel could sustain his voice without a draught of water. Every time Valorian took a breath, the shadows flickered and the rhythmic heartbeat of the She-Beast grew louder.

"There!" Danika hissed as she pointed across the lava pool. Finned backs rose and fell in slumber. Snouts, tails, claws and scales wound together in a heap.

"There are more over here." Bron gestured toward the back wall. He turned back to his army. "Leave them be."

A hulking shadow stirred deep within the back of the cave. Bron raised his hand to halt the troops. He gestured for a torch. One of the soldiers ran back into the tunnel. He emerged with one of the torches they'd left behind. The last embers simmered, casting a dim light. The soldier handed Bron the torch, then filed back into line a little too eagerly.

Bron stepped forward, holding the torch in front of him. A massive, scaly mound of flesh rose to the ceiling thirty feet above their heads. A tail, wider than Bron was tall, coiled around the body. Tucked above the tail's end lay a snout as large as the princess' royal carriage with teeth like swords jutting haphazardly in crooked directions.

"What are you waiting for? I'll cut the beast's throat." Danika raised her sword.

Bron grabbed her arm, holding her still. "She's no use to us dead. We must draw her into the crevice and throw her body into the lava core."

"We're so close. We can end it now." Her face glowed in the reddish light, her flushed cheeks slick with sweat.

"No. If we leave this place as is, another She-Beast will rise. 'Tis only a matter of time before they breed enough fry to overtake our land. We would only delay the inevitable." He leaned down and whispered so only she could hear. "Your father once told me to purge the evil at the source or else you treat the symptom and not the disease." Bron placed a hand on her shoulder. "The wyverns' reign must end now with the destruction of the vile mountain, and I mean to end their reign myself."

Danika stilled with the mention of her father. She glanced hungrily at the She-Beast then pulled her gaze away and nodded. "My father's wisdom speaks even now. How will we draw her to the crevice? We could no more move the mountain itself."

Bron turned to Valorian. "Can you convince the She-Beast to move with song?"

Valorian finished his phrase, letting the note taper beautifully into the echoes. "I can. But my song will awaken both the She-Beast and the hatchlings. Controlling only her actions may be beyond my abilities." Movement stirred from the sleeping fry, and he picked up the song where he'd left off.

"'Tis why I'm here." Bron signaled to the army, proud to finally be of service amongst all this minstrel glory. They spread in a semicircle around Danika and Valorian and raised their swords. "Protect the minstrel and the princess. Hold your ground."

He raised his sword to the She-Beast and nodded to Valorian. "Make it so."

Valorian's song changed from a lulling drone to a twisting melody, each note pricking his consciousness as if the notes didn't quite belong. Bron's legs twitched. He shifted on his feet but every position was uncomfortable.

The blasted music. It affected him, too.

He shook his head to rid the melody from his thoughts and stood his ground.

Movement stirred around them as the fry awoke. They opened their eyes and stretched lazily by the lava pool. One by one, they eyed the soldiers. Some of the soldiers took a step back. Bron heard one whisper, "They think good ol' ma has brought them more meat."

Bron steeled his voice. "You're soldiers of Ebonvale. Hold your ground."

One of the hatchlings hissed and lunged at the front line, extending its claws. A soldier blocked the hatchling's attack with his shield, while another stuck his sword in its back. The hatchling squealed, and everyone except for Bron covered their ears.

The other hatchlings lunged in mass horde at the soldiers, but Bron kept his position. In the dim glow of the reddish light, the She-Beast opened her eyes.

She raised her head slowly as if taking in the scene. Her lips stretched back from her jaw, exposing the full set of her jagged teeth. She hissed, and the air gusted into Bron's face, scaring his cheeks.

Bron glanced at the crevice, noting the distance from him to the edge. He turned his gaze back on the beast and brandished his sword. "Come meet your doom."

Fast as lightning, the beast extended its neck and snapped its jaws. Bron ducked, as the snout closed over his head, and then again as the beast pounced again to his right. The beast's nostrils fumed as it opened its jaws wide. Its stomach pulsed as it fanned the fire inside its gut. Bron stepped backward toward the crevice and brought down his visor, preparing for the flames.

Air rushed around him as the flames engulfed his body, traveling over Garish's armor. Bron held his breath, waiting for the surge to end. At some point the beast had to breathe again. The victor would be the one who could hold the longest breath. The She-Beast expelled her air to propel the fire, whereas Bron held air in his lungs and rationed it bit by bit. The flames died, and Bron took in a deep breath of dry, hot air. He raised his visor. "You'll have to do better than that."

The She-Beast hissed and uncoiled her tail. Bron jumped to his stomach as the tail knocked several soldiers to the ground. They fell on their backs and hatchlings swarmed over them. Danika rushed to their aid, slicing the fry with her sword.

The giant wyvern's tail separated Bron from the rest of his men, which was exactly what he wanted. He had to keep her attention and lure her to the crevice without her attacking any more of his men. He sliced the air with his sword. "Come on, you foul beast, you hellbound fiend."

The giant wyvern squirmed forward from her alcove. A clawed foot hit the lava rock, shaking the ground so hard Bron used his sword to keep his balance. She studied him, tilting her head back and forth as a boy might study an ant crossing his path. Penetrating wrath emanated from her dark eyes.

Danika's voice echoed over Valorian's song. "There are too many of them. We can't hold out much longer."

Bron needed to lure the mighty beast to the crevice. He sprinted forward and zigzagged as her jaws snapped. The reek of the beast sickened him as he drew close and sliced his sword. The blade cut a gash in the scales just above her clawed paw. Greenish liquid sprayed across his armor, sizzling like acid.

The wyvern pounced and Bron fell back. Each step she took rattled his helmet and his teeth. He scrambled onto his feet and raced toward the crevice. In the distance he heard Danika shout in horror. "Nooo!"

He knew what he had to do. Time suddenly stretched before him, each second like a lifetime. He thought of his pa working in the field and his ma baking pumpkin bread. He could almost taste the spice on his tongue. He saw Hule wearing the armor they'd made from old pots and the loving look on Artemus' face before he died. So many people that mattered to him.

Lastly, as he raised his sword, he remembered back to the first day he spotted Danika, watching the trials from the stands, her golden hair glowing like a natural crown.

The wyvern leaped toward him and Bron stabbed his sword into its gut, slicing open the belly of combustible gases. The mass of the beast fell into the crevice, the forward momentum tugging him with the beast before he could let go of the hilt.

"Helena and Horred, take me home."

Bron closed his eyes as he fell, hearing the shrieks of the She-Beast as she fell with him. He hit a hard surface, knocking the air from his lungs. He expected to be dead, melted by lava. He moved his limbs, hearing shouts from his army as they fought for their lives. Bron opened his eyes.

He lay on his back on a small plateau, ten feet from the edge of the crevice. Hope soared in his chest then fell once again as he realized he had no rope. The lava rock was slick with no handholds. He had no way to reach his men. Valorian's voice broke into a croak above. The minstrel couldn't hold on much longer.

A crack like thunder rattled Bron's bones. He gazed into the lava pit hundreds of feet below. The lava boiled with the She-Beast's spilled entrails. The mountain shuddered around them and the crevice cracked open wider. Stalactites fell from the cavern ceiling, splashing up lava as they landed below. A satisfying sense of resolution came over Bron. He'd achieved what he'd come to do. The mountain would blow.

"Bron! Thank the gods you're still alive." Danika's head appeared over the rim. "Let me find you some rope."

His heart melted. He hadn't thought he'd ever see her again. "You don't have time, Princess. Get Valorian and the soldiers out." Behind them, Valorian's voice cracked and died. A muffled sound came from his direction, as if something had knocked the air from his lungs. "Princess, help!"

Bron collapsed to his knees on the plateau. Below him, the lava rose inch by inch, fueled by the She-Beast's combustion. "Princess, you must save Valorian. You must choose."

Her head disappeared over the ridge.

Good. She'd made the right decision. He was proud of her, but that didn't hide the emptiness in his heart. Bron breathed deeply and closed his eyes.

"Danika Rubystone, I will love you forever."

Peace settled over him. His time had come.

Chapter 32

Resurrection

The remnants of the army huddled by the tunnel's mouth with their back to each other to hold back the swarm of hatchlings. How many were there? They kept coming in an endless tide. Two heaps of their bodies piled on either side of her. Their acid blood had burned her sword down to a stick.

"Go!" Danika shouted over the rumbling. "I command you! Regroup by the boats." They'd fulfilled their oath to Ebonvale. The cavern teetered on the verge of collapse. To ask them to stay would be madness.

She searched the chaos for Valorian.

The minstrel stood with his sword up, surrounded by hatchlings.

Maybe she'd spoken too soon.

No. There was no way for the army to reach him without thinning out the ranks. If she ordered them back, she'd kill them all.

She shouted to Valorian. "Hold on! I'm coming." If only she could split herself in two. Scrambling over cracked stalactites, she searched the debris for her travel bag.

The bag rested on a cracked eggshell. The hatchlings had dragged it and torn open the leather. The contents lay scattered. They'd eaten all her food rations.

Danika sprinted to the bag and dug inside. She clasped her hands around a length of rope. Thank Helena and Horred she'd stuffed it into her bag. Hoping the rope was long enough, she ran back to the crevice where the lava rose.

Bron knelt with his eyes closed. Had the same warrior who'd slayed the She-Beast, the Necromancer King, and carried all of the metal up from the shadows of Darkenbite given up?

Danika tied the end of the rope around a ridge and dropped the other end down to Bron. The rope landed on his shoulder, and he opened his eyes, staring at her as if she'd grown wyvern wings.

"Take the rope, you lug."

"What are you doing? You don't have time to save us both."

Danika glanced over at Valorian. The hatchlings had him pushed up against the far wall behind the whale skeleton. He swiped at them, but he wasn't as good a swordsman as Bron, and there were too many even for her to hold back.

"I choose you. I cannot live without you. If you don't take this cursed rope, I'll die here with you."

That did it. Bron clutched the rope and started to climb. Another quake rattled the cavern. The sound rumbled in her ears as chunks of the ceiling fell around her. Danika only had enough time to block her head with her arms and hope the falling rocks didn't hurt too much.

At least they had succeeded. Ebonvale would go on.

The quake subsided. Danika coughed as a dust cloud wafted around her. The rope twisted down into the crevice, unmoving.

Had Bron let go?

She dared not look over the rim.

The rope twitched, and Bron's strong hand came up. Relief weakened her knees as she rushed to grab a hold of him. A distant rumble promised more cave-ins.

"Hurry!" Danika pulled with all her strength until Bron cleared the lava pit. "We don't have much time."

"Where's Valorian?" Bron's chest heaved.

Valorian! Danika scanned the debris. Chunks of rock from floor to ceiling covered the place where the minstrel had stood.

Tears stung her eyes and she shook her head, pointing to the cave-in.

"No." Bron rushed to his feet. "Don't tell me he's in there."

"'Tis the last place I saw him."

Bron rushed over and began throwing chucks of rock. Behind them the lava had overflowed the rim of the crevice, and hot magma oozed toward their feet.

"Go!" Bron picked up another chunk and threw it before the lava to stall the flow. "I'll follow."

"You cannot stay here!" Danika tugged on his arm. "We have to leave now."

"I cannot leave him after he saved my life this very same way."

"Then we die together, the three of us. Right here. Right now."

As if to reiterate her sentiment, another quake rattled the cavern. Bron held Danika close as more debris fell on top of the pile. Behind them, the lava swelled, filling the cavern floor. The heat became unbearable, cooking their skin from the inside of the armor out.

"I'm the Princess, and I command you to come with me. If you stay, you abandon your sworn oath to protect me."

"Helena's Goblet!" Bron's face cracked into a scowl. He threw them both toward the tunnel. "Run!"

They followed the strewn torches as the tunnel shifted. The lava flowed behind them, surging forward with each new explosion. Exhaustion brought Danika to her knees. Her throat burned, her lips split, leaking blood down her chin, and her skin felt like a layer had been removed. Valorian was dead by her hand because she'd chosen Bron. The horror of the mountain's onslaught overwhelmed her.

"I cannot make it."

"You have to make it." Bron hauled her up. "You are the sole reason why I'm not back in that cave, searching for Valorian. On your feet, soldier."

She stumbled forward, half blind by the smoke, coughing and wheezing. If it wasn't for Bron's steady hand on her back, she'd lose herself in the chaos.

Daylight shone at the end of the tunnel, bright and pure, unlike the reddish hell they'd left behind. With escape so close, Danika found a last fountain of energy and broke into a sprint. The tunnel caved in behind them, leaving only enough room for lava to seep through.

They reached the plateau and Danika gulped in the fresher air. The barren lava rock was no meadow, yet the sulfur-to-oxygen ratio was much lower than inside. Magma dripped from the plateau around them, creating red streaks down the lava rock. Large chunks of flaming rock spewed across the smoky sky. Dead wyverns lay in heaps around them, the lava melting their remains.

Bron scanned the terrain. "Where is my army?"

"I commanded them to leave and regroup by the boats." Danika searched the lava rock for any sign of silver armor. "There!" She pointed to the far ridge where helmets peeked from the lava rock like silver spoons. "They escape as we speak."

Bron glanced back at the opening as it filled with black smoke. He froze as if an invisible cord had snagged him and wouldn't let him go.

Danika put both arms on his shoulders and shook him. "Valorian is dead, Bron. You are not going back for him. I need you with me."

Bron blinked as if waking from a dream, then bent to find the rope he'd tied to hoist them up was still there. "Grab a hold of me!"

The mountain rumbled beneath them as Danika held on to Bron. Using his upper body strength, he lowered them down the rocky ledge. Lava flowed around them in red, orange and yellow streaks. Danika searched for any dry spot to land. "Over there. I see a clear path to the far ridge."

Bron kicked against the rock and they dangled past a lava river to the other side.

"The rope will not reach. We'll have to jump." Bron maneuvered them closer to the clear area.

Danika steeled herself. If she could confront the She-Beast, she could jump over steaming lava. "I'm ready."

Bron released the rope and they tumbled onto the rock. Danika skidded when she landed, rolling toward the lava. She flailed her arms and the skin on her fingers tore as she tried to grab a handhold. The molten red-orange came up quickly, burning her face from inches away. Bron reached out and grabbed her arm, pulling her back. "That was close."

Danika breathed with relief. She sat up and scanned his body. His leg bent at a strange angle, making her heart stop. "Are you hurt?"

He unbent the leg, testing the muscles. "No. Are you?"

"Not yet." Danika scanned the area around them. The lava rose quickly, blocking so many ways to escape. "We have to keep running."

"I know." Bron pulled himself up, looking wearier than a plow horse at the end of harvest season.

They leaped over streams of lava, working their way to the far ridge where the army had gone. The muscles in her legs screamed and ash covered the inside of her mouth until she could taste nothing except smoke and blood. Her lungs burned with each breath. She'd lost her sheepskin somewhere in the heart of the volcano, and Bron had nothing besides his sword.

"Just a little ways farther." Bron must have seen her faltering. "Then we can slow down."

Slow down? Danika wanted to lie down, curl up and forget the dreadful memory of Valorian's voice calling to her to help. This time she'd slighted him to the death.

"Princess? Can you make it?"

"Aye." She trudged ahead. The strength in Bron's features carried her on. If she couldn't force her body on for Ebonvale alone, then she'd do it for him.

They reached the ridge and disappeared into the crevice between the lava rocks, working their way to the other side of the island. The atmosphere rumbled with the volcano's wrath and gray smoke covered the sky. Ash fell like snow around them, and their boots left imprints on the ground along the way.

Danika moved in a blur, feeling as though she wandered in an ashy neverland stretching on eternally. If it wasn't for Bron, she would have fallen to her knees and collapsed, letting the ash cover her in a dry, heated grave. Hours passed, or maybe days. She couldn't tell. The gray twilight endured and no sign of the sun or stars came through. The lava rock, the ash and Bron's steady hand on her back remained constant.

The crashing of waves echoed from the distance, bringing Danika out of her trance. They'd reached the sea separating them from the first island. That meant one thing: the ships would be waiting for them with water and a soft bed. They'd be waiting to take them home.

"Look. The tide is out." Bron jogged up ahead. "We can make it across."

Danika stumbled forward, following his footsteps in the ash. This stroke of luck seemed too good to be true. Helena and Horred were on their side.

She reached the shore, wading into the water. The lava rocks protruded from the surface in haphazard steps to the peninsula. Bron offered his hand. "Come, I've found the best path."

She followed him, allowing him to pull her up to the higher inclines. It took all her energy to hurl her weary body forward. The gray twilight darkened as they crossed. Night had come.

Panic rose inside Danika. Had the ships already left?

She grabbed Bron's arm. "How many days?"

His shoulders slumped. Even the great warrior's strength was failing. "What do you speak of?"

"How many days have we been gone?"

"Tomorrow will be the third day."

"Is that all?" It seemed like forever ago they'd disembarked on their quest.

"Aye."

"That means we have two more days to get back to the ship."

"An easy task, Princess." Bron reached the shore and sat on an outcropping of lava rock. He pulled off his boot and emptied the water from the heel. "It will take another day, if not less, to cross this island. Two people travel faster than an army."

"Even without food and water?"

"That I can remedy." Bron pulled off his helmet and set it down by the rock. Next, he unlatched his breastplate.

Danika blinked in shock. What was he doing? Had he lost his mind? This was not the time for romance. She'd said "water," not his naked, hard body.

The metal clanged as the breastplate hit the ground. He pulled out a flask no bigger than his palm from the folds of his undershirt. He must have stuck it to his chest before he put the armor on.

Danika frowned in repulsion. "That's for liquor."

Bron smiled as though he knew she'd react in disgust. "Aye, but there's none of that in mine. Many a battle I've fought when I've lost my sheepskin."

He offered her the flask. "Try a sip."

Danika took the smooth, silver flask in her hand. In a world where everything was covered in ash, soot and blood, the silver shone perfectly. She brought the rim to her lips and sipped. Water. Pure, fresh, untainted water. Her mouth reveled as the water flowed down her throat. Remembering to save some for him, she passed the flask back to him. Only then did she think she'd just put her mouth where he must have put his a hundred times.

It's not like they'd never kissed.

Bron took the flask and brought the edge to his lips. After he drank, he closed the lid and slipped it back into his shirt. "We'll rest here for a bit then walk throughout the night. We can reach the ship by dawn on the third day, just to be safe. That is, if you're up to it?"

A ship with food, water and a soft bed? Did he have to ask? She nodded and sat across from him, stretching out her aching legs. "Aye."

They sat in silence. After what had happened to Valorian, talking about anything else seemed trivial and disrespectful. She didn't want to bring up the cave-in and, from the looks of it, neither did Bron. A heavy weight had fallen on his shoulders since he'd left that cave. Would Valorian's death always be a thorn between them? Would it drive them apart?

The desire for comfort from his gentle touch came over her. She leaned against his arm. If she could borrow his strength just for a moment...

Bron pulled away, shifting on the rock to leave a hand's width between them. "Use the ridge for your support." A cold, unyielding resistance turned his voice to stone.

What had she done? By saving his life, she'd lost his love forever. Tears burned in her eyes. "I don't understand."

"Valorian is dead." Bron rubbed his hand over his face. "I've failed in my life debt to him."

She turned toward him, but he avoided her gaze "You have not failed me."

"I've failed Ebonvale. I've failed your father. And worst of all, I've failed you. If I hadn't said how I felt on the ship, then you wouldn't have sacrificed Valorian for me."

A growling rumble like underground thunder came from behind them, followed by a series of loud explosions. Bron jumped to his feet and grabbed his helmet and breastplate. "We should start moving."

Danika followed, though her whole body protested and their conversation was not over. She had to convince him Valorian's death was not his fault. It was hers. She'd made the choice to save Bron and sacrifice Valorian. Somehow he had to believe it. Weariness and shock had stolen her reason, and the words to express herself could not come.

As night fell, the volcano's wrath lit the sky with red fury. They used the bloodshot haze to find their path. Empty sheepskins, scorched travel bags and damaged weapons cluttered their path. They passed in the army's footsteps. Some men had survived and waited for them at the ships.

Thoughts of the survivors comforted Danika in her grief for Valorian and the other men who'd lost their lives. Monks would utter their names for centuries to come and etch their likeness in the great temples. They were heroes of war, much like Helena and Horred, and now they stood with them in the place where time had no meaning.

Was Valorian at peace? Would he forgive her? She could only hope.

They passed the night, following the tracks of the soldiers to the other side of the island. As dawn broke, and the sun peeked from a smoky horizon, the masts of the *Destiny* and the *Fortune* claimed the coastline.

The crew, the soldiers and the minstrels clapped and cheered as Danika and Bron emerged from the ridge. Many had made it back to the ship. The sight brought tears to Danika's eyes.

"Long live the Princess," they chanted as Danika made her way to the ships. The chant grew until Bron joined in. He knelt by her feet and bowed to her. His gaze would not meet hers, and his voice fell lifeless from his lips. "My lady, you have triumphed over all."

For Danika, it was a melancholy victory. They'd defeated the She-Beast and reduced the wyvern brood, but they'd lost so much. She'd lost so much. How could she return and tell Valorian's father she'd sacrificed his son to save her bodyguard? How could she live without Bron's love?

One of the minstrels broke from the crowd. He bowed before her with fear in his eyes. "Any word of Valorian?"

Danika shook her head and the crowd grew silent around her. She'd prepared a speech on the long trek back, smoothing over each word like a pirate held a treasured jewel. She'd speak of Valorian's courage, his compassion, his determination to make Ebonvale and the House of Song safe. Lastly, she'd speak of his wish to unite both kingdoms. Collecting her thoughts, she cleared her parched throat to begin.

"Look! Over there!"

Danika whirled around, following everyone's gaze.

A single soldier climbed down the ridge. With armor as black as soot, slumped shoulders and a noticeable limp, he looked as though he'd barely survived.

"Who is it?" someone else called out.

They stared, mumbling their fallen comrade's names, each one hoping the returning soldier was their friend.

The figure brought his hand up and took off his helmet. A long stream of nut-brown hair fanned out in the breeze of the sea.

"That's no soldier." Danika's heart sped. "It's Valorian."

Chapter 33

Pleasure and Pain

"It's the Prince!" a man shouted as the soldiers and minstrels ran to Valorian with sheepskins, bandages and food.

"Long live the prince!"

As the people chanted around her, Danika couldn't believe her eyes. A mix of relief, joy, guilt and regret threatened to bring her to her knees. She'd had a chance to help Valorian, and she chose Bron instead. The Prince of Song had seen her choice. He knew the true nature of her heart.

Bron rose from beside her with stoic acceptance. "You should go to him."

"I cannot." She could no longer hold together her façade. Not if he knew she loved Bron. "To go to him would reek of a lie."

"Go for Ebonvale's sake, Princess." Bron's voice came out hoarse and pained.

"No." She turned to Bron. She was her mother's daughter after all, but this time it didn't shame her. She followed her heart. Placing her hand on his breastplate, Danika whispered, "I've made my choice."

Bron gazed at her hand with a mix of guilt and pain. "And so it may undo us all."

They watched together as Valorian approached. Minstrels surrounded him, tending to his wounds and giving him water. Despite all of the commotion, his gaze found Danika's.

She bit into her already dry and torn lip. How could she ever face him alone again?

As he grew closer, she mouthed the words, "I'm sorry."

He nodded once. His features tightened, and she couldn't tell if it was from the strain of the trek or her betrayal. "I'm relieved to see you are safe, Princess," he whispered.

"My thanks to you and your minstrel army. Without them, we would not have achieved victory." She bowed, hoping her one action wouldn't tear their kingdoms apart. When she gazed up again, she didn't get her answer. Valorian had already left for his ship, without extending an invitation to her.

Danika's knees weakened and she swayed.

"Come." Bron placed his arm around her as if he took full responsibility for her actions. "Today you must sail with Ebonvale. The soldiers need you."

They both knew he spoke a lie.

They sailed onto the deep blue sea as the volcanos erupted behind them. The healers helped Danika to her cabin and attended to her wounds. After they'd bandaged every cut and soothed her burned skin, she stayed to rest out of respect for Valorian, despite her urge to talk sense into Bron. She didn't want to be seen tramping about with her bodyguard. The time to unite her kingdom with the House of Song had come and gone, and now all she could do was ensure no further damage between their relations. Besides, Bron avoided her like the plague of the undead, staying below to comfort the wounded soldiers.

When the ship had traveled a safe distance away from Scalehaven, a knock sounded at her door.

Danika wrapped the sheets around her undergarments. Was it Bron? "Come in."

A servant girl with a tray of bread and cheese bowed before her. "You must be hungry, my lady."

Disappointed, Danika nodded. "Thank you. Leave it by the chest."

Movement stirred in the corridor behind the servant. A healer came in with a tray of ointment and bandages. "Come to check on you, Your Highness."

"My goodness, you only tended to me this morning."

The old woman smiled. "Aye. You're the princess, love. I can't have you getting an infection. Do you not want to be healthy when you greet your people?"

Danika laid back on her bed in acquiescence. "That will be some time, though, won't it?"

The healer unwrapped a bandage around her arm and winked. "It will be sooner than you think. The minstrels have sent out carrier pigeons to alert Brimmore of our victory and our arrival."

"You mean there will be a crowd to greet us when we dock?"

"A crowd unlike any other, love." The healer leaned over her and spread ointment upon her lips gently.

Danika squirmed under her sheets. What would Valorian say to his father? Would the crowd suspect a newly flamed discord between Ebonvale and the House of Song? Were they forever cursed to slight each other one way or another?

"Are you in pain, Princess?" The healer gazed down at her with compassionate eyes.

"No, no. I'm fine." Danika breathed to calm herself. For now, she had to catch some rest. Who knew what the future would bring.

* * * *

Days passed, and Danika gazed out her window at the endless horizon of sea. Bron didn't come to her and she'd never felt so alone. Was he as dead to her as her father? Was she cursed to follow in her mother's footsteps? Would she end up an old woman, scorned and alone?

"Land ho!" The call roused her from her dreary thoughts.

They'd reached Brimmore's Bay already? Danika scanned her room. She'd left all of her gowns aboard Valorian's ship. All she had to wear was her battle-scarred armor. That was fitting, wasn't it? She'd much rather her people and the people of the House of Song see her as a fierce warrior, not some dainty princess to be auctioned off to the highest bidder. Such notions would have resolved this dispute in the first place.

A knock sounded on the door and she jumped. "Who is it?"

"Lefina Squires."

Danika breathed easy. It was only the girl servant. "Come in."

Lefina walked in, bearing a tray of eggs and bread. She immediately looked away and closed the door as Danika was in her undergarments. "I have news from our sister ship."

Danika's heart sped. She'd heard nothing the whole journey. What could Valorian want other than to disgrace her?

"My lady?" The servant girl stood, tapping her toe.

Danika must have been gawking. "Perhaps you can help me strap this armor on?"

"Of course." Lefina walked to the bed. She looked just a bit older than Nip. Suddenly homesickness tightened in her chest. She hoped the boy had fared well with Muriel. He didn't seem to enjoy castle life with all of its tea parties and politics. But she had other worries at hand.

Danika handed Lefina the breastplate. "What is the news?" She tried to keep her voice even as her heart skidded.

"Prince Valorian wishes to speak with you before you address the crowd."

Danika froze. The time of reckoning had come. Her hands shook, and she balled her fists. "Oh, he does?"

"Yes, my lady. He wishes for you to visit his ship when we dock."

She'd have to face him. Alone. Danika shuddered. What words could he have for her that weren't angry or hurtful? She'd betrayed him. If he'd done it to her, she would have surely let him have it.

Lefina clasped the armor behind Danika's neck. "Your hair, my lady?"

Danika glanced in the mirror. A rat's nest sat on her head. "It could use a brushing, yes."

As Lefina brushed and braided her hair, Danika slipped on her boots. She steeled herself, knowing she had to face the consequences of her actions. Even if it meant disgracing herself in front of everyone. She only hoped she wouldn't bring down Ebonvale along with her, losing everything her father had achieved.

"There. You are ready." Lefina brought the mirror from the desk.

Danika looked at her reflection. Her cheeks were still burned and red, but her lips had healed well, and Lefina had braided her hair in a natural crown, like a true queen.

"You look well rested, my lady."

"Thanks to you." Danika smiled at the girl and handed her two rolls from the tray. "You may go back to your quarters and prepare for docking."

"Yes, my lady." She curtsied then left Danika with her turbulent thoughts.

Instead of mulling her destiny over, Danika decided to meet fate head on. She climbed the steps to the upper decks. The fresh air hit her face with a cool, misty breeze. She'd never take clean air for granted again.

The city of Brimmore stretched before them. People stood on ladders, removing the boards from the windows, and a crowd gathered at the docks, waving Ebonvale's purple and green pennants, and music played from the House of Song. Joy danced in the air and spread across their faces. If only they knew how many had died, and the precarious place Ebonvale stood with the House of Song.

The crews of both ships worked hard on the rigging, using the sea gusts to steer the boats toward the dock. Bron stood on the stern, flanked by his men, his gaze set upon the city. Danika wanted to go to him, but she knew their docking in front of the crowd would be the worst possible time. Valorian had requested her, and she owed him one conversation.

They set anchor, and the crew laid down the planks to the dock. Danika took the first steps off the ship, eager to set foot on her homeland. After so many days aboard the boat, the dock felt solid and comforting under her feet.

Her moment of respite was short-lived. Valorian had already walked ashore. He waited for her by his ship. He stood with arms crossed, wearing the fine minstrel clothing he was accustomed to. Seeing him brought a fresh wave of remorse. But, she did not love him. That was more clear now than ever before. She would not have his hand for their kingdom's unity or she'd be living a lie. She'd only ever give herself for love and there was only one man who had it, whether he followed his heart or not.

She summoned her courage. If she could confront the She-Beast, then she could talk to the Prince of Song one last time. Danika adjusted her helmet as if for battle then took long strides toward Valorian.

Valorian bowed at her approach. "My lady."

"Your Highness."

His lips tightened. "I trust your voyage home was enjoyable."

Shame heated her cheeks. Did he think she slept in Bron's bed the whole ride home? "Enjoyable, no."

He raised an eyebrow.

"Valorian." She took a deep breath. "I harbor great remorse for what happened. I could think of nothing but what I'd done. I was wrong to lead you to believe--"

He placed a finger to her lips. His face softened as he cupped her elbow. "Come, let us speak in private before our emotions unravel us both."

Valorian led her to a quiet alcove where the other minstrels carrying their supplies off the ship wouldn't overhear.

"I've had a lot of time to think these past few days."

Danika swallowed hard, listening carefully and expecting the worst.

Valorian glanced at the gathering crowd then at Bron's ship. Her ship. Her choice. "Like I said before, I do not see what is not there. Your actions have showed me enough."

Danika shuddered, thinking of Valorian alone in that dark cave. "I cannot imagine what you've been through."

"Please, do not trouble yourself any longer on my account." His words came out bitter.

Danika cringed and Valorian's face softened. For her, his anger could only go so far.

He watched the minstrels unpacking the boat. "Only a hard-hearted fool would keep you from love." He gazed at her wistfully. "Even though this might come back to haunt both our people, you are not bound to me or the House of Song."

Valorian scanned the people congregating at the docks and then their mingled army disembarking from the ships. "We have proved together we provide a much stronger united front. So many have died, why start a civil war between us? We would be foolish to fight amongst each other when necromancers awaken armies of undead and beasts that breathe fire still roam this world. Let us unite not by marriage but by treaty." He knelt before her, offering her a scroll. "While I rule, you will always have the House of Song's army, should you need it."

Danika unfurled the scroll. He'd written a peace pact in beautiful, calligraphed letters between both kingdoms, to be signed by the King of Song and the King of Ebonvale, whomever that should be.

She stood speechless, every wish of hers coming true. They had their unity and their victory, and she had the option to choose Ebonvale's rightful king. "And you shall have Ebonvale's army in return."

Valorian stood and smiled sadly with acceptance shining in his eyes. "That is all I can ask for. Who knows? Maybe the next generation will have better luck." He winked, looking more like himself than he had since he'd come back from the dead. "Come, let us provide a united front to our people to usher in a new, golden age."

Danika took his arm and together, they walked to greet the crowd. People cheered, throwing their hats. Little boys played with wood carvings of knights and dragons, and maidens swooned over the incoming army. Hope shone in their faces where despair and fear had been, heartening Danika. Ebonvale would rebuild, and her kingdom would move on. Her father would have been so proud. As for what her mother would say, Danika would have to ask her. She looked forward to their reunion with a renewed sense of love.

Valorian spoke first. During his speech, Danika's gaze wandered over to Bron. As always, his stoic face showed no emotion, but she could have sworn she saw hardness in his eyes, turning her heart cold.

Had guilt and disgust eaten away at his love until there was nothing left? She wanted to throw her arms around him and tell him of Valorian's forgiveness. Most of all, she wanted to ask him the question she'd been longing to ask ever since she kissed him at her father's grave. Every heartbeat seemed an eternity.

Finally, the speeches ended. As people greeted the returning soldiers, Danika said her goodbyes to Valorian and his minstrel army and made her way to Bron and the Royal Guard.

The Chief of Arms stood alone on the pier, his gaze searching the sea. The ships bobbed with the incoming tide, and seagulls stood on the beach, cracking open oyster shells. Danika approached him. This time he did not seem to hear her footsteps, dismaying her even more.

"Bron?"

The warrior turned and smiled sadly when he saw her. "A lovely day for unity, is it not?"

"Aye."

Bron put his hand on the pier, idly scratching lines in the wood with his fingernail. He didn't meet her eyes. "You and Valorian have made up, then?"

Danika tried not to smirk. The jealousy in his eyes raised her hope. He did still care. "No, he's offered a peace pact between our kingdoms. Marriage was not part of the bargain."

A shocked expression came upon Bron's face. "You speak the truth?"

Warmth spread through her. "Every word of it. Valorian forgave me He let me go. I can follow my heart as I wish."

Bron shook his head and gazed at his boots like a flustered schoolboy. "I didn't expect this. I don't know what to say."

She took his hand, running her fingers over his calloused. She'd had a long time to think about what she'd say, and to renew his honor, it had to be good. "My choice wasn't your fault. I know you told me your feelings back there on the boat. But, the truth is, what you said had no bearing on my decision."

She took his face in her hands. "The truth is, I've loved you all along."

Bron blinked as if in disbelief. Pain, desire, then joy swirled through his gaze. He shook his head. "I cannot marry a princess. I'm a farmboy with no land or title to my name."

"You're a hero who's saved not only me, but our kingdom." Danika pulled him close, not caring who saw or the gossip to follow. She touched his breastplate, running her fingers along Ebonvale's crest whimsically. "Tell me, what are your thoughts on becoming king?"

Epilogue

Muriel opened a velvet sack and pulled out a long string of pearls. "My mother bestowed me with these on my tenth birthday. She claimed my father took them from the sea and stranded them together." She wore Danika's pink silk gown instead of her plain handmaiden's cottons. Danika had insisted her half-sister dress like an equal.

Muriel smiled. "We both know the truth behind that tale."

Danika touched the cool, smooth surface of the large center pearl. The oily white sheen glistened in the rays of sun filtering through her triangular chamber windows. "They're beautiful all the same."

"Which is why I want you to have them." Muriel opened the clasp and held each end to Danika's bare neck. "As a wedding gift to wear when you walk down the courtyard."

Warmth spread through Danika's heart like a rising sun over Ebonvale's now-peaceful lands. She smiled and shook her head. "I cannot accept such a keepsake."

"Nonsense. I want you to have some part of me with you. We're sisters, remember? Besides, you're not traveling to any distant kingdom anytime soon. I'll still see them on your lovely neck."

Danika smoothed her wedding dress, humbled with gratitude. If her destiny had taken another course, she'd be standing at the House of Song and marrying Valorian. "Thank Helena for that."

Muriel fastened the necklace around Danika's neck. "You are content with your choice?"

Danika thought of Bron's eyes widening in surprise as a trace of a smile worked its way into the corner of his lips after she asked him to be her king. His gaze had smoldered as he drew her close. His response still sent a tingle down her arms and legs, *"If it means being with you, then yes."*

She couldn't have picked a more worthy man to be king. Danika smiled. "I am more than content."

"Good. I always thought you and Bron--"

A knock sounded.

Muriel whirled around with annoyance. "Who could it be at this hour? Everyone should be setting up the courtyard and taking their seats."

Had Nip lost the rings?

Danika adopted her formal tone. "Come in."

Ariella stepped in and bowed. "There is someone here to see you, my lady."

Muriel put her hands on her hips. "Who would interrupt the princess's preparations for her wedding?"

The young handmaiden winced. "She wouldn't say. She had the messenger's seal so I let her in."

Danika's chest tightened. Had the wyverns returned? Or the army of Sill? "Let the messenger in."

Ariella bit her lip and glanced at Muriel. "She wishes to speak with the princess alone."

Muriel shook her head adamantly. "I do not like the sound of this. Right before the wedding? Could it be an assassin from the House of Song come to take revenge for rejecting Valorian's hand?"

"Don't be ridiculous!" Danika stood and turned to the servant girl. "You did well, Ariella." The princess glanced at her sword resting against the side of her bed. She'd learned from Bron to sleep with her weapons like loyal lovers. If she moved toward the blade, she'd only upset Muriel more. Besides, she could reach the other side of the room in seconds if she had to.

Danika took Muriel's arm. "Go now. Leave me with my visitor." She nodded to Ariella. "Admit the messenger."

"I will stand outside this door." Muriel straightened as if she'd had as much practice with hand-to-hand combat as she had with embroidery. "If I hear one strange sound, I'm bursting in."

Danika raised her pointer finger. "You will do nothing of the sort. One of us has to live to rule the kingdom."

Muriel's face dropped and her mouth opened in shock.

Danika squeezed her arm. "I'm only jesting. Now, see to the final preparations. Make sure Bron hasn't changed his mind."

Muriel sighed. "He'd sooner stab his heart with his dagger." She gave Danika a hard stare. "You know where to find me."

"Indeed." Danika waved her away. "Off with you!"

As Muriel left, a hooded figure wearing a torn black robe entered. The smell of pine and cherrywood blossoms drove Danika to step back in shock.

The messenger threw back her hood. Graying, white-blond hair spread from her mother's face in a wild tangle. Sybil smiled. "I received your invitation."

Danika had sent the messenger pigeon with mixed feelings and little hope. "I didn't think you'd come."

"And miss my own daughter's wedding? For that I'll endure a thousand gossiping tongues."

Danika suppressed a wince. Her mother might have to if so much as one person recognized the former queen. "You should keep your hood on." Although spoken out of love, Danika's words came out with a dagger tongue. She wished she could find the compassion in her heart to be kinder to her mother, but the anger still worked its way in from time to time.

She'd stayed behind for Danika. Sybil smiled as though her daughter's acid tongue dealt no pain. "I intend to, only if the hood doesn't restrict my view of my gorgeous daughter." She walked around Danika in a circle, admiring her gown. "You look lovely."

"'Tis your wedding gown."

"I remember." Amusement flashed in Sybil's eyes. "However, I have reason to believe you are a lot happier wearing the white silk than I was." She squeezed Danika's arm. "You chose wisely, my dear."

Relief came upon Danika in a downpour. Knowing her mother favored her choice meant more to her than she thought it would. She hadn't confided in anyone, not even Muriel, about her choice and what it meant to reject the hand of the Prince of Song. Only her mother would understand. "'Tis not the best decision for Ebonvale."

"A content queen with a peaceful, open mind to rule is more precious to Ebonvale than a ruler with unrest in her heart."

"I certainly hope so." Danika had a sudden flash of herself as her mother, running away from the House of Song back to Bron. How disastrous that would have been for kingdom relations.

"I speak only truth." Her mother leaned over and kissed Danika's cheek. "I'm proud of you, daughter. Your actions have eased so many wrongs in my blighted heart."

Tears brimmed in Danika's eyes. Her mother's visit had rekindled so much of her love, but the pain held her words back. Her mother turned to leave, and Danika's chance of expressing gratitude slipped away. Could she bring herself to fully forgive?

As Sybil reached the door, Danika stepped forward and blurted, "Mother, wait."

The old woman turned around and raised an eyebrow. Interest flashed in her good eye. "Yes?"

"I could use an advisor. Someone who has gained wisdom from experience." Danika opened her heart to hope. "How about you stay a while."

Meet the Author

Aubrie Dionne has been a fantasy lover all of her life. She wrote her first poem in elementary school about how she'll never get to see a unicorn. But, that doesn't stop her from dreaming and writing about every fantasy creature she can conjure up. A fan of Lord of the Rings, she dreams about visiting the elves in Rivendell and having Legolas teach her how to wield a bow.

When she's not writing, Aubrie teaches flute and plays in orchestras, making up stories to go along with the music. You can find her on the web at http://authoraubrie.blogspot.com and www.authoraubrie.net.

Acknowledgements

I'd like to thank Renee at Lyrical Press for continuing to believe in my work. Also, my editor, Paige Christian, for squeezing out those important extra words from my imagination. My agent, Dawn Dowdle, comes next for supporting me through thick and thin. My beta readers, Brianne Dionne and my mom, Joanne, deserve a heartfelt thanks for listening to all of my ideas. Thanks goes to my husband for sitting with me at my author table at Barnes and Noble and pretending to be the author of girly books while I had to go to the bathroom. Also, my brother, Austin, for being the best salesperson I could ask for at the arts and crafts festival last year. Cherie Reich is my author bff forever, and she deserves more thanks than I can give. My flute teacher and mentor, Peggy Vagts has my thanks for supporting me in everything that I do, whether it be flute or not.

Turn the page for a special excerpt of Aubrie Dionne

Nebula's Music
Each note brings her one step closer to the truth.

When the cyborg Nebula plays the piano she experiences memories from a time before her creation. These memories—which involve a captive rebel fighter being held on their ship—bring with them complex human feelings and awaken a desire for her to discover her origins.

Radian is the long-lost love of the woman from which Nebula was made. He's vowed to avenge his finance's death and rescue her sister from the Gryphonites, a fierce race out to enslave the galaxy.

Nebula grapples with her identity and how much of who she is comes from someone else's past. She is not the woman that died, yet she is undeniably drawn to Radian.

Together Nebula and Radian seek to rescue his fiancé's sister and end the Gryphonites' cruel reign. But can Radian learn to love again and can Nebula accept a past made from someone else's memories?

On sale now!

Chapter 1
Memories

Nebula's fingers struck the keys of the Steinway and a cascade of chords tinkled down like falling stars. Above her, the dusty, reddish-blue galaxy hovered through the window, illuminating her pale skin in mottled hues. The other crew members sat poised in the shadows, watching her performance in silent awe as the crescendo of Rachmaninoff's piano concerto resounded throughout the hall, echoing off the glass hull of the ship. Though she lacked the emotional swells, Nebula knew the technique would be fluent and flawless.

As her finger struck a particularly poignant note, a distant memory flashed in her mind. Daises bloomed in an open field, bowing to a light wind underneath a sky of gold. Nebula closed her eyes, trying to hold onto the flighty notions. She hadn't ever seen a sun. At least, not from the surface of a planet. Still, the farfetched images returned each and every time her fingers touched the keys, causing a black void to ache in the center of her being. She felt like she missed a vital part of her identity, as if she were made incomplete. The emptiness was one of the only emotions she'd experienced in her short existence.

The note resolved, and the idyllic scene disappeared when the angst of the chord dissipated into resonance. As always, the fragments of thought were insistent and ephemeral. They visited when her fingers brushed the keys but never lingered.

Nebula's hands flowed off the piano and fell to her sides, and there was a surge of applause from the crowd. She gave a modest bow and walked off stage to the reception area to greet and thank the guests as they dispersed. Next time, she would program Mozart. The decision to do so was instant, almost as quick as it had taken her to download the Rachmaninoff from the circuit board of the computer mainframe.

As the first audience member approached her, warning lights flashed around the deck. The captain's tenor voice came through the speakers. "Code six. All senior officers on the control deck."

The crowd scattered as everyone rushed to their stations. Nebula slipped into the dressing room beside the stage. Considering the ramifications of a code six threat, she slid off her black, sequined concert gown and stepped into her United Planets in Action uniform, fastening the silver buttons with her nimble fingers. She took the elevator to the main deck and placed her cold hand on the panel to gain access to the control room. A green light blinked above and the doors parted, dissolving into the sides of the threshold like melted glass.

The control room surged with chaos. Angstrom ran between screens, collecting coordinates and inputting data. His tube-like hair stuck out at all angles and she could tell he'd come right from bed. Oso clutched three sets of headphones over his three sets of ears, listening intently to the communications tower. Captain Ritter talked in heightened whispers with his first in command, Venus, whose glowing blue face told Nebula she was afraid.

Beyond all the activity on deck, what caught Nebula's attention was the main sight panel. A Gryphonite Warbird hovered off the front bow, firing at a small cargo freighter of unknown origin. No. Nebula focused on the side of the vessel. It was a rebel ship, further complicating matters.

"Nebula! Good, you're here." The captain left Venus's side while the first in command was in mid-sentence and sprinted over. "I need the probability factors of the Gryphonite ship attacking us if we defend the rebel freighter."

Nebula's gaze glossed over as she accessed the inner recesses of her mind. "Sixty-five point six three percent to one with no defense of the freighter. Seventy-eight point three seven percent to one after freighter assistance."

Captain Ritter's bright eyes narrowed, the skin crinkling around the corners and showing the oncoming signs of middle age. "I thought so. What are the odds of the Warbird overtaking our speed?"

Nebula leveled her gaze at the construct, taking in all possible angles, the engine capacity and the probable weight. "The chance of successfully outrunning the Warbird is ninety-four point two four percent."

The captain smiled at Nebula like she'd become his best friend. Nebula frowned, unable to interpret his rush of favoritism. All she did was calculate the odds. Captain Ritter whirled back to Venus, and Nebula understood the smile was not for her at all, but for his first in command. "Looks like you've won."

Venus held her hands to her heart. "Thank the gods."

He turned to the crew. "We're not going to save the freighter, but we'll save them." He drew in a quick breath and sighed. "We're going to phase out the people on the freighter. By the time the Gryphonites board their ship, hopefully we will all be long gone."

Oso turned, his eyes black and intense. "But sir, they're rebels. This will put us at odds with the Gryphonite-UPA alliance negotiations. The rebels are considered outlaws. We would be aiding terrorists."

Venus stood by the captain. "Oso, these are people in need of help. You and I both know those savages will use the rebels as slaves. Besides, under the terms of the UPA agreement, they aren't supposed to attack anyone."

Oso lifted an eyebrow. "And what if the rebels attacked first?"

Nebula stepped forward. "The odds of a rebel freighter attacking a Gryphonite Warbird are one hundred ninety-nine to—"

"Enough, all of you." The captain raised his hands to his head as if the banter was clogging his ears. "Let's just get those people out of there and be on our way."

Nebula analyzed the situation. Chances were the crew could evacuate the rebel freighter and jump to flight speed in enough time to evade the Gryphonite Warbird, but the captain was running a risk. Venus, as always, was the sympathetic thinker, and Oso, the logical, self preservationalist. She noted both parties' disagreement for the log.

The captain tapped his fingers. "Angstrom, how are you doing on those coordinates?"

Angstrom's tube hair bounced as his head whipped around. "Almost got them, sir."

"Nebula, I need you to go to the phase chamber to greet and assess the victims."

"Yes, Captain." Nebula raised her hand in the formal UPA salute. As she walked back to the threshold, the captain grabbed her slender arm. In the dilation of his pupils, she saw doubt. "Log everything."

Nebula made sure to hold his gaze. "You know I will."

"Yes, yes." He spoke mostly to himself and turned back to his crew. "Oso, prepare for optimum flight speed. Let's hightail it outta here."

Nebula did not wait to hear his reply. The glass doors closed behind her in a whisper of wind. She rushed through the corridors to the phase chamber. A new mission loomed, and missions always brought her pleasure, if one could call it that. They gave her a sense of accomplishment and filled the void, the dark place where the impossible memories liked to hide.

* * * *

When Nebula entered the viewing room, the phase chamber was empty. The ship shuddered and the floor tipped under her feet. The Gryphonite Warbird must have fired a blast at their hull. Nebula's mind turned to her calculations. Two more blasts at that power would breach the shields.

She did not have time to consider it further as particles twirled in the phase chamber below her like dust motes in the sun. The people in the rebel freighter were being channeled onto their ship. Nebula estimated thirty or so beings and waited patiently until their forms solidified.

As their bodies came into clarity, she identified mostly humans and a few other closely related life forms. They all wore the bold red streak of the rebel defenders on a sash across their chests and were equipped in blast-proof vests with laser holsters at their sides. Thank goodness Angstrom had filtered out the weapons.

They were not happy to be brought on board without their consent. A young, punk-styled rebel beat his fist in the air. "Hey, what's going on?"

A woman with flaming pink hair and tattered fishnet sleeves snarled at the viewing box. "What do you think we are? Tourists?"

Nebula took the intercom in her hands. Her bland, ambivalent voice was perfect for such hostile situations. "Remain calm. We of the Flightship Freedom have saved you all from certain and immediate slavery under the claws of the Gryphonites."

She felt the deck move underneath her feet, not from a blast but from the propulsion into optimum flight speed. Oso must have maneuvered the vessel out of the blast zone. Coldhearted as he was, he was an excellent navigator. Nebula logged the time and the tactics used. Her probabilities had all proven correct.

The rebel punk looked at her through the glass. "I demand to speak with your captain."

Nebula pegged him as their leader and continued in her monotone voice. "Captain Ritter will be with you in a moment. Right now we need to determine if anyone requires medical assistance."

"What we need are some answers," the rebel leader called back, "and a real person to speak to, not some walking corpse."

Nebula felt the sting of the slight like the first time she'd felt cold water hit her face. The crew members of the Flightship Freedom had always treated her with respect, but these people were flagrant outlaws with cutthroat reputations. They were civilians who'd decided to take matters in their own hands, not trained professionals like those around her. She blinked a few times, bit her lip and remained silent. She had no programmed response for discourtesy.

The retorts came at her in a wave of curses and accusations, forcing her to shut off the intercom and silence the voices in the room below. Their arguments were beyond her hands now. She pressed the button to the control deck. "Captain, you are needed in the phase chamber immediately."

Nebula tried to control the rush of the strange new feeling and catalog it as it coursed through her. It was the bitter slap of prejudice. She wanted to understand the roots of the vagabonds' discrimination. Scanning the crowd, she studied their features and every gesture, as if they were a different species.

The pink-haired woman huffed and sat against the wall, crossing her tattooed arms over her legs. Behind her a man emerged from the crowd, stealing Nebula's attention. He had dark features like a Romanian gypsy and large blue eyes tinged with sadness. While the others were aggressive and bloodthirsty, this man possessed an inner tranquility, as if his fate was already decided and he was a reluctant passenger along for the ride.

Although he had the punk appearance, with his black hair spiked and dyed in cobalt highlights and an outlander's cloak, Nebula could sense that more was lurking underneath the rough facade. As her gaze took him in, a wistful melody echoed in her mind. Every line in his face spurred another note, as if he were somehow connected to her music. Nebula shook her head, but the soaring sounds came back, insistent. She resisted the urge to turn away.

It was impossible yet there he was, staring back at her as if he recognized her. His face changed from fierce defiance to shock. He pushed through the other rebels. When he was just feet below the viewing room, he looked up, mouthed a word that began with an "m" sound and held up his hand, as if reaching for his own salvation.

Nebula's finger hovered over the intercom speaker. If she turned it back on, maybe she could hear what he was saying.

Just then, the doors opened behind her and Captain Ritter came in, followed by a group of guards. "Nebula, are you okay?"

She pulled her head out of the trance she was in and shifted away from the glass. "Fine, sir."

"Report."

"There are thirty-one rebels, mostly human with three other humanoid races. The leader is the man front and center. They are hostile, sir, and demand they speak with you."

The captain rubbed his head. "Great. We go and save them and now they want to wage war here instead. All right. Good work, Nebula. You are dismissed."

While the captain instructed the guards, Nebula lingered in the viewing chamber just a moment longer than protocol, surprising herself. There was no way she could have known that man, and yet his face drew her in like a puzzle demanding to be solved. The black void ached inside her.

Nebula left seconds later, walking faster than she normally did down the corridor to her room. She knew there was no way for her to speak with him. At least not until later, after the rebels were processed, filtered of contaminants and questioned by the captain.

If the man ignited the music, and the melodies spurred the memories, he could be connected to her past. Nebula didn't know anything about the woman she once was, or if the mental pictures she sifted through were true memories of the past. What she did know was how to access the memories, and now who to look for. This time she would be welcoming the visions instead of questioning them. This time she would get answers.

Nebula entered her room in a rush and sat on the bench in front of the Steinway. She struck the keys, hesitant at first, then gained speed and force as she progressed, trying to find the melody that sight of the rebel summoned in her thoughts. She searched for the recollections lurking in the haunting tones, the glimpses of a past she couldn't possible have, yet belonged to her as intrinsically as her own name.